SING GODDESS THE WRATH OF THE FONZ;

SMOKEPIT FAIRYTALES PART II

TRIPP

This book is dedicated to the men and woman of the First Marine Division, service members everywhere, and the Veterans of Iraq and Afghanistan.

CONTENTS

Diane,

The man who owns Guinness, the guy who owns Budweiser, and the owner of Coors all walk into a bar.

The Budweiser owner orders a budweiser.

The Coors owner orders a Coors.

The Guinness owner orders a water.

"What are you doing?" Asked the Budweiser and Coors owners.

The Guinness owner says,

"If you aren't going to drink beer, neither am I."

— Trump

ACKNOWLEDGMENTS

Thank you to Erin Shaw, Christopher O'Quin, and to all the regulars at smoke pits and smoke decks, bars, Sailors, Marines, Soldiers, and Airmen around the globe for inspiring the nonsense put together in this story and Parker Chlovechok.

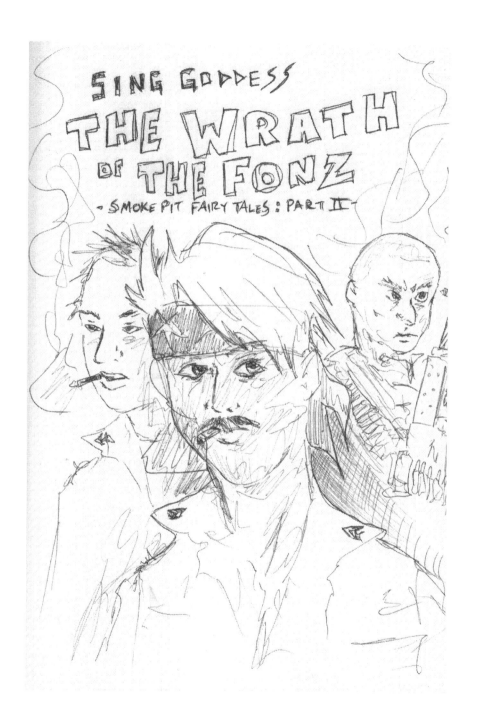

SING GODDESS
THE WRATH
of THE FONZ
~ SMOKE PIT FAIRY TALES : PART II ~

Tripp

00 THE EPIC CONTINUES

"So, does that mean we *can't* die?" Doc's shaken voice asked.

"I don't know. Apparently the only people to eat the damn wolfberries were that Noah guy with the unpronounceable name and his family. I don't think they passed it on. Or else by now there'd be a metric shit ton of immortals."

"Well, do you think we could find him?"

"Doc, even if this all true and not just a weird fucking coincidence, we're not Sherlock Holmes. And what the fuck are we going to do, take leave to Iraq and try to hunt him down? We don't speak Arabic and why the fuck would that guy stay in Iraq for eight thousand years? If, and I mean *if,* this is all real than that dude's probably living in Ottawa smoking pot with Osama Bin Laden's daughters."

"Then what do we do, man?"

"I don't know. I don't know if there's anything we *can* do. And what would we be doing anything about? It's not like we're superheroes. Knives still cut and the shit still fucking hurts. The only difference, I can think of, is that we healed all the way from injuries, that at best should have crippled us for life, and we don't get new scars."

Doc sat quietly for a minute. "Should we test it?"

"What?"

"Like test if we're immortal."

"I know what you meant dude."

"Well…"

"No, dude! Fuck no."

"Dude, this is some heavy shit."

"Yeah. I don't know why the fuck we're so willing to accept this, but when I heard the story, it all just felt so real."

"Dude, I got the same thing going on." Doc rubbed a hand through his thin hair. "What the *fuck?*" He was still battered and bruised from the car accident the other night. "Man, if we *are* immortal, it's the worst fucking kind of it."

"We just better make sure not to get buried alive." I joked, trying to lighten the mood.

"Bro, that fucking cave, or temple or what the fuck ever it was, was fucking terrible. And there's legitimately this ancient fucking text that fucking outlines it!" Doc's phone started to buzz again. "Dude I don't know what to even fucking think right now." He picked up the phone but didn't answer it, "I gotta go."

"Where?"

"I don't know. I should go talk down Kristy, but I need to clear my head first."

The next few weeks were blurry. It was December and the entire Department of Defense was getting two back-to-back four-day weekends, so no one wanted to get any work done. I was happy about that attitude because I didn't want to work either, I didn't even want to think. I couldn't get how that old Epic and what happened to me in Iraq were so similar through my head. I probably would have thought it was humorous if I hadn't had a solid reason to be dead.

1 HOLIDAY MASSACRES

It was Christmas Eve. Penelope was throwing a party. Virescents obviously didn't share our holidays, but they got excited about the big ones like Christmas and New Years. It was San Diego, so Penelope got a small palm tree and decorated it with glass balls and lights instead of an evergreen. Red and green ribbons, and stars hung from the ceiling. She had ornaments hanging from the ivy on the walls. I thought the paper cut snowflakes were funny. It was sixty three degrees outside. No matter how shitty life got, I still had California to bask in. Ginny and Glædwine had helped her get things set up for the party. I was okay with Penelope spending time with Ginny, but Glædwine put me just a little bit on edge. But I was glad to be around people. My thoughts only tried to murder me when I was alone, and my bruises disappeared, so that was good.

I was standing on the balcony with Éclair smoking a cigarette. Elvis was singing us Christmas carols through the radio. "So, you cleared shit up with Ginny?"

Éclair rolled his eyes. "Yeah…" He took a deep swig of the black Virescent wine Thom brought. "It was bad man. I had to pretend to cry and everything."

"Really, dude?"

"I mean, I love her dude, ya know?"

I raised my brow.

"Don't judge me."

"Whatever, dude."

"Yeah, so what's with the little blonde chick being here?" Éclair asked.

"I don't know dude. For some reason Penelope wants to be friends with everybody I fucking know."

"That was the same chick that…"

"Yup."

"Bleh. Is Doc coming tonight?"

"He should be. But I think he's still fighting with Kristy."

"Yeah, she's kind of a bitch."

"You have no idea, dude."

"No man, they'll be at the barracks and I can hear them yelling from across the decks. Then I had to go pick him up from LA that one time."

"Yeah, what was up with that? I was on duty and couldn't go." I lit another cigarette.

"Apparently they went up there to check out some record store and he said something about Filipinos and she left the store and drove the fuck off. He said you were busy and I had to fucking drive up there and drag his ass back."

"That's fucked up man. I don't know why he deals with that shit."

"I don't either man. But it was fucking cold driving up there in your jeep."

"It's got a heater."

"It doesn't have a roof, how's a heater any good?"

"I just wear a jacket in it."

We headed back inside. I didn't know most of the people in attendance. Thom, Fay, Frince and Ginny were talking over sugar cookies. Penelope and Glædwine were still pulling things out of the oven. Éclair and I mixed another round at the counter where the liquor was sitting. I mixed a Dead Nazi, the peppermint schnapps made the drink taste like Santa's blood.

I turned around mixing my drink with a plastic spoon.

"Hey, what's up man?" Jerry greeted me.

"Nothing much, dude. Haven't seen you for a while. How's it hang'n?"

"Not too bad."

"Yeah?" I was half nervous to talk to him. I told myself not to be, he probably didn't know how I felt about his wife.

"Yeah, you know, keeping busy with work and all."

"Yeah? How's that going?" I saw Éclair standing by me out of the corner of my eye. "Oh by the way this is Richard Éclair." I looked to Éclair "This is Jerry, Glædwine's husband."

They shook hands.

"So how *is* work going? Glædwine said a little bit about it, but I don't pay attention to what she's saying half the time," I lied.

"Well, we're working on some pretty interesting stuff. We finally built a program that understands the Virescent digital language and Windows. We're over the hill as far as research goes."

"Windows?" Éclair asked. "Why not Mac or Linux?"

"Because we're working for the government so we can't be too efficient." Jerry chuckled. "But anyway we're starting to work with Norfolk-Grumman and Lockeed-Martin building prototypes for Earth-Virescent Machines."

"Like what?" Éclair asked.

"A lot of it has to do with systems that increase survivability in space, but the arms teams are building some really cool stuff. Like the Russians are building this thing called the 'Putinbot'. They're saying that it's for construction uses, but it's a sixty foot tall robotic suit."

"Huh?"

"Imagine a Russian built robot from a Japanese cartoon. We think it's pretty much a giant walking tank."

"Should you be telling us about that, man? That seems like it should be classified." Éclair asked.

"Notice how I wasn't talking about American or British projects." Jerry said.

"So there is a US-UK one?" I asked.

Jerry made the quote symbols with his fingers. "*No.*"

"Well, alright then," I said. "I always thought that Vladimir Putin was a James Bond Villian."

"He pretty much is." Jerry took a sip of his drink.

"So, we had this stupid Christmas party at the shop the other day," I said to Éclair.

"Yeah? How'd that go?"

"I wrote a poem for it, and no one understood it."

"*You* wrote a poem?" Jerry jeered.

"Yeah, you wanna hear it?"

"Sure."

I pulled out my wallet and unfolded the paper I had it written on. "Jerry you were a Marine for a bit right?"

"Yeah."

"You'll like this."

I held up the paper to read:

It was the night before Christmas as I laid in my tent

No power for the lights, No heat for the vents

Garza hung stockings his wife sent with care

Besides that and a calendar the walls were all bare

The Marines were all shivering Cold in their cot

Dreaming of warmth and places we're not

My sleeping bag green my beanie tan

Most people don't know it's cold in Afghanistan

Then somewhere outside there rose quite a racket

We repelled from our cot to see what had happened

We opened the flaps to look out of our tent

When who did we see? It was First Sergeant!

He looked straight at us and then with a shout

He 'Devil dogged' us and called us all out

His nose was runny under his shaved head

He was huffing and puffing and then he said

"This is a mess! How'd it get this bad?

The trash on the ground is making me mad!

Everything's out of order, nothing is clean!

Is there no limit to the garbage I've seen?"

Then us Marines in the star's light glow

Began to see where this was going to go

First Sergeant said, as he scanned all around

"I don't like what I see laying on the ground!"

Then he pointed to us, the four of us all

He said with a grimace "You're going to police call!"

We picked up the butts to the cigarettes left

And we emptied the trash and swore under breath

We swept on the decks, no dust did we leave

What a crummy way to spend Christmas Eve

Then we took off our neck gators and beanies

Because warming layers "Aren't for Marinies"

We finished the clean up cold in the sand

Then the First Sergeant who didn't lend a hand

Cracked a smile and walked out of sight

He said "You have post tomorrow, Merry Christmas, Good night."

Éclair laughed. "That's fucked up."

"You wrote that?" Jerry asked.

"Yeah."

"That's good man."

The three of us walked out to the balcony. Éclair and I lit cigarettes and Jerry pulled out a pipe.

"Where'd you get that pipe, Gandalf?" I joked.

Jerry brandished it as if it were of no consequence. "Oh, I've had it."

"That thing's cool man." Éclair peered at it. "I like how it's carved to look like a wizard or a sultan."

"Yeah, see how it's light tan? When I got it, it was white, the stone it's made of absorbs the smoke and after a few years of smoking it the whole thing will turn brown."

Éclair admired the pipe. "That's pretty sweet dude."

The glass door to the balcony slid open and Penelope grabbed my arm. "Hank, come in."

I stepped in, closing the door behind me. "What's up, babe?"

Two tall Virescents stood before me. They looked as if they were in their forties, so I had no idea how old they actually were. "Hank, these are my parents. Chardance and Binnette."

Chardance was tall with dark emerald skin. He had a short cropped orange beard and slicked back glowing hair, his pupils were a demon's scarlet. He was the handsome gargoyle on a Visigoth cathedral with a white three piece suit covering a muscular body.

Binnette was almost angelic. Her golden hair was curled and folded over the top of her head. She had an attractively healthy body weight, I had to fight to keep from staring at the proof that Penelope's bust size ran in her mother's family.

I extended my hand. "Good Evening, nice to meet you."

Chardance gave me a firm handshake. "It is a good evening." His accent was a little thicker than most other Virescents I had talked to.

"Penelope's told us a lot about you," Binnette said, shaking my hand.

"Well, hopefully nothing good."

Binnette laughed at my joke, Chardance didn't seem amused.

Penelope's folks gave me the, *who's this dating my daughter?,* interview and I minded my manners. They didn't dig too deep. I wondered how old someone had to be to not have a potential suitor shaken down by the parents. I speculated that since Penelope was eighty-eight, parents probably stopped caring when their kids are about five hundred. Either way, the conversation was pretty dull. Chardance left to get wine long before Binnette was done. I caught my break when I saw Doc and Kristy through the window walking up.

I met Penelope at the door to let them in.

"Hey! Merry Christmas!" Penelope greeted them.

"Hey! You too!" Kristy said, hugging her. "I love your sweater!"

"Thanks! I don't remember quite where I got it."

"It's nice, I brought casserole."

"Wonderful!"

The girls walked to the kitchen. Doc and I grabbed a drink.

"Well, they got friendly." I poured a rum and coke.

"Yeah, apparently when your girlfriend drove Kristy home that night from the bar they had some conversation and now they're best fucking friends."

"Penelope's like that. She wants to be friends with everyone and their mother. So she's snagging all my friends."

Doc took a glimpse around the living room, "She sure went all out."

"Yeah, this is their first Christmas that they actually know what's going on. We'll see if it keeps up. She's excitable."

"She's got a mean backhand too," Doc chuckled.

We all drank into the evening. Instead of making the rounds, wishing everyone I didn't know a Merry Christmas, I stuck to the people I at least knew a little. The seven or eight of us that knew the Christmas carols sang along when the familiar ones played, and we all picked at the ham and sweets.

Chardance, Jerry, Éclair and Ginny, Fay and Frince, and Doc, and I smoked cigars Chardance brought on the balcony. The night was cool, but didn't require more than a sweater. The San Diego lights illuminated the air in a beauty that couldn't be beat by any other unnatural lights.

"I do rather enjoy cigars," Chardance said.

"Yeah, I'm surprised as many Virescents picked up smoking as they did." Ginny said. "You guys didn't have tobacco before Earth did you?"

"No," Chardance shook his head, "and I'm not fond of cigarettes or a pipe, but a good cigar seems to do the trick."

"That's because you haven't had the right kind of pipe tobacco," Jerry commented.

"Perhaps." Chardance blew a smoke ring.

"Yeah, and if you think American cigarettes are bad, let me tell you about these Iraqi smokes called Pines," I said.

"Holy God, those things were terrible," Éclair groaned. "I ran out of Marlboros in Al Kut and had to smoke those fucking things the rest of the deployment."

"It's not your fault, dude," Doc said. "Nobody brings enough cigarettes on their first deployment."

"What was so bad about them?" Fay asked.

I answered her, "Well, I'm not sure how things are on other planets, but on Earth everybody makes things, but there's always someone who makes things the best. And someone who makes total shit of a product. Good wine comes from France, good rice comes from South East Asia, good tobacco comes from North America." I rolled the cigar in my hand. It was a Cohiba. "And before the embargo was lifted Cuban cigars were what all Americans wanted to get their hands on. They're usually good, but most of the excitement was over the fact that they were illegal."

"Why was that?" Frince asked.

"Political bullshit," I shrugged.

"Hey, Hank, you remember that Afghan foot bread?" Doc asked.

"Dear Lord that was good." I chuckled.

"Yea, you guys seemed to have fought a lot of wars recently," Frince said smugly.

"Eh." Doc, Éclair, and I shrugged.

"What were they all about anyway?" Fay asked. "You guys seem to get pretty heated over the subject."

"Well, they tell you it's about freedom," Éclair started, "but no one actually goes for that."

"How so?" Frince asked.

"It's about the brothers you're there with," Éclair answered.

"Hmm. Okay." Frince judged.

Éclair, Doc and I stared at him.

"What's wrong with that?" Doc asked.

14

"Nothing. I just haven't heard that one before. Usually it seems people have fought under the banner of freedom, and not just on your world. But is freedom really worth laying in a hole with your own guts in your hand?"

The only reason I didn't throw Frince of the balcony after that sentence was because Penelope was having a good night and I didn't want to ruin her party. Although I wasn't sure Éclair or Doc weren't about to do it themselves anyway.

"Frince, man," Jerry said out of the blue. "Have you ever served?"

"No…" I could tell he wanted to say something snide like *Being in the military is for the slime of society and the poor,* but sensed that being thrown off a fifteenth story balcony wasn't outside the realm of possibility. "But I can't think of anything so terrible that could happen that I'd feel the need to take up arms."

"So you'd rather be a slave than fight?" Jerry asked.

"I'd rather be a slave than die. I'd certainly rather be a slave than mauled for a word."

"So 'Freedom' is just a word is it?" Doc asked angrily.

"It could represent an idea, sure. But even then, that idea you call 'freedom' who decides who gets it afterwards? Who exactly decides how much of this 'freedom' that people get, if any at all? Definitely not a foot *soldier.*"

I glared at Frince and tightened my lips.

He continued, "What could the enemy be doing that's so terrible that I should be okay with going and fighting him? Whatever he's doing he's not doing it to me or even anyone I know. And war is never for what the people sending you over there say it is. It's for the respective governments' profit. It doesn't matter who's war it is or what it's supposedly over."

"So that's why you had to leave your planet?" Éclair asked. "Because you're a race of fucking bitches that'd rather turn tail and pussy out instead of stand and fight like fucking men would?"

"What did you say?" Frince asked offended. He and Éclair stared each other down.

Doc and I looked at each other, then Éclair, then Frince, and then slowly put our drinks on the railing.

Without taking his eyes off Éclair Frince taunted him, "Do you want to go little man?"

Éclair, Doc, and I flicked open our knives, almost in unison. Fay looked like she was about to cry and Jerry switched the position of the beer bottle in his hand, turning it into a weapon.

Ginny just looked annoyed.

"Listen, spinach dick," Éclair said in an angry, but calm voice, "I've killed more people than you've fucked. You don't want to go anywhere with me. I've got nowhere to go but Hell, and right now the only thing between here and there is a slit throat and a fifteen story fall."

Frince stood silent. He was nervous, but didn't look like he was backing down.

"Alright, everybody calm down," Chardance said, frustrated. "We're not all nancies like France here."

"Frince."

"Shut *up* you vagina! It doesn't matter what, or whose, war it is, it's the warrior who wants to fight for the glory of battle and wants only more so to do it with his brothers. When you're old and decrepit and picking out the flowers to go in your stomach, have fun explaining to your children and their children's children how you were a coward that never did anything with his life."

"I'll fight you *all*," Frince's voice started to shake.

"Oh, please. From what I can tell, you just pissed off four men with daggers who all fought in war, probably together, who are about to stab and beat you until you're wailing for death, and they'll then only give it to you by hurtling you towards the ground below. Then, since you've shamed *our* people enough, I'll have half the mind to tell the authorities that *you* threw the first punch." Chardance turned to Fay, "Get your girlfriend away from here before she gets hurt and don't let us see you again."

Fay grabbed Frince's arm and dragged him out of the apartment.

"I do apologize for that," Chardance said.

I put away my knife away, "Why? He was being the tool."

"Because you humans tend to bundle people of the same color into groups and I don't want to be associated with an ignorant ass like that. I don't even know a good word to use to describe people like that."

"Pussy would work," Doc said.

Éclair said, "Or faggot."

"I was under the impression 'faggot' meant homosexual," Chardance went back to his cigar.

"Eh," Éclair shrugged.

"It is, but I've personally never heard anyone use it to call someone gay," I said, "but people do get their panties in a twist about it."

"Yeah that whole community gets mad about that. You can't even really say it without an uproar," Ginny said. "Even if you're not describing gay people."

"Huh." Chardance puffed.

"Oh hey, also, I was never deployed," Jerry commented.

"It's okay dude, you showed up." Doc patted Jerry's shoulder.

I looked in through the window, Kristy and Penelope mean mugged us from the other end of the apartment.

"I was a soldier once," Chardance stated. "Frince was only half wrong, but he was a complete buffoon."

"What was the deal with flowers in his stomach?" Ginny asked.

"It's a burial tradition. Before one dies they choose a plant and its seeds are put in their body after they pass. We wrap our dead in a soft coffin and bury them shallow. The seeds use the body for nutrients and the plant grows. Instead of a field of headstones, we'll have a garden or an orchard to remember the deceased. In our olden times people were buried along the sides of the city walls and vined flora would be planted with the body. Apparently it was very beautiful."

"Interesting." Ginny took a sip of her drink.

Penelope slid open the balcony door. "What the *hell* was that?"

"Frince was being rather obtuse," Chardance said firmly. "so, I politely asked him leave."

"Politely? They didn't seem like they were sent out with manners."

"He was offending the company around him and was given the opportunity to leave without being drug."

"He was being a real bitch," I concurred.

Penelope huffed, "Hank, come inside for a moment." I followed her to her room. "Do you have to ruin every party you attend?"

"Woah, don't pin this on me. Frince started it, and your dad gave him the boot."

"Well, would he have started it if your friends weren't badgering him?"

"Hey, you fucking invited them, not me. I know you want to be friends with everybody, but personally I think most of *your* friends are shit heads."

"*My* friends are shit heads?"

"Yup. Especially Frince and Fay. I mean your dad's cool, but the people your age need to be knocked down a fucking peg."

"Well at least they don't go around starting fights with everyone."

"*Frince* started it!"

Penelope moved her face to half an inch from mine and scowled at me from under her eyebrows.

"What?" I taunted her.

"I've been friends with those two longer than you've been alive."

"I really *don't* give a shit."

Penelope stuck her index finger into my shoulder and tried to push me back.

18

I looked at the red-nailed green bean prodding my shoulder then back into Penelope's eyes, there was a storm brewing in those seas. "Are *you* trying to fight me too?"

Penelope's brow dropped lower and she poked me again harder.

"How much have you had to drink tonight?" I tried to smell the alcohol on her, but I was a hair too tipsy to do so.

She drove her nail into me until it started to hurt. I grabbed her hand just hard enough so she couldn't pull it away. When she failed at yanking it back she shoved her opposite shoulder into my chest. I caught her arm and lunged, tackling her onto the bed.

"Penelope, listen, that wasn't my fault, Frince was being a dick pissing everyone out there off and you're not helping the situation. And if you're worried so much about your party getting ruined then you should probably stop acting like a bitch."

"What?" She barked.

She scowled at me, trying to jerk herself free. I hadn't been in a fist fight with a woman before and I didn't want to start that kind of lifestyle off with the woman wearing my ring. I wasn't sure what I could do or say to calm her down, so I pressed my lips onto hers. She forced her bottom lip onto mine as if she were trying to bite me through them. I put my body weight down on top of her, pinning her harder to the bed. Penelope reached out with her teeth and bit into my bottom lip just hard enough not to break the skin. I shot my hand up and yanked a fistful of her hair. Her legs wrapped around me and squeezed my waist. The skirt that could have been made for an elf slipped up her legs, revealing the lacy bands holding up her thigh highs. She ripped open my pants and pulled my cock out, it was already at half-mast. She squeezed it far beyond the barrier between pleasure and pain. I performed the same operation on her right breast. She flinched a little in pain. I let go of her chest and slapped her hand off of my dick. I gripped my shaft and used the head of it to slide the bottom of her panties out of the way. I found the right hole and lined it up with my cock. Then with one strong thrust I shot the whole thing in… dry.

Penelope let out a yelp and I clamped my hand over her mouth. It didn't feel good for me either, but this was war. I started driving long hard pumps until her juices lubricated the friction. Penelope crept her finger up the back of my shirt and dug her nails into my back; I felt little droplets of blood form and ooze down my back. With the momentum of my thrusts I

19

slowly slid her to the top of the bed, pound by pound. When we arrived, Penelope was still clawed into me. I took the handful of her hair and pulled her head to the side and drilled her so her head banged into the headboard. I pounded her up until she couldn't go higher and the board was hitting the side of her face. As she increased the pressure of her fingers I increased the hitting of our hips. Eventually, between the moans of pain and passion, she understood the method to the madness and relaxed her hands. I pulled back off of her and threw her legs to the side. I clawed her hips and pulled her ass to my crotch and reinserted myself. I continued my attempt to break her pelvis.

Penelope looked back at me. Her mouth was open with her bottom lip hanging down. She could only hold her eyes open half way. She whimpered, "Hank…"

I pushed her face down into the pillows. Penelope reached back and put her hands on the sides of my hips. Beads of sweat formed over Penelope's body and the nectar from inside of her soaked our legs. She ran her hand under me and started cupping and stroking my balls. After one particularly hard thrust she squeezed them like she was squeezing a lemon. I pulled out far enough to break her grip and immediately shot back full force. Only this time it was into the other hole. Penelope screamed but pillows and Christmas music from the other room muffled it. I expected her to try to push me off but she lifted her hands to grab the top of the headboard. I went for broke. Penelope took one of her hands off the bed and slipped a couple of fingers inside of her slit. I grabbed her face and curled my fingers into her mouth. Penelope tried to suck the skin off. After a few minutes she relented her assault on my hands and her head started going limp and the pitch of her moans rose and came faster and quivered. It sounded like she was trying to say my name, but she still had a mouthful of my fingers.

I listened to her breathing and at the deep breath she always took before she came I pulled my dick out and held her hands away from her crotch so she couldn't finish the job herself.

"Not fair!" She wined, still face down with her green ass in the air.

"You're right, it's not." I poked her butt cheeks with the head of my cock. "Are you done fighting with me?"

"Yes." I saw a smile from the side of her face. "You win," she panted.

I took my hand off of hers and wrapped it around my shaft.

"My pussy feels like it's bruised."

"Yeah? Your ass is bleeding too."

"Hank, why don't you always fuck me like that?"

"Because I don't normally fucking hate you."

"I think I need to fight you more often."

"Oh yea? Well, I got something to fight about."

"What's that?" She said looking back at me smiling.

I grabbed her by the bangs and shoved my cock all the way down her throat, just once. Her eyes grew wide and her arms flailed. Then pulled it out, gripped it and pulled until white pearly ropes of cum shot into her face, effectively gluing her eyes shut.

"God Damnit, Hank!"

"Don't start fights with me over shit that ain't my fault." I pulled up my pants and tucked my shirt back in.

Penelope felt around looking for something to wipe her face with.

I tucked my hard on into my belt and awkwardly made my way to the balcony trying not to let people see the bulge in my pants.

Finally alone for a moment I fell into one of the metal chairs around a table that wasn't big enough for anything more than a few glasses and lit a cigarette. I was still breathing hard and I'm sure I looked like I just got out of a fight.

Halfway through my cigarette the Glædwines slid through the door. Lovis set fire to the end of a Marlb and Jerry lit his pipe. "Good evening," they said, placing glasses of yellowish brown liquid on the table.

"Yeah. Merry Christmas."

"That too." Lovis sat in the chair opposite mine. "So, I just had an interesting conversation."

"Cool. Me too. You go first." I exhaled a thick plume of smoke.

"I was talking to that guy Thom, and apparently he doesn't like Penelope being with you."

"Okay, Thom's Penelope's brother, that's kind of to be expected."

"His train of thought is that you're going to die several centuries before she does and he doesn't want her to get hurt," Jerry informed me.

I thought for a second. "I can see that, but I think a good counter argument would be that I'm an enlisted Marine and we're *probably* going to get divorced anyway, so his logic is a bit off."

The Glædwines smiled. "Yeah I'm pretty sure he didn't consider that," Jerry chuckled.

Penelope limped out to the balcony. She was wearing a different sweater and her makeup was gone except for a quick dab of eyeliner. She looked like she may have ran a comb through her hair. She carried a red velvet Christmas stocking in her hand.

"What's in the sock?" I asked as Penelope sat down. She leaned to the side of her chair as to not be sitting flat on her butt.

"Christmas presents."

"Yeah, how are you people so cool with Christmas but freak out over birthdays?" I asked.

"Eh. One can't help what they see on TV." Penelope extended two fingers towards me slightly separated.

I looked at her questionably.

"Cigarette please."

"You don't smoke." I waved her off.

"I do when the right things happen." She smiled.

I passed her a Lucky's. She took one excruciatingly deep drag. The smoke from her one exhalation filled the balcony. She handed me back the cigarette.

Lovis Glædwine leaned over the table and looked at Penelope's hand. "I don't think I've seen your ring." Penelope gave Lovis her hand and she looked closely at the rose jeweled band. "That's very nice." Lovis smiled, but it looked forced. She glanced at me for a second then looked back at Penelope. "You're a very lucky woman." She let go of Penelope's hand. That whole situation made me feel uncomfortable.

"I think I'm doing alright."

By the time I lit my third cigarette most of Penelope's guests had left, including her parents and the Glædwines. Doc, Éclair, Ginny and Kristy were out with us smoking before they went home for the night. People stuck their head out and thanked Penelope for her hospitality, she told them they're welcome and Merry Christmas Eve.

"So..." Ginny said, "we got together and got you three something for Christmas. Something similar because the three of you seem like you're the three best friends on the planet."

"Like the Three Musketeers," Kristy added.

"Please don't start calling us that," Éclair begged.

Penelope pulled three small boxes out of the stocking, each with red wrapping and 'Hank,' 'Richard,' and 'Wilson' written with a golden pen on top. "We got together and decided these are the best things the three of you could share."

We each took the box with our name on it. Opening them we found brand new lighters with words engraved on the front. Éclair's and mine read "I FUCKING LOVE THE MARINE CORPS AND THE MARINE CORPS FUCKING LOVES ME!" Doc's was the same, only with "Navy" instead of "Marine Corps."

"Sick!" Éclair yelled as he inspected his lighter.

"This is pretty bad ass." Doc wrapped his arm around Kristy.

I grabbed Penelope's hand and smiled at her.

Then we were alone. Penelope had brought back a blanket from when she locked the door after everyone was gone and we cuddled under it on the metal chair on the balcony smoking cigarettes and looking at the city. Somewhere along the night Penelope had put on a Santa hat, I flicked the ball at the end between cigarettes.

"Hank."

"Penelope."

"I want to have more sex like that. Like wild animals battling for the last scrap of the zebra."

"There's something wrong with you, woman."

Penelope lit one of my Lucky's with my new lighter. "You love me."

"I do." I did. I did not however have the words to describe it. When I held her in my arms it felt like the galaxy was pouring warm milk directly into my soul from all reaches of the cosmos. When I wasn't near her, I felt like a child on a ship who's favorite stuffed animal had fallen into the sea. And although I didn't show it, when she was angry towards me my heart felt like the screaming victims of Mount Vesuvius being burnt alive in the unholy fires raining on Pompeii. And when it was cold outside, and she was curled up on my chest, I almost felt at one with the universe. I didn't care about the world, I didn't care about myself, I didn't care about the war. But how do you tell someone you feel like that without sounding like a complete faggot?

"Hey, how's your booty?"

"It'll be okay." She took a drag off her cigarette. "You know sometimes I feel like I'm robbing the cradle sleeping with someone as young as you are, but you're finding ways to surprise me."

"Well sometimes I feel like I'm robbing the grave sliding it into someone as old as you."

Penelope smiled up at me from under the Santa hat. I reached down and drug my lips across hers. She flicked her cigarette to the street below. She rustled around under the blanket as we kissed. Penelope slid her long beautiful legs through the holes under the armrest of the chair. Straddled over me she found the end of my arm, put her panties in my hand and whispered in my ear.

2 LATVIAN VIKING

A few years passed. Doc married Kristy and Éclair married Ginny.

I married Penelope and bought a house in Ramona. The drive to work was a pain in the ass, but I didn't mind. Our home was small but we had a decent amount of property. Doc and Éclair helped me add a few rooms to the house. The studs for the walks in the bedroom were made of trees that were still rooted in the earth, as were the olive trees I used for bedposts. We had a few pictures on the walls, but most of the additionally constructed rooms were covered in ivy, at Penelope's request. I built myself an epic man cave out of the basement. It had green walls, a full bar stocked with every assortment of liquor and wine. I found an old jukebox that played records, at a garage sale, and fixed her up next to the bar. The biggest pain in the ass to make was what I called the armory. I dug out a space adjacent to the basement and effectively built a ten by ten safe, giant lock and all. My guns were illegal in the state of California so I kept them and all my ammunition along side a few boxes of MREs and water in case of an emergency inside. Penelope made fun of me for it, but I told her I was prepared for when the zombies come.

Eventually the Marines from Motor T were let off the hook for Kelsey's murder. As far as the general public was concerned the case was still open. I kept waiting to see it depicted on one of those unsolved crime shows. Éclair, Doc, and I went on with our lives and figured we'd be okay as long as we stayed cool.

I kissed the right ass to get orders back to Division. They had made me the NCOIC of the photo section. I abused my power to go to the field to be with the Marines, instead of sending the younger generation to go out and get their training. I had made the cardinal mistake of marrying a chick before I dated her through a deployment, but I didn't think it was a big deal. There weren't any current wars and I was reaching my service limitations. I was ready to get out of the Marine Corps at the beginning of the next year. I did, however, want to get in one last rodeo before I made the transition to the monotony of civilian life. I talked my Warrant Officer into sending Éclair and me with Two-Seven to Latvia for six months on the Black Sea Rotational Force. Before going to Latvia I hadn't seen much of Doc because he had gotten orders back to Two-Seven as the senior line corpsman for Weapons Company, so it was good to catch up with him.

The battalion was held up in a series of old Soviet barracks on a Latvian army base a few miles northwest of a city called Daugavpils. The buildings were gray, stone, and cold. Faded Cyrillic signs were posted on the walls. The only color, besides the green the Marines were wearing, appeared as dark red streaks running down the sides of the buildings, faded rust from their iron accessories.

There were a few local vendors that worked on base providing the Sailors, soldiers and Marines an alternate option to stuffing our faces than the chow hall's cold bland slop. Doc, Éclair, and I sat in a small dirty booth with our grunt buddy Stevens waiting for some Latvian fish. It was February and we were a little less than a month into our six-month training evolution.

"Dude, I am so glad they brought back Nineteen-Elevens." Stevens said, sipping a plastic cup of ice water.

"Right?" I agreed. "You ever had to shoot someone with a nine mil?"

"Yeah, you have to put three or four rounds into their ass before they fall down. People bitch the nineteen-eleven's only got eight rounds, but one forty five blows a hole in ya big enough to fist fuck."

"I wish we had that shit in Iran." Éclair mumbled. "Those guys were so hopped up on drugs they didn't even feel it when they got shot half the time, and you'd have to waste most of your ammo on the same guy."

"That's 'cause you don't know how to shoot." Doc laughed.

"Yeah, all that two in the chest one in head shit goes out the window when they're fucking running sideways," Éclair defended himself.

"Then thank God for machine gunners." I rubbed my arms. "It's fucking cold here man. When are we getting happy suits?"

Stevens' face twisted in thought "I think before that field op next week."

"That's going to fucking suck." Doc complained. "Cold, wet, and fucking hungry? Fuck it, send me back to Iraq. Why the fuck are we here anyway?"

"It's the same thing as what's going on in Australia with their rotational force," Éclair said as the waitress set our food on the table. "Thanks," he told her. "We're just here to poke at Russia and say 'Look assholes these guys are our friends and *we're* here and haha you can't come do this in Canada.'"

"No, dude." I unwrapped the napkin around my silverware. "They tried that in Cuba and it almost started World War Three."

"No, that's what he's saying," Stevens said, defending Eclair. "If we put a bunch of troops somewhere close to countries we're not really friends with then it's okay because no one can do anything about it. Anyone else does it and we're going to have to fight you. America's the new empire, bro."

I shook my head. "Yeah, but I wish we'd just fucking embrace that instead of doing this half assed shit." I took a bite of the fish covered potatoes in front of me. "You know, I'm glad this little restaurant thing is here. I'd fucking hate to *have* to eat at the chow hall."

"You're telling me, man." Stevens said, shoveling food into his face. "I thought the chow halls on Pendleton were bad, but fuck." He pointed his fork at me. "But, you've got that girlfriend there."

"She's not my girlfriend, dude." I imitated shooting him the bird with my ring finger and it's golden band with runic inscriptions.

"She's cute, though. She looks like she's an MP. And she's always smiling at you man. You should go talk to her."

"I don't speak Russian. And even if I did I really have no interest."

"Why not?" Stevens asked.

"Dude, Hank's wife's fucking hot," Éclair said.

I nodded my head and showed Stevens the background photo on my phone of Penelope sitting on a rock by the beach in short-shorts holding my M14.

"Good call." Stevens smiled. "I'd wife that too. The green doesn't bother you?"

"Na. And she's going to look like she's seventeen for the next hundred or so years, so I'm always going to have a hot wife."

"I can dig it. Have you ever seen an alien fucking crackhead?" Stevens asked.

The other three of us shook our heads.

"They look weird man. Their skin gets super light green and they're all spotty. They look fucking inhuman."

"Well technically they are." Éclair chuckled.

We finished eating dinner and smoked a cigarette outside the barracks. The sky was that dark gray that never gets black in a snowy winter. There was about six inches of white powder and ice on the ground. The fat fluttery flakes that were falling didn't look like they were going to halt their assault any time soon. My boots were soaked from the snow. My toes were ice.

"I fucking hate snow," I grumbled. "I hate snow, I hate ice, I hate the cold." I inhaled my nicotine. The fog from my breath was heavier than the smoke I exhaled.

"It's not that bad," Éclair said.

"Yeah, sure it's not you fucking yankee." I shivered.

"Don't hate me because you can't handle the cold." Éclair laughed.

"No, but seriously, what kind of fucked up shit is this? Isn't Europe *Second* Mardiv's responsibility? Why the fuck is a battalion from Blue Diamond, from fucking Twentynine Palms, doing cold weather training in fucking Latvia?"

"It's supposed to be a UDP type thing," Stevens said, "but yeah, Sixth or Eighth Marines should be here and we should be in Okinawa."

I grumbled and flicked my cigarette into the ashtray. "I'm going to go call my wife for a few minutes. You guys wanna watch a movie tonight?"

They agreed to the entertainment and I kicked through the snow to the payphones. Yeah, fucking payphones. I punched in Penelope's cell number.

About half an hour later I walked back to the barracks. I was excited and a little scared. I wasn't planning on stopping at the smoke pit, but I saw Fonzie burning a cigarette. He had made his way to sergeant and was now a squad leader in Fox Company. Fonzie was one of the few people still left in the battalion from when we were in Iraq. Almost everyone else I knew either died, switched units or got out. I knew Fowler had gotten to Staff Sergeant and had a platoon in Gulf Company, but I hadn't seen him yet.

"FONZIE!" I ran up to him and slapped his shoulder.

"Hey, bro, what's up? You ready to go freeze your balls off next week?"

"Yeah, whatever. Dude. I'm gonna be a dad!"

"Awe, congratulations man!"

"I know, right!" I pulled out a Lucky's.

"You know if it's a boy or a girl?"

"No dude, my wife just found out like two days ago!"

"You married a Virescent, right?"

"Yeah!"

"How's that work?"

"No clue! Hopefully it's not a fucking egg I have to make a nest for and shove up my ass or anything." I lit the cigarette.

"Yeah, but…" Fonzie made a circle with the fingers of his left hand and stuck his right index through it. "I didn't even know we could breed with them."

"I didn't either, but I wasn't too worried about it, I figured if it happened, it happened, and it happened, so, yeah!"

"Ya got names picked out?"

30

"No, but we should be home a few months before she pops it out, so I got time."

"Cool, bro."

"YEAH!" I snuffed out the cigarette from which I only took one drag and went as fast as the ice and my boots would let me back to the barracks. I flung open the door to the open squad bay. Rows of bunk beds lined the grey crumbling walls. Doc, Éclair and Stevens were bullshitting about something, but I didn't care to listen. "Dudes! Penelope's pregnant!"

"Is it yours?" Stevens joked.

I punched him in the ribs.

"It was a joke man, chill out." Stevens rubbed his side.

Doc and Éclair congratulated me. "What are you going to do now?" They asked.

"I have no idea." I tried to think of just what the hell I was going to do with the rest of my life. "I have no fucking idea, but I probably have to reenlist now."

"Yeah, should have worn a rubber man," Éclair said, "now you're gonna be stuck get'n fucked by the big green weenie."

"Yeah, I don't really know how that whole thing works," Doc said, confused. "I mean she's legitimately from a different solar system. I don't think you two should be able to produce offspring."

"I guess we'll see what color it is when it comes out."

"No, dude." Stevens nodded. "I've heard about humans and Virescents having kids."

Doc continued, "yeah, but I think there's something wrong with the whole situation. I mean we're not even the same species, it's like a bad SciFi movie. Things in real life don't just work out because the director wants them too, there's gotta be a reason for things."

"Directors don't write movies, dude," I corrected him. "They just tell people to parade around in front of a camera like a nance instead of getting a real job."

Éclair laughed. "Yeah, but even if it's not a *real* job all those fuckers are laughing their way all the way to the bank. Fuck, I think I'm going to do that. I'm going to get out of the Marine Corps and go be an actor, *pretend* to be a Marine and be a fucking millionaire."

"Yeah, let me know how that works out." Doc rolled his eyes, "But yeah, you guys wanna watch this movie?"

Éclair got his laptop and placed it on the rack across from Doc's. The four of us squeezed together on Doc's bed and Éclair opened the file named 'Thule.'

For three hours we watched a terrible film, filled with plot holes and shooting mistakes. My mind kept drifting to my wife and what I was going to do with her in the future.

"That was the stupidest ending to a movie I've ever seen." Stevens barked as the credits started to roll.

"Yeah, and why did the people in the first village not know that the castle belonged to the king?" Éclair asked.

I stood up, my legs were asleep from sitting on a single sized mattress with three other men for three hours straight. "I don't know man, you'd think that they'd notice that kind of shit when they wrote the damn script."

"It was a good movie though," Doc said.

"It was better than staring at the ceiling for two hours," Éclair griped. "Anyone else up for a cigarette?"

"Yea, I'll go with you." I dug my hands into my pockets to make sure my smokes were where I left them. "Hey, did you notice the island had the same name as that Virescent wine?"

That night I layed in my rack trying to go to sleep, but not wanting to. I was excited, I was going to be a dad! I thought to myself, *how cool is that!* Then I thought about how I was going to afford that. I shrugged it off. We couldn't drink while we were in Latvia unless we were granted liberty. It was one of the first time in years I went to bed sober.

The nightmares came back.

3 THE JUDGMENT OF PUTIN

We didn't get happy suits, but that was just as well. As cold as it was, when we got moving we built up a sweat. The sleeping systems were warm enough for the night and we moved throughout most of the day. We didn't really go to the field. We were away from the barracks out in the woods, but we had aluminum Quonset huts to sleep in and they gave us hot chow for breakfast and dinner.

The first night in the field I laid in my sleeping bag on the concrete floor of the bivouac just warm enough to not involuntarily shiver. As I dozed into slumber I found myself dreaming I was running in formation with Lovis Glædwine, Gunny Chanceworth, and Satin Sheets. I don't know why Satin was in the Marine Corps in my dream, but you know how they are. We were all in our green short shorts and shirts running through the Pendleton hills. My throat was raspy and as we ran my cough grew more steadily. I fell out of a formation in which I was the only male. Nightmare already. Satin and Glædwine kept running and Gunny Chanceworth waited for me at the top of a hill. When I reached her she asked me if I was okay and I told her yes. We ran about fifty more yards and I started to vomit. I couldn't control the mushroom soup escaping my mouth. The stomach acid burned through my teeth and they fell out. But then there was a sharp pain in my head and new teeth grew. Long, sharp fangs. Chanceworth put her hand on my back. I twirled around and clawed off her face, killing her in one strike. Then in my dream I watched Satin and Glædwine run. They stopped, saying they thought they heard a scream. I stalked up close to them through the brush and stood at the top of a hill looking at them as they stood below. When they saw me they turned and ran in fear. I sprinted after them and tackled Satin to the ground. I started choking her and eating her hair. Glædwine found a stick and tried to hit me. I grabbed the branch and broke it with one hand. I then stabbed Glædwine in the chest, she fell to the ground and a pool of blood soaked the sand around her. Satin was screaming, I couldn't tell her to be quiet because my mouth was still stuffed with her hair. I picked up a fist sized stone and smashed in her skull.

I woke up to someone saying, "wake up bitch, fire watch," to the Marine sleeping beside me. I tried to go back to sleep but couldn't.

The next morning I stood in line for chow with Éclair and Doc. In the field Marines eat by order of rank, lowest to highest. Éclair had picked up sergeant so we were both in the middle of the line.

"I had a dream about Gunny Chanceworth last night."

"Ugh," Éclair said in disgust, "I'm sorry dude."

"Wet dream?" Doc joked.

"Noooooo," I replied.

"That's not funny, Doc." Éclair said. "That chick is so haggard it ain't even funny."

"She can't be that bad if Hank's having dreams about her." Doc smirked.

"No dude, it's bad." I shook my head.

"Yea," Éclair nodded. "She looks like someone tried to make a Mister Potato Head out of wet Play Doh."

"Gross."

"Like this chick is *so* fugly…" Éclair continued, "I'd bet that her pussy has cleft lips."

"That's fucking disgusting. I don't even know if I want to eat anymore." Doc turned his head away from the food trays.

I looked at Doc. "Dude, you went down on a hooker and you think that's gross?"

"Wait, what?" Éclair asked.

"It was before our first deployment…" I said.

Doc sighed, annoyed. "I was going up to see this mama-san in Orange County at this massage parlor. I'd go see the same chick every weekend. I was just *destroying* my wallet. But Eventually I started talking to this chick I'd see every weekend. It got to the point where I'd fuck her for free, while she was on the clock. And I would get into it. I'd eat her ass and everything…"

"You were giving a hooker rim jobs?" Éclair asked.

"Yeah," Doc said, embarrassed. "But anyway, I told this chick that I was going to marry her and take her away from this fucking life of prostitution and take her home to Oklahoma and end her story like a fairy tale. So the day finally rolls around and she comes to meet me at the courthouse. I don't show up on time and she starts calling me, and I didn't pick up because by the time the date comes I'd been in Afghanistan for a week."

"Dude, that's *all* kinds of fucked up!" Éclair laughed. "Oh my God that's terrible!"

We had our breakfast scooped onto our recycled cardboard trays. The eggs were one mass of greenish-yellow clay. When the cook scooped them out, it stuck together like expired jello. I couldn't verify that the sausage tasted like cat turds, but they looked like it.

We sat down with our backs to the huts, we weren't allowed to eat inside the living area. The wind wasn't bad that morning, but we still had on our beanies and warming layers. The weather had been messing with us since we got to the field. Towards noon it would warm up just enough to melt the snow and the rest of the day we'd have to trek through mud so deep it almost reached our knees. Then at night it would freeze and snow about a foot. The ground would be full of rock hard ditches that were camouflaged by the loose powdery snow. Doc saw at least five Marines a day for rolled ankles.

I finished my meal and lit a cigarette. "So have you heard of those space cruises?"

"Yeah," Éclair's eyes lit up, "they look fucking legit, but they're expensive as shit."

"I'm supposed to go on one when we get back."

"What? How the fuck are you affording that?" Doc asked.

"Penelope's parents hooked it up. But I don't know if I'm going to be able to go."

"Why not?" Doc asked.

"Because Penelope's going to be pregnant as fuck."

"Awe, that bites." Doc whined for me.

"Well maybe you'll get another chance." Éclair put his tray on the ground and pulled out a pack of Marlbs.

"It'll probably be good to wait," I continued. "I read that they're starting to use all the Virescent technology to terraform some of the moons around Saturn and Jupiter, and Mars."

"So if you wait twenty years you can go visit them?" Doc asked.

"Yeah."

Éclair and I got our gear together and linked up with Fox Company. We marched a few miles into the hills to an assault course where we met with a Latvian Army company. The course was crude. There were a few blown out concrete buildings, whose only purpose was to be shot at and cleared. Between the buildings, wood pallets were constructed into obstacles. The Latvian soldiers and Marines took turns tearing through the course. We would be doing the same thing for three days, only on the third day we were to use live ammo. We ran through the mock village trying not to rip our feet off in the divots hidden under the snow. Éclair and I only ran it once then we started taking photos and video of the event.

First Sergeant DeLeon told us that we weren't marching back. The AAVs had made it to the area and we were going to ride. We were excited until forty-five minutes after the tracks were supposed to show up and we were still standing in the snow.

One of the Latvian soldiers came over to our company and held up a soccer ball. He smiled and tried to ask, "football?"

Nearly an entire squad of Marines shrugged and met a group of Latvian soldiers just outside the assault course. They dropped their gear and ran around on the unforgiving terrain kicking the ball back and forth. The Latvian team kicked our ass.

"This blows." Fonzie barked from the side lines.

"I know, man. It's so fucking cold my dick crawled back up inside my body. I got a total mangina right now," I said, shaking.

"No bro, this game."

"Oh." I looked at the men running around the field. "Well, they're all white."

"Huh?"

"I mean that's cool for Latvia, but we've got a bunch of Mexicans here, I don't know why they're not out there stomping those mother fuckers."

"Bro that's racist."

"Am I wrong?"

Fonzie sighed and took off his jacket. "Rios! DeLaGarza!"

The Marines shouted back, "yes, Sergeant!"

"Drop your shit we're going in."

"Aye, Sergeant."

I rubbed my arms in a vain effort to keep warm. "Now whose the racist?"

"I'm Salvadorian bro."

"Same difference."

Fonzie muttered something in Spanish and ran with the two other Marines to the field and started turning the tide. They kicked around the ball, hooking and weaving for about eight minutes in the falling snow. The score was tied and the players all stared each other down.

"GET ON YOUR SHIT! THE TRACKS ARE HERE IN TWO MIKES!" First Sergeant DeLeon yelled at the Marines playing soccer.

A Latvian solder picked up the ball and smiled. The rival teams shook our hands and dispersed. We loaded on the tracks and drove through the ice and snow back to the camp.

Fonzie, Stevens, Éclair, Doc and I stood outside the huts smoking cigarettes, waiting for the chowhall to open.

"So, what's the deal man?" Fonzie asked me. "You gonna stay in?"

"I don't know man. I don't know if I want to. I mean, sure if there was a war going on, but this peace time Marine Corps bullshit is fucking stupid. I'm going to put in a reenlistment package, and if it goes through, awesome. If it doesn't, then fuck it, I'll go be a stay at home dad for a while. My wife already makes a shit ton more money than I do so I'll take care of the kid and let her go back to work."

"That's kinda fucked up." Fonz chuckled.

"Well here's my thing. The military's downsizing because nothing's going on and congress is too fucking stupid to acknowledge that they have to bulk up every time there's a conflict. They're kicking out all the war vets because we're too hard to handle, and Headquarters Marine Corps sees us as dangerous. But instead of having the ball sack to say 'Fuck you you're fired because you're not being a drone and blindly following bullshit orders like a good little boy' they're just making it ridiculously hard for sergeants to stay in. And the sergeants nowadays, us, are the generation of Marines that grew up in a war zone."

"I feel ya, bro," Stevens said. "Those faggot admin and supply fucks get all the time in the world to pick up and Marines with jobs that actually do shit are getting our shit pushed in."

"Yeah, and they're fucking treating us like shit and their priorities are all fucked up. Like a fucking four deployment, nine year sergeant can't get a housing allowance, but they'll pay for your sex change," I barked.

"They won't do that," Fonzie retorted.

"Dude, look it up. They've done it to like four people already. All of them were chick to dude, but they're getting Uncle Sam to pay for it."

"Yeah it's like the breast implant thing," Éclair said, defending my argument.

"That's all kinds of fucked up," Fonzie said.

"But, fuck it. Where I stand now, my kid'll be born before I get out, so I won't have to pay for that. Then I'll put in a package and make it look like shit so they deny it and then they'll have to give me that fifty thousand dollar severance package."

Fonzie shrugged, "at least it's a plan."

Stevens lit another cigarette, "yeah but that medical shit's a real thing man. That's one of the reasons I joined."

"I joined to fucking kill people, but go on." Fonzie poked fun at Stevens.

"I'd been dating this chick since high school and she got some weird fucking bone disease that we couldn't pay for. So I joined the Marines and married her. She spent about four months at the Naval hospital and now she's almost better," Stevens smiled. "Whole thing's working out."

"The whole thing worked out with your hole thing?" I joked.

"Yeah yeah, haha," Stevens replied.

Lance Corporal Rios came running up to us from the other side of the huts. "Sergeant Palacios! Sergeant Palacios!" He said, distressed.

"What, boot?" Fonzie demanded when Rios came to a halt.

"Bama got stuck to the water bull," Rios huffed, trying to catch his breath.

"What?"

"He was drinking out of it and got stuck."

Fonzie had a confused look on his face and rolled his eyes, "alright."

The troop of us followed Rios over to the Water bull. I never understood why we called it that. It was a big metal water tank on a trailer, and looked nothing like any kind of animal, especially a bull.

The spigot on the back had a Marine's lips stuck to it. When he saw Fonzie his eyes grew wide with fear. Fonzie crossed his arms and glared at the poor lance corporal stuck to the metal water tank.

"What the fuck is this?"

"Mmmhmhmhm hmhm hmhm." Bama tried to reply.

"Are you supposed to be drinking straight from the bull?"

"Mm hmh hmhmh."

"That's the only water source that the fucking company has, you stupid fuck! And now we're all going to get your fucking germs!"

"Hm mhmh."

Fonzie took a deep breath. "I have half the fucking mind to just let you fucking stay there overnight."

Bama shook his head and pleaded, "Hm mhmh hmhm mh!"

"No, it's fine, the rest of us can just eat fucking snow. We'll hydrate off that."

"Hmhm mhhhm!" Bama's eyes started to water.

"Pull yourself off."

Bama tried pushing. His skin stretched and he relented.

"Hey Doc, how do we get this guy off?" Fonzie asked.

Doc kneeled down next to the young Marine. "You already try pushing water and spit to your lips to get yourself loose?"

"Mn mhn."

Doc inspected the situation up close and stood back up, "Well, cold water isn't going to help. We don't have any way of getting hot water…"

"I got it." Stevens walked up to the bull, whipped out his dick, and put it above Bama's lips.

Terror filled Bama's eyes and he ripped himself off the spigot. He fell to the ground, but half his lips stayed attached to the bull. Bama looked at the line of blood leading to the bull in shock.

"You stupid mother fucker." Fonzie glared at Bama. "Rios."

"Yes, Sergeant."

"Clean Bama's shit off the fucking thing and don't let anyone get fucking water until Doc says it's okay."

"Aye, Sergeant."

"Bama, stand the fuck up."

41

The Lance Corporal jumped to his feet and stood at parade rest. There was enough of his mouth missing that his teeth could be seen.

"I got him dude," Doc said to Fonzie. "Come on, kid." Doc took the Marine away to the medical tent.

"He's probably going to have to be sent home," Stevens' observed.

"At least to Germany." Éclair agreed.

"Fucking, stupid fuck," Fonz growled. "Hank, was I that fucking retarded when I was a boot?"

"I don't think we had time to be stupid when we were boots. We were too busy trying not to get killed."

The day of the live fire assault course rolled around. Before we went to the range we packed our gear and stowed it in the tracks. We were going to go straight back to the barracks from the field that day.

The dog and pony show started. A company of US Marines and Latvian soldiers worked side-by-side bounding through the obstacles, firing at the green plastic targets that popped up along the way. Most of the exercise went off without a hitch. None of us really thought it was anything spectacular, but the group of officers watching us all had hard-ons. The general for US forces Europe and most of his staff were watching us from a tower behind the course. Our Regimental commanding officer and the battalion's CO and XO and the sergeants major all watched alongside a handful of foreign officers.

The assault ended and the officers ordered us to circle around them so they could tell us how awesome we performed. I guess they didn't realize we had been doing the exact same thing for almost a week straight, move for move. It was warmer on Pluto and we were all wet form lying in the snow. I don't even remember what the general talked about, I just remember wanting him to shut the fuck up.

When we were dismissed we loaded in the AAVs and headed back to base. I sat on the hard metal bench in the back next to Éclair and Stevens. AAVs weren't as loud as helicopters. You had to yell to talk to anyone, but at least the sound wasn't drown out.

"Did you see that army staff sergeant up there?" Stevens yelled.

"Yeah, man," Éclair screamed back. "She had some *big* ol' titties."

"They probably had the giant blue vein running up top," I hollered over.

They laughed.

"No, but seriously!" Stevens started "I want to make a shower that rains KY jelly and just rub my dick in her face! I'd hit that *so* hard that whoever pulled me out would be declared the next king of England!"

"If I wasn't married I'd wrap her titties around my neck, let her be the big spoon, find a cave and hibernate for the winter like a bear," I said, "those things were huge. I'd be okay with using her like a tauntaun!"

"Dude, being an attractive female in the military has to suck," Éclair screamed. "Just imagine being surrounded by a bunch of sex deprived maniacs. Those chicks *have* to know that everyone that sees them wants nothing more than to fuck them in the ass!"

We got four days of liberty that weekend in Daugavpils. I didn't really let loose and go wild like I would have when I was younger. I was content with getting a few souvenirs and postcards for people, then finding a hole in the wall bar and getting drunk while I shot the shit with Doc and Éclair. I didn't feel the need to go causing trouble and chasing women, I had a woman back home and didn't feel the need to cheat on her either. Unlike half the other assholes there.

We found a pub that looked like it used to be a house. The walls were gutted out of the middle and a bar was placed over a hard wood floor. The bricks were probably originally red but over years of constant smoke turned brown and black.

"Why can't there be anywhere in America like this?" I lit a cigarette.

"You mean smoking inside?" Éclair asked.

"Yeah. I mean, it's a fucking *bar*. I'm not here to make good decisions, let me fucking smoke."

"As much shit as they get, third world countries are usually pretty awesome," Doc observed.

"Yeah, but Latvia's not really a third world country." I said. "It's old Soviet. I think that makes it second world, right?"

Éclair was staring over my shoulder. "You guys ever listen to Donna El Rey?"

"Sure..." I said slowly.

"Why?" Doc asked.

Éclair pointed behind us. "She's on TV."

Doc and I turned around. The volume was down, but we could tell she was singing. Her hair was flowing over a thick fur coat. Her eyes sparkled alongside giant, diamond earrings. The camera cut over to a bunch of people in black tie attire.

"Is that President Menelaus?" I asked.

"Yeah," Doc shook his head. "Is that his wife?"

"I think so," Éclair said.

"Goddamn, dude." I wanted to turn around and grab my beer but my eyes were fixed on the image of the first lady. If you took Satin's face, Penelope's attitude and Kennedy's body, the frankenwoman would only be half the beauty of the woman on the TV. "That is honest to God the most beautiful woman I've ever even seen a picture of."

"Yeah man, she's hot," Éclair said in a daze.

"How have I not seen her before?" I wondered aloud.

"I dunno. How much TV do you watch?" Éclair asked.

"I don't. Just movies, cable's fucking expensive man." I stared at her until the camera cut back to Donna making sweet lyrical love to a microphone. "What's her name? I'm going to Google that shit when I get service."

"It's something stupid." Éclair thought for a second, "Helen VonTroy Menelaus."

"Huh." I finally grabbed my beer. "That sounds familiar, I guess."

"Maybe you heard it on the radio," Doc said.

"Yeah, that's probably it."

44

We got up and sat back down at the bar to be closer to the TV. We asked the bartender to turn up the volume and ordered another round.

"Dude," Éclair said. "Look at that. They're sitting with Putin."

"I can't believe that guy's still around," Doc sipped his beer.

"Look at the flags behind them."

Behind the President and First Lady, and a few other people in tuxedos and eveningwear that we didn't' recognize, was the Russian flag, the Stars and Stripes, and the Latvian colors.

I waved the bartender down. "Hey," I pointed at the TV. "Are they here?" I pointed down at the bar.

The bartender looked at he screen then back to me. And said something in Latvian.

I pointed back at the tube, "Lativa?"

"Ah." He nodded, "Da, Latvia."

"Riga?" I tried asking if they were at the capital.

The bartender shook his head, "Daugavpils."

"Holy shit, dude." I smiled at Doc and Éclair. "They're here dudes."

We kept watching the TV and drinking. Putin and Menelaus both got up and gave short speeches, smiled and waved. We missed out on what they said. The broadcast was dubbed over in Latvian and the subtitles looked Russian.

Doc raised his glass, "Here's to peace and tranquility in our region. May there forever be content in the nations we both call allies." His brutal sarcasm continued, "Blah Blah Blah, there's no new cold war and the U.S. and Russians can go to bed tonight dreaming of each other's cocks in their mouths."

"I wonder what the fuck this is about," Éclair said. "It's gotta be a pretty big deal."

"I dunno," I grabbed my beer. "Maybe they all have a mutual friend getting married and this is the reception and they hired Donna El Ray to hold security."

"Why would Donna El Ray be a bodyguard?" Éclair asked.

"I meant sing." I filled my lips with a cigarette.

The event went on. One shot showed Putin laughing with Helen and a few other women. Putin had his hand on his chin like he was considering a world changing decision, even though he was laughing with a group of beautiful women. One of the women looked like she made a joke and used her breasts as props. Putin laughed and handed the woman an apple. The channel showed random clips and shots from whatever event was happening for about another hour.

"It turned out that it was a wedding reception," Doc said, pointing to a shot of a woman in a long white dress and veil.

"Yeah, but who the hell's getting married that this many important people are there?" Éclair asked.

"No clue."

The program ended and we drank until we forgot how to speak English. The bar closed at one, which was okay because our curfew was zero two. That was just enough time to catch a cab back to base and rack out. The warmth from the alcohol helped me fall asleep in the cold barracks under the snow.

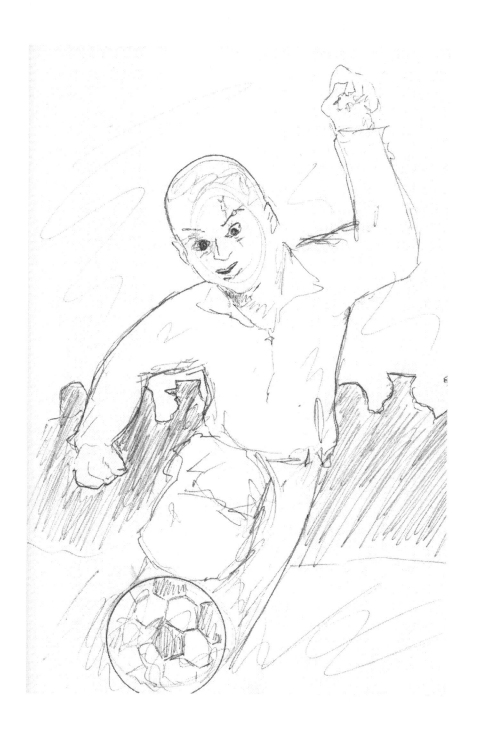

4 IVAN AND THE MECH

"WAKE THE FUCK UP! GET OUT OF YOUR GODDAMN RACKS!

Someone was screaming at us to get up, and it wasn't the voice of a lance corporal getting someone up for fire watch. I opened my eyes and the lights burned a hole through the back of my head. I winced and covered my face. My body felt like it was in the ocean and the world was spinning.

I was still drunk.

I looked at my watch, it was zero four and I'd only been asleep for about an hour and a half. "What the fuck?" I muttered.

I half sat up and saw First Sergeant DeLeon screaming "GET YOUR FUCKING CAMIES ON! HURRY THE FUCK UP AND GET TO THE AUDITORIUM!"

"What the fuck man?" Éclair rubbed his head.

"I don't know, dude."

First Sergeant grabbed a Marine walking to the head. "DON'T BOTHER SHAVING JUST GET YOUR SHIT AND GET DOWN THERE!"

I looked at Éclair. "Fuck dude, what happened?"

We scurried to get our clothes on. I kept falling over. My entire universe was a gloomy fog. We made our way to the building behind the company offices. The room looked like it used to be a basketball court, but only the bleachers still stood in the empty space. Everyone was seated on the flimsy sheet metal benches, hunched over from lack of sleep and hungover. We were called to attention, the battalion commander walked into the room. Lieutenant Colonel Amcmnon seated us before our wobbling got the best of us.

"Good morning, Gentlemen." The light colonel addressed us.

"Good Morning, Sir." We groaned in response.

"I know we just set you out on liberty, and I'm sorry to have to awaken you this early on your days off. However, a situation has developed. About an hour ago Russian Federation forces stormed the Latvian, Estonian and Lithuanian borders. Considering that's less than fifty miles away from us, we're officially about to be *in the shit*.

"This battalion has received orders to evacuate civilians from Daugavpils. Now, we do not have current information on where Russian forces are, but they *are* heading this way. I don't know if any of you are aware, but the President of the United States and several senators and other members of the staff are in Daugavpils as we speak. Never mind who butt-fucked the intelligence on Russian military movements and let that much of our government get that close to what could potentially become a front line, we're going in to pull people out. Our main objective being American civilians. There's already a SEAL team extracting Mister Menelaus, we're just picking up the rest. Your company commanders will relay to you the information on your specific missions. We may have to harden the fuck up on this one. Semper Fi, gentlemen. I'll see you out there."

The Marines broke up into their companies. Éclair and I decided to tag along with Fox since that's where the most familiar faces were.

Captain Sancho, Fox Company's Commander, tried to give us a motivational speech, but I wasn't sober enough yet to tell for sure if the whole thing was actually happening. After the Captain left, the Executive Officer, Lieutenant Toshi, briefed us the what, where, and how of the mission. We drew our weapons and ammo and loaded up in the AAVs outside.

We tracked towards the city. The hatches on the top of the vehicle were opened for the Marines to have their rifles at the ready, pointed outwards. I was at the front of the hatch letting the cold air and snow hit my face in a vain attempt to sober up.

"I'm not sure if I should be scared or excited," Éclair shouted from behind me.

"What?" Doc asked from the darkness.

"My dad was in the army during the cold war, so I've always wanted to shoot commies, but I ain't killed anything besides jihadists yet," Éclair said over the engine.

Doc's eyes were bloodshot, as were the rest of ours. He shook his head at Éclair. "Hopefully they don't have close air support."

Daugavpils started coming into view. The city glowed orange and black. The architecture was silhouetted by fire. Thick black smoke rose into the sky. A red aurora from the flame's light bounced off the snowy clouds and fog illuminating the night sky. The view started to sober me up. I had never seen anything like it. I was used to fighting people in God forsaken shit-holes in desert mud brick villages. Combat where civilized people who didn't have sex with animals lived, in a place with steel, glass, and lights… that never crossed my mind as something I would ever see.

We hit the outskirts of the town. The ramp at the back of the track fell and the Marines darted out. Each platoon was to disperse, search for civilians and bring them back to the AAVs where they'd be taken further west. Enemy situation was unknown, but we could hear gunfire in the distance.

There was a detachment of Latvian soldiers herding people into trucks already, and driving them away.

Fox Company split into squads and started combing the city. Each with some sort of vehicle trailing them, we had a Latvian high-back Humvee. The power was out, but the fires from the buildings kept it bright enough that we didn't need to use our night vision. My sight was still a little blurry from the night before.

"Hey," I nudged Fonzie. "Remember Al Najaf?"

"Yeah, bro. But this shit's eerie. I really hope they don't make us try to retake the city alone."

"Yeah, I'd like to just grab these fuckers and leave."

"No, but with just one battalion…" Fonz stepped over a crumbled concrete lamp post that had fallen in the street, "there'd be no sense in having everyone killed in a fight that was far beyond uneven in numbers. We don't even have armor."

"Thanks for reminding me."

We passed by a shop with broken windows. Glass was shattered across the sidewalk. There was a small family inside. One of the Marines extended his hand to coax them out. We put them in the back of the truck and kept walking. I tried to take photos of it, but it was too dark.

We skirted the streets looking and listening for movement. A man came around the corner a block or two down. He was in rain boots, a bathrobe and a leather jacket. The man ran until he saw us, he stopped dead in his tracks and stared at us in horror.

McMillian put his hands in the air and yelled "American!"

The robed man eased his stare but stayed weary. McMillian waved him over.

"American?" The man shouted.

"Yes!" McMillian yelled back.

The man crept up to us. He kept looking over his shoulders. He had bags under his eyes and a thousand yard stare. He wrapped his arms around McMillian and cried something in Latvian.

"It's okay man, it's okay," McMillian comforted the man. "You speak English?"

"Little." The man nodded his head and took his arms off the Marine.

"We're taking people out of here, we're taking them west. You understand?"

"Yes, yes."

"We're trying to find people who can't get out on their own. Can you point us to where more people might be?"

The man pointed southeast. "Apa... Apra...Apartment!"

"Awesome." McMillian escorted the man to the truck and helped him in the back.

We couldn't see the sun because of the clouds, but its light brightened the eastern sky. It wasn't comforting, neither was the burning ash that fell alongside fat snowflakes.

"Sergeant Palacios!" McMillian said. "Hey, Sergeant Palacios!"

"What is it?" Fonzie griped back.

"The truck is getting pretty full. Think we should send it back?"

Fonzie halted the squad and radioed the company.

I took the first photo of the day. Buildings burned the sky behind Fonzie as he radioed higher for information. I took another picture of the truck. It was packed to the brim, there weren't too many more people fitting inside of it. They were all miserable. Dirty, tired, scared, they just lost everything they probably had, and their lives changed forever. I took another photo of Doc looking over the Latvians in the back of the vehicle, seeing to any medical issues they may have.

Fonzie grabbed Corporal Flynn. "Hey, give one of your lances a radio and send him back to the rally point with the truck."

"Aye, Sergeant."

Doc hopped out of the vehicle and walked with us.

Fonzie looked back at the squad as the truck full of Latvians disappeared into the city behind us. "Alright Marines. Tactical column on me."

The squad got into a loose formation and started heading down the grimy alleyways. Using the main road would have been a poor choice as far as cover and concealment went.

"Sup, dude?" Doc whispered beside me, keeping his eyes on the windows looking down on the alleyway.

"You're looking at it man. I just hope I don't get mugged."

Doc chuckled, "Yeah."

After the alleyways and through the city we bounded across streets and parks until we saw a complex of hotels. They were dirty and riddled with bullet holes.

I looked over at Doc, "Where's Ivan?"

"I don't know, man."

"There's bullet holes and shell casings everywhere. Did they just do a fucking drive by?"

"I don't know, but it's freaking me the fuck out."

The squad started clearing through the buildings. They were all shelled. We found a lot of people in there, none of them were still alive, and fewer were still in one piece. The roofs were caved in or collapsed. The walls were Swiss cheese. Everything was charred.

"This is fucking worse than fucking Tehran." Flynn muttered.

I shot back at him, "Yeah, I didn't make it that far."

"That was fucking bad. But this is going to beat that into the dirt."

"I don't know about all that," I started taking pictures.

"Sergeant Allensworth!" Flynn barked at me. "Are you fucking sick? Why are you taking pictures of all this shit."

"S2's gonna wanna see this," Fonz defended me. "Keep doing your job, Kodak.

Flynn stood there in shock.

"People are going to need to see what those communist fucks are doing." I said.

"Eh."

"Flynn," Fonzie called to him. "Quit hassling him, I think I found someone."

The Marines ran over to Fonzie and started helping him pull someone out of a pile of rubble. The man groaned as we pulled concrete and rubble off of him. I saw a hand lift from the debris, I grabbed it and hoisted up the man's body.

He was on his feet but still looking down at himself.

I put my left hand on his shoulder, "Don't worry man, we have a corpsmen that'll check you out."

"Oh thank Jesus you're American," he said. "I was starting to think I'd never get out of there." He lifted his head back to the ceiling.

I dug around in my flack jacket and handed him my canteen. "You thirsty, dude?"

"Yeah, I'm…" He looked me in the eye and stopped. He glared at me as if he knew me. He opened his mouth to finish his sentence, then I recognized him and closed his cock holster with my fist. He fell to the floor with a thud.

"Woah! What the fuck comcam?" Fonzie yelled at me.

I tightened my fists in my Kevlar knuckled gloves and took a fighting stance over the man's body. He was holding his bleeding face and swearing. "Fonz, you remember that chick I was talking about on our first deployment."

"Sangin?"

"Now Zad."

"That Satin bitch that left you for…"

"Don't call her a bitch!" The man on the floor said holding his face.

"No fucking way!" Fonzie smiled.

"Yeah, fucking way."

"HA! Aye Dios Mio, you were so fucked up about that."

I glared over at Fonzie.

"I'm sorry, dude. It's just hard to imagine a chick leaving you for a fat fuck like that."

"Hank?" He stared at me confused. "What the fuck are you…"

"Real fucking coincidence, right, Bryan?"

"Dude, that was almost ten years ago." He fingered the blood oozing from a laceration on his face.

I took a deep breath in and put my hand out to him to help him back up. He looked at me distrustfully. "I'm not going to hit you again."

"Bullshit." He spat a glob of blood onto the floor.

I grabbed his arm and forced him back up to his feet.

He looked at me with mild shock.

"Is there anyone else around here that you know of?" Fonzie asked.

Bryan didn't take his eyes off me. "My *wife* should be with some of our associates about a mile away."

I glared at him, he smiled a little, and my heart sank. "She's here, too?"

"Yeah," he said snidely.

I pointed my thumb at him. "Hey Doc, you wanna put some quick clot on this fat fuck's face."

Doc came over and pulled out some ointment and gauze.

"What's quick clot?" Bryan asked.

Doc started rubbing the ointment into the cuts on Bryan's face. "It's a powder that immediately stops bleeding."

"That's a thing?"

"Yeah."

"Is it alien?"

"No, it's been around for years, but you don't want it."

"Why not?

"It burns."

Bryan winced, "I think I can take a little burn to make my face stop bleeding."

Doc looked over at me frustrated. "Hank, this is the guy Satin left you for?"

"She didn't leave him," Bryan said. "She *came to me* before the two of them even started fighting."

"Okay, dude." Doc pulled out a packet of quick clot. "Lie down."

Bryan laid back on the rubble covering the cracked floor.

Doc opened the little green bag of powder. "Close your eyes, you don't want this in them." Doc spilled the white contents of the packet onto Bryan's cuts and immediately tossed the bag and pressed down on the wounds."

Bryan screamed. His body twisted in pain trying to push Doc off. Two other Marines and myself held Bryan to the floor. Doc let go of Bryan's face and the rest of us got off his body.

"What the fuck was that?" Bryan screamed, in agony. He grabbed his face and grimaced. Instead of lacerations Bryan now had powdered covered scars decorating his head.

"It's supposed to be for cauterizing arterial bleeding. It burns your flesh back together," Doc stated.

"Then why the fuck did you use it on my face?" He growled.

Because fuck you I thought to myself. "You told him to do it."

Bryan glared at me with an intense hatred for every ounce of what I was.

It started to snow harder. It started to *fucking* snow harder. It wasn't enough to just be colder than all fuck and there be a foot of snow on the ground already, it had to fucking snow *more*. Our squad mustered in the plaza after our search of the hotels. Bryan was the only person we'd found in enough of one piece to still be alive. On our way out I yanked a wool jacket out of a shattered closet and threw it at him.

Since I technically knew Bryan, Fonzie stuck him with me. We formed back into a column and starting patrolling through the alleys and streets. We didn't see anyone for a long time. No civilians to evacuate, no enemy soldiers to shoot, not even a fucking feral cat.

"Hey," Bryan tagged my shoulder.

"What?" I asked annoyed.

"So, what's going on? What's going to happen?"

I didn't look at him, I kept my head and eyes ahead, searching for people and watching for the enemy who had yet to show themselves. "We're going to move a bit further out then we're going to link up with the trucks and they're going to drive you back to some fucking base where you'll be evacuated to Germany or France or some fucking place where you'll probably be taken back to the States."

"Well what about the other people?"

"Huh?"

"Like Satin, she's out there too somewhere."

"Well, I'm not leading the patrol so I can't just go get her."

He looked at me with anxiety in his eyes "But..."

"We're not the only people walking around looking for people. There's more than an entire battalion of US Marines walking around looking for fucks like you out here in the cold."

"Oh, well that makes me feel a little better."

"There's also a lot of Latvian army guys marching around. They'll probably finder her, then lose her, and not even remember what happened."

He looked at me with a blank look on his face, "Why are you so cynical?"

I shot him daggers. "Shut the *fuck* up."

We moved into a hotel lobby. It was a nice ritzy place, minus the blown out windows, glass and wreckage on the floor, pools of blood, and body parts.

"I don't trust this place," Flynn muttered. "I don't know about you guys but getting waxed because a brick fell on my head isn't exactly the way I want to go out."

"That's not getting waxed," McMillian said. "Waxed would be if the brick got a buffer and chewed you up."

Flynn looked at McMillian. "What the fuck does that even mean, dude?"

Fonzie gave the hand signal to halt and get down. Everyone found cover, besides Bryan, who stood there like a moron. I yanked him down by the belt and whispered angrily, "when we all get down, get the fuck down or you're going to give away our fucking position and get us killed."

Fonzie talked into the radio on his shoulder.

"What's going on?" Bryan asked me.

"I don't know, he's probably talking to the company about pick up."

Fonzie raised us back up. "We're going to loop around south and link back up with the company. Enemy Situation has not been distinguished."

The squad started following him out of the building and down the street. We had moved about two klicks when McMillian screamed "CONTACT LEFT!" and started pouring rounds from his M4.

Russian lead chipped holes in the concrete walls around us. We all scattered and dove for cover behind anything we could, dumpsters, cars, and rubble. Bryan stood in the street too shocked to move. I tackled him to the ground, "You dumb fuck!" I rolled off him and returned fire to the enemy. It was still snowing. My fingers were frozen and wet. My hands ached as I pulled the trigger.

Fonzie barked at us, "Fall back! Building number four on the left! Flynn throw a smoke!" He pulled a grenade out of his pouch screaming, "FRAG OUT!"

Flynn yelled, "SMOKE OUT!"

The grenades popped. I grabbed Bryan and we ran back to the decrepit building. I pushed Bryan through the door and turned around to provide suppressing fire for the other Marines. Fonzie and McMillian found cover near the entrance and fired at the enemy. The squad sprinted behind us into the building.

Fonzie led us out the back of the building and we bolted through the labyrinth of backstreets and alleyways. The Fonz called in the contact report over the radio. No one had any idea where we were. Everything was gray, nothing was written in English. We were fucking lost in that concrete jungle.

Fonzie slowed to a trot and looked into a busted window. "All right everyone in here. QUICK!" He counted us as we moved through the window to make sure we hadn't lost anyone.

McMillian led the way in, muzzle first. Doc and I helped Bryan in next, then the rest of us scrambled through. We moved through the debris to a back room, out of sight from unwelcome eyes.

Fonzie huddled us together. "Athena's on the way, we're going to hold tight until then."

"Who's Athena?" Bryan asked.

"It's a CAAT platoon," I answered.

"What's that?"

"It's the guys with the trucks, missiles, and machine guns."

"Sergeant Palacios," McMillian called.

"Yeah?"

"What's that noise?" McMillian asked.

"I hear it too," Flynn said.

Fonzie gestured his head, "McMillian and Kodak. Go to the roof and check it out."

McMillian and I found the stairs and shuttled up a few decks. We walked in slowly, rifles at the ready. Ivan could have been anywhere.

McMillian crept over to the window, being careful not to stand in front of it so no one could see him. I heard him grumble under his breath, "Fuck fuck fuck fuck fuck."

I looked at him worriedly, "What?"

"Come here."

I edged over to the window and peered out. "What the fuck?" I whispered. Walking down the street, if you would call it walking, was a sixty-foot tall iron monster. It looked like an evil Norse god made a person out of a tank. It had a body, arms, legs, and a head. Its face had one big glowing red eye. It was carrying a rifle about the size of a howitzer and there was a big red star painted on the left shoulder. It was bulky and crude but nonetheless terrifying. "How the fuck are we supposed to fight that?" I looked at McMillian. The metal monster's eyes scanned the streets. A squad of Russian soldiers patrolled behind it. I pulled out my camera and snapped a few photos the thing.

McMillian and I raced down the stairs back to Fonzie.

"Sergeant, you're not going to believe this shit." McMillian panted.

"What?"

"There's a fucking transformer out there."

"What?"

"I don't know, a transformer, or a fucking Gundam, or mecha-godzilla, or a god damned metal gear, I don't know what the fuck it was."

I pulled up the picture on my camera and showed it to Fonzie. His eyes grew in astonishment. "Well, that's just a fucking glorious fist fuck fiesta ain't it?"

"Sergeant, it didn't look like they were searching buildings," McMillian noted.

"Alright," The Fonz looked around the room. "Okay, we're gonna climb up these stairs, quietly. Then we're going to hide out until these ass baskets pass and make movement later."

We climbed to the top floor and perched. Fonzie called in a SALUTE report and gave the COC our current situation.

We sat there for about twenty minutes, staying clear of the windows and keeping the stairwell covered. Doc pulled an MRE out of his pack and started eating his main meal.

I looked over at Doc, "Really dude?"

"Chow's continuous man."

Half the other Marines followed suit and pulled out something to gnaw on.

I opened mine and offered Bryan the main meal.

"Thanks." He took the green plastic sac of slop. "What is this?" He asked curiously.

I handed him the spoon from the pouch. "It's food, eat it."

He grimaced at me. I guess he didn't like being told what to do. I opened another packet and bit into my crackers.

The wind blew through the holes in the walls, chilling us to the bone. I had on my gortex top, but my pants, face, and feet were wet from the snow and I made the cardinal mistake of not bringing extra socks. I watched as the graying sky turned dark. The few fires still burning illuminated an obscure haze through the snow. I took a couple of pictures of us waiting around. The only light was coming in from the window.

Doc came and sat next to me. "This looks like it was someone's apartment."

"Yeah." The photos that used to be on the walls laid covered in dirt and broken glass. A family portrait of man and his wife and children sat on the floor. I picked up the frame and brushed away the shattered shards. "I wonder if these guys got out or if the commies wasted 'em."

"They're not communists anymore," Bryan corrected me.

We ignored him. I glanced over at McMillian, who was watching the window. He looked at Fonzie, "Sergeant, I think they're gone."

Fonzie peered out the window. He then stuck his whole head out looking around. "Yeah, we'd better get moving." He radioed in that we were oscar mike.

We slid back down the stairs being careful not to stomp and make a racket. We didn't know how close the reds were, and we didn't want to advertise our presents. The squad scurried across the road outside into another alleyway. The Fonz looked back at us, "If you can help it don't step in snow, we don't wanna give Ivan a trail." We nodded our heads in compliance.

After an hour of silent creeping through the streets we came upon a church. The west side of the roof was blown out letting in the sun's setting light. The altar and the pews were blown to splinters. A statue of Christ with his hand out as if bidding welcome stood out of a pile of strewn about planks. The statue of Mary was laying on the floor, cut in half, with a dud artillery shell protruding from her chest. I snapped a few photos of the Marines looking at them.

CRACK!

BOOM!

"CONTACT!"

The squad leaped to the floor as Russian Machine guns rattled above us, ripping away what was left of the flimsy church. I was curled in a ball on the ground holding my Kevlar to my head. I looked up and Bryan was standing there paralyzed in fear, too overwhelmed with shock to move. I was too fucking hung over for this shit. "Mother fucker!" I jumped up and again tackled Bryan. But when we hit the deck, instead of feeling the thud of two bodies hit the floor there was a blast, sharp pain, then silence and darkness.

I awoke to Doc slapping the shit out of me. "WAKE THE FUCK UP HANK!"

I looked around with a glazed stare. The Marines were all still firing towards the enemy. Doc was wrapping gauze around my left arm and McMillian was tightening a tourniquet around the leg on the same side. Fonzie was screaming into the radio while shooting and swearing at Ivan. Jesus and Mary were still standing out of the rubble. There was something on the wooden lacquered floor that looked like spaghetti, really thick chunky spaghetti, but without the noodles.

Doc was trying to talk to me. I couldn't hear him. There was a loud ringing in my ears. I couldn't find Bryan. *Did they give him a weapon and have him hold security?*

"Doc," I looked over at him.

Doc said something. It looked like he was telling me I was going to be okay, but I still felt like there was a gremlin fucking a dog whistle in my ears. I looked down at myself, I was drenched in blood and I was shaking violently. I didn't know if the temperature had dropped while I was out or if I had lost that much bodily fluid.

I was starting to be able to hear again, "Doc."

"Yeah buddy what is it?"

"Where's Bryan?"

Doc looked at me with a frightened look in his eyes. "Dude, when you dived on him y'all landed on a grenade." He motioned back with his head. "That's him on the floor."

"Doc, there's nothing on the floor but spaghetti..."

"Yeah."

I stared at what was left of Bryan. "Doc, I swear I didn't do that on purpose."

"I believe you, man." He patted me on the shoulder. "You lost a lot of blood but you're going to be all right."

Fonzie turned around, "Break contact!" He pointed out the doorway we came in from. "Bound back, five hundred yards!"

Doc and McMillian helped me to my feet. "Can you limp it man or do you need help?"

"I can do it, man," I said, huddling, trying not to get shot in the head. Doc let me go and I face planted into the hard wood below.

"Damn it, Hank." Doc picked me up and slung me in a fireman's carry, I passed back out.

When I stirred back from the darkness Doc and a Marine I didn't recognize were loading me into the back of a Humvee. I guess we linked back with the rest of the platoon. That gave me a warm and cozy. It was still freezing out and snow was piling up higher on the ground. It was night, but because of all the white flakes it was still easy to see.

"Doc, are we out?" I felt a little better being awake this time, the hangover was gone, but my limbs were in agony.

"Yeah." He patted my shoulder. "And you need to lose some fucking weight fat ass." He chuckled.

I smiled and raised my middle finger. I heard gunshots and tried to look behind me. "Where's Ivan?"

"Across the block."

Marines started yelling and I could hear fire coming from just outside the vehicle. Doc looked around the corner of the vehicle. "FUCK!" He grabbed me by the flak and threw me into the alley the truck was parked beside. Doc jumped on top of me and the vehicle erupted into a ball of flame.

"What the fuck?" I screamed at Doc.

"Giant metal robot!"

A couple of Marines tried to pull the Marines out of the burning truck, but they were mowed down by Machine gun fire. I saw a couple of assault men from CAAT across the street prepping a SMAW. The Marine holding the tube swore and the other shouted commands. The missile fired towards the Russian metal demon. It was outside of my line of sight, but I heard an explosion, then a loud creak and a crash shook the ground around us.

I forced myself to my feet and peered around the building to see what happened. The robot looking tank had it's legs blown off and was on it's back trying to balance itself. Its head rotated towards us and it grabbed the rifle it had dropped. It pointed it in our direction, but before it could fire, another missile hit it in the shoulder severing its arm. I didn't know at the time if it had a pilot or a crew, but I remember thinking *I hope they like bayonets shoved in their guts.*

Doc grabbed my arm and hoisted me over his shoulder. I pulled my rifle around to my back and pulled out my pistol. "Ya think this time might be it, Doc?"

"Hank…" He looked at me probably thinking about Gilgamesh, "Dude, if you get blasted, who's gonna put cigarettes out on me to prove Keanu Reeves is the greatest actor of all time?"

I coughed up, "It's Brad Pitt." Doc helped me get to the end of the alleyway. "Hold on. Let's see if I can do this without face planting." Doc let me go and I leaned against the Swiss cheesed concrete wall. I pushed myself off. "I think I got it."

"You sure?"

"Yeah." I put my pistol back and unslung my M4. I gimped though an alleyway and we linked back up with Fonzie's squad upstairs in the next building. Everyone was firing at the cyclic, Ivan was fucking everywhere. I reached for my camera, but there was a hole torn through the body and the lens was cut in half. I yanked out the memory card and tossed the camera away.

Fonzie had his ear to the radio relaying information as he sent Ivan lead. He circled his hand in the air. "Athena's in the street! Fall back on the trucks!"

The squad rushed out of the room and down the stairs. I followed trying to shove my memory card into a pouch. The card fell, I kneeled to grab it. Pain shot up through my leg and I fell. I gritted my teeth and grabbed my leg. "Damn it!" I banged my Kevlar on the floor with my head and picked myself back up, snagging the card on the way.

On the way down I must have made a wrong turn. Instead of finding a bunch of Humvees filled with pissed off Marines I found a platoon of Russian soldiers and a giant Soviet walking tank from hell. It pointed its canon-sized rifle at me. The machine's eye flashed as I turned to run.

BOOM!

5 ALONE AND UNAFRIAD

The round burst into an orange fiery cloud behind me. I was thrown back first through a window, which had to be the only fucking article of glass still in one piece in the whole city, and down a flight of stairs.

I plummeted down the stairwell and slammed into a wall. My head and back felt like the Incredible Hulk skipped dinner and a movie and went straight for the gang bang. I looked around the room in a daze. There was a screaming woman being held down on a table by three Russian soldiers. They stared at me in shock. Before they could react I drew my nineteen-eleven and blew a barn door out of each of them.

I dropped my arm. The woman stood up crying and backed away from the bleeding corpses around her. I was too tired and broken to do anything after that. I could only take short, sharp breaths, but I managed to squeak out "U.S. Marines… here to help."

The right side of my body was covered in black soot and the backside of my neck and uniform were shredded from the window. I didn't seem to be burned though.

The woman started to calm down. She walked to me slowly. "Umm, are you alright?" She asked through her tears.

I peered up at her from under my Kevlar, "Define 'all right'," and rested my head back against the wall.

"I don't know. Alive?" She kneeled down beside me and looked over my tattered body.

"Sure," I gasped. "I've been through worse." I had a coughing fit and hacked up a decent amount of blood. "Hey, get away from the stairs, we don't want Ivan to look down and see us." I rolled onto the floor and crawled out of sight of the stair well.

"Ivan?" She squinted.

"The fucking Russians." I took off my helmet and gloves and rubbed my eyes and temples. Everything hurt. I blinked my eyes hard trying to get all the crud out of them. The forced tears were cold against my already frozen face.

The woman, who I haven't gotten a clear look at, sat down next to me, "What's going on out there?" She asked.

I mumbled, "A fucking war."

"Thanks," She said, frustrated.

"Some Latvian dude probably butt fucked Putin's sister and now he's here for revenge. I don't fucking know. We're just here to grab civilians and get the fuck out of dodge."

"Oh, so you're here to take us home?"

DING DING DING! GRAND PRIZE WINNER! "Yup." I tried to take a swig from my canteen, but the water was all ice. I chucked it across the room.

"Have you already evacuated people?"

"We've got a few truck loads."

"Do you remember anyone's name?"

"Yeah, they all ended up being from my fucking book club."

She kept sobbing. I felt a little bad for being a dick, or as bad as I could feel as banged up as I was. "Who are you missing?" I tried to console her.

"My husband's out there somewhere."

I finally cleared my eyes and got a decent look at the woman, it was *her*, eyes bluer than the ocean, skin whiter than milk, hair blacker than my soul. "Satin?"

"What?" She looked at me confused. "How do you know who I am?"

"You don't recognize me?"

She took a careful look at my face.

"Oh *my* God." She looked at me in a state of shock.

"Holy shit, right?" I tried to smirk.

"What are you doing here?"

"Killing dirty Russian snowmen that were going to rape you then cut your head off."

"I mean in Latvia."

"Uh, a 'thank you' would have been nice."

She stared at me, not the least bit entertained.

"We're here part of the rotational security forces in the Baltic. What are *you* doing here?" I coughed up more blood.

"Bryan and I came here for a wedding."

"Who the fuck is getting married in *Latvia* that you'd be here for?"

"Peleus and Thetis Achilla."

"Yeah… who the fuck is that?"

"I'm not really sure. We just came here with Menelaus."

I winced.

"The president." She sneered.

"Okay?"

"Bryan's a senator."

"WHAT?" I spat up more blood in a coughing fit. Then tried to stop myself from whimpering from the pain in my chest. "He's too young to be a senator!"

"No the age is thirty. He's the youngest one the country's had."

"Well, that's fucking nice." I coughed again; there was a little less blood this time. I mumbled, "Fucking faggot."

She snapped back at me, "It seems to be working better than whatever you're doing!"

I wanted to scream at her. I wanted to say *At least* I'm *alive right now!* But I didn't want her to know that it was my fault Bryan wasn't Bryan, as much as he was pasta. Okay, well I did a little bit. But bleeding out on the floor of a dirty basement in East Europe wasn't much better.

"So what you're telling me is you *don't* want me to take you back to get the hell out of here. Because if you want to spend the rest of your life half frozen to death while being ass raped and tortured by soulless, dwarf-dick communists be my fucking guest!"

"That's not what I'm saying," She said frustrated. "He's just done very well for himself, no thanks to *you*."

"No thanks to me? What the fuck did I do?"

"That bullshit you pulled calling the dean and telling him we were together obstructed his education for about a year," she fired back.

"Really? That shit worked?"

"Yes, asshole, he got fired from his job as a teacher's assistant, and expelled from school, and since one of the university's programs was paying for his apartment, he got evicted too!"

"Shitty." *HAHAHA!* I needed a morale boost.

"That's all you have to say for yourself?" Her tears had turned to anger.

"Listen, I was angry, and I had a gun. Then you fed me the ammo."

"What the fuck did you expect to happen? You were being a whiney little bitch, always like 'baby baby please don't leave me' crying on the phone and shit. Fuck you! You're the fucking asshole here!"

I sunk back down, "well maybe I was being a bit craven."

"A bit? Do ya *fucking* think? You were being the *biggest* bitch!"

"Yeah, okay, got it." I tried to wave her off and she started slapping me. I covered my face with my arm and let her hit me. I didn't hit her back, but I did shift so she hit the Kevlar plate in my flack jacket. She gave up the assault and glared at me.

I looked at my watch, or where it used to be. I had a fucking hole in my sleeve over my wrist and the timepiece was gone. "Great." *That was a nice watch, too. I guess that's my fault for bringing it to the field.* "Well, I'd love to just sit in this basement and fight with you all night but we have to fucking leave."

She looked at me, angry that I had the audacity to disregard her like that.

Painfully, I forced myself to my feet.

I looked down at Satin, "I'm going to take you across the street, throw you into a truck, drive you to the Latvian army base, and then chuck you into an airplane, and never see your pasty white ass again." I put my hands in the air demandingly. "Will that one work for you?"

Satin crossed her arms, "It will."

"Awesome." I pointed my thumb over my shoulder. "Let's go." I limped to the stairs and started hobbling up.

"Are you going to be make it with that limp?" She asked.

"I made it down here didn't I?"

"You fell down here. You didn't use your legs."

I shot daggers at her.

"Are you at least going to take your helmet?"

"Death would be *more* than welcome right now, I'll be fine without it." I pulled my beanie on.

I made the painful climb up the stairs and put just enough of my face past where the doorframe used to be, to see if Ivan was still around. The giant walking tank was split open and dinged from heavy machine gun fire. CAAT must have gotten him. The cockpit was open and the pilot was laying half of the way out. A stream of blood stained the armor from him to the ground. There was gunfire in the distance, but I couldn't figure out which direction it was coming from. The ringing in my ears was too loud. I signaled for Satin to follow me and limped as fast as I could across the street.

We moved into the alley from where I came then to the street on the other side. No one was there.

"Where the fuck is everyone?" I put my left hand up to the side of my face. "We are *so* fucked!"

"What's happening? Where's whomever we're trying to find?" Satin inquired.

"Fuck," I muttered. "I don't know."

"Well, where's that army base about which you were talking?"

"I don't know where the fuck we are."

"How do you not know where we are?"

"Because it's dark outside, and foggy, so I can't see really bright lights and can't orientate myself by where the sun is and I was passed out when I got carried over here." I spread the fabric over my skin below my tourniquet so she could see a wad of bloody gauze. "I landed on a fucking hand grenade and was out for a while. Okay?"

"If you landed on a grenade how are you alive?"

I knew the answer, but I wasn't going to tell her. "How about we don't bitch at each other right now. We've got more important problems."

"Fine."

I walked on the sidewalk close to the buildings down the street in what I thought was the right direction. "Stay out of the middle of the road so they don't see you and keep your eyes open for a convenience store or something."

"What do you want out of a convenience store?" Satin asked.

"One of those novelty tourist maps. If I can find where we're at on there I should be able to get us the fuck out of here."

We walked straight on that road for at least an hour in the bitter cold without one word spoken until Satin said, "Thanks for saving me from those guys."

"What?" I looked back at her. "Oh, uh… no problem." I turned back around. "Fucking communists. They're worse than Al Qaeda."

"All of them or just the Russians? Who aren't actually communists anymore, by the way."

"All of them. I don't give a shit. Once a commie, always a commie." I don't know if she was bored or trying to get her mind off the cold or if she was scared but she started talking. I doubted if she really cared.

"So, what have you been up to?" She shivered. "Since I last saw you."

"Went to Afghan a couple of times, then Iraq, and Iran. Married a Virescent, got a sweet car and nice house and I'm about to have a kid. I was finally starting to be happy with life, then this shit happened and there's a good possibility I'm never going to see that shit again."

"Oh, I'm sorry about that."

"No, it's cool," I said sarcastically. "I was about to get out of the Marine Corps and just fucking live, but I'm okay chucking my life into inherent danger. It's cool. It's real fucking cool." I spat half a mouthful of blood and saliva without looking back to address her. "What about you? You married that dipshit?"

"Yeah, he's actually really great," She whispered.

I wasn't feeling a bit of sorrow for his death at this point. "No I mean, you left me for *him?*"

"Yeah, you were being a complete asshole."

"Not until you starting screwing around with him," I shot back at her.

"You didn't know if I was doing that, you were speculating."

"Well you *were,* weren't you?" I demanded.

She didn't answer, but I could feel her eyes darting me down.

"What was so great about that fat fucking ass anyway?"

"First off Hank, he's not an ass. He's kind to me and very caring and sweet."

"So you're telling me I wasn't?"

"Well," she paused and took in a deep breath, "He was also there for me. You were God knows how many miles away gallivanting around the desert with an M16. I needed someone close to me. And you drove me away."

"Yeah, I guess we're not all qualified to make sacrifices," is what I said, but I was thinking was, *Fuck you, you selfish, two-timing succubus fuck.*

"Wait!" She halted me. "*I'm* the one who can't make sacrifices?" She said angrily, "what about you? Everything was *always* about *you*! Just look at *this*!"

"How is this about *fucking* me?"

"The whole Marine Corps thing was! You joined because it's what you wanted to do, and you just left me behind like I was nothing."

"That is not fucking true at all. I left home to go serve my fucking country and you didn't want to come along. I fucking asked you to come out to California with me, and woman, you said 'no'. Don't pin being separated on me. You are the one who didn't show up. You ran off in another direction."

"I was eighteen. I wasn't about to go off and ruin my life."

"So, I would have ruined your life, huh?"

She didn't have an answer to that one.

"It's cool, I'm glad you didn't."

"Then why did you plead so much?" She asked indignantly.

"I would have wanted nothing more *then*, but now you're a prissy little know it all, and I wouldn't be able to please you, not with this paycheck anyway. I get it, it's cool," I barked maliciously.

"I needed to find myself," she rebutted.

"*Find* yourself?" I stopped walking and faced her. "That's bullshit! That's fucking unadulterated, whitewashed bullshit. Where were you that you had to go find yourself?"

"I didn't know who I was."

I just stared at her with a bewildered look on my face, "who were you? Sybil? Did you have multiple personality disorder?"

"No, I was just a kid, and I didn't want to be stuck never knowing what could have been."

I didn't respond to that. I knew that when we were together I was a moron. I mean who wasn't a complete fucking idiot when they were nineteen, but just because I made stupid decisions doesn't mean that it didn't hurt. Satin was right in her decision and in the end, everyone is really just looking out for number one. Could anyone blame her? It really is funny how something so miniscule in the grand scheme of things can cut someone's world apart.

Satin interrupted my thought process, "and you're not the only one who makes sacrifices Hank."

"Really?" I said sarcastically. "How often do you see your family?"

She opened her mouth to answer me.

I cut her off, "when was the last time you couldn't communicate with anyone you cared about because you were on the other side of the world and you had no way of knowing if they were OK?"

"Hank, that…"

"When was the last time you got shot, stabbed, blown up, or fell on a grenade?"

"Han…"

"When was the last time you saw your friends crying for help in a bloody mess on the ground and no matter how they begged to not be taken into the darkness all you could do was stand there impotently and watch them die?"

"Hank, that's not fair."

"No, that's the world we live in. That's the goddamned problem with America, everyone's out for themselves, and they want everything given to them. No one wants to work for anything anymore. They live locked up in their castles and ignore the rest of the world outside. They don't understand that things are so fucking good in the States that homeless people in Detroit have it better than the middle class in some other countries. They think a bad day is when they have a flat tire in the rain. Well the world doesn't revolve around Satin Sheats. And for you, say'n that you didn't want to wonder what could have been to then run off and marry some disgusting fuck before you were even done with me. *The* fuck?"

She looked at me meekly, "the world doesn't revolve around you either Hank."

I leaned in close to her face and looked here square in the eye. Slowly and quietly I said, "Fuck you."

Neither one of us said anything for a good minute. We continued walking.

"You used to be a happy person, Hank."

"I used to not be freezing in the cold not knowing where the fuck I was, hoping some snowman wasn't going to sprout up and unload an AK into my nut sack with a woman who fucking hates my fucking guts."

"I don't hate you, Hank."

"Then what would you call it, Satin?"

"I don't know," she murmured. "You just put me through a lot. I thought you were going to come and show up at my place, stab Bryan, and stalk me from the bushes or something like that."

"Yeah, I don't make enough money to just fly across the country for the sole reason of kicking someone's teeth in. Fuck, things probably would have turned out better for me if I had though."

I turned around and walked for a few more minutes until I spotted a small row of stores. "That place over there looks good." I pointed toward a souvenir shop. "You'd think there'd be more shit like that around here."

"*One* would, yes," she said, correcting my grammar.

We walked across the street and started rummaging through a store, "hey, if you're hungry now would be a good time to eat something, if you can find anything."

Satin looked around the store and grabbed a bag of chips.

I found a map of the city by the postcards that were knocked over onto the floor, and a bag of some kind of jerky.

"Will you be able to find a way back?" She asked.

"As long as I can match a street sign with something on here." I bit into a piece of jerky I found and walked out to a street sign. "All this shit looks the same to me." I compared the lettering on the sign to the lettering on the map.

Satin put her finger on the map and said, "here we are."

I marked the map where we thought we were and starting looking for the base. "Okay, I think I know where to go."

I noticed Satin was quivering from the subzero hell we were in. All she had on was a thick sweater, a beanie, and a scarf.

I took off my flack vest and my gortex coat and offered her the jacket. "Here put this on, it's got holes in it and it's soaked in dried blood but it should help with the cold."

"Are you sure?"

"Yea, take it you're going to need it. The weather's going to get worse before it gets better." I put my flack back on, I still had a lightweight fleece on under my blouse, it didn't help too much, but the plates in my flack jacket blocked the wind.

We moved west through the city, the snow started to fall heavier. The wind blew through my bones. We couldn't move too fast. The hole in my leg and the coughing up of blood didn't favor moving swiftly. I started to worry about frostbite or ice forming in a wound. I was attached to my body parts, in more than one way, unlike what I had just found.

"Shit," I said looking down at an arm that looked like it used to belong to a Marine.

"What's wrong?" Satin asked me.

I looked back at her, she was miserable. Her bangs were frozen, her glasses were covered in an icy glaze, and her lips were chapped and cracking. I motioned to the arm. "This." I looked around, spent cartridges and blood caked the pavement. The arm was holding a radio. I bent down to inspect it. I opened the shoulder pocket on the arm and pulled the kill card out. It was one of Fonzie's guys.

"What's that?" Satin asked me.

"It's kinda like a dog tag that you keep in your pockets so, if like, here…" I presented her the arm, "you can find out what poor bastard it belonged to."

Satin looked like she was going to puke.

"This guy's in my platoon." I picked up the radio it had called for help. "Any station any station this is Combat Camera. Any station any station this is Combat Camera, over."

I looked at the radio's battery life. It was almost dead. The radio gave a slight hum and the speaker rang, "Combat Camera this is Fox Six Actual, send your traffic."

"Thank you God in heaven!" Satin whimpered.

I pressed the button on the radio, "Fox Six, I got separated from my platoon about five hours ago, I am escorting one civilian and my location is at Third Ave and Fifth Street. I don't have coordinates over."

"Stand by..."

"What's that mean?" Satin asked, "Are they coming to get us?"

"No." I kept looking at the radio. "They just told us to hold on."

Satin looked anxious.

"Hey, let's get out of the road, we don't need to get spotted." I guided her to the opening of an alley.

"Combat Camera this is Fox Six."

"Send it."

"Fox Two is currently two klicks to your north west."

"Roger, copy all, tango, out." I looked over at Satin and smiled for the first time that day. "We got a ride."

"Thank God!"

We headed north through what alleys we could and streets when needed. When we turned west I told Satin, "when we get close we're gonna make an iron cross so they don't shoot us."

"What's that?" she inquired.

I made the gesture for her. "Just put your arms straight out with your palms toward them and walk slow."

"Ok…Hank."

"Satin."

"When you get home, give me a call."

I glanced over at her, "I guess you really do have to lose to know how to win."

"It was nice to see someone I knew out here, *even* if it was you."

"Satin, it's been so long that we don't even really know each other anymore." I tried to make her think I was shrugging her off.

"And in Hell, even old acquaintances are welcome."

It didn't take us long at all to get there, even with my gimp leg. We put up the iron cross and walked into the intersection slowly. I didn't see the trucks.

We stopped walking in the middle of the road. A few Marines popped out of a doorway. It was Stevens! "The *Devil*'s been at work today hasn't he?"

I looked him in the eye, "He wouldn't be much without his *Dogs*."

Satin and I headed to the doorway of the half destroyed building. Satin went first. Stevens said, "Dude you look like shit."

"Blow me."

He patted me on the back and helped Satin in. She turned back to look at me, I took a step into the doorway and I heard a loud crack. I saw blood splatter on Satin's face. It all of a sudden got really hard to breath. Satin looked horrified. I looked down and saw a good deal more blood start pouring out of my chest.

One of the Marines screamed "SNIPER!" I fell on the ground. The Marines drug me inside and started firing in all directions.

Doc was there. He pulled me further into the building. He took off my flack jacket, opened my blouse and cut off my sweater and skivvy shirt.

The floor was cold, and all I could see was gray, I thought I was going to die of hypothermia. I hoped that time it would stick. Doc put a piece of plastic over the hole in my chest and duct taped it to me. He looked down at me, "Hey buddy, you're going to be okay."

I grabbed the shoulder strap on his flak. I tried to tell him *Fuck my life.* But instead I laughed and rolled my head back.

I heard a loud crash and the building shook. The machinegun fire intensified. The Doc closed my blouse and flack. "Try to stay warm, man."

The pain mixed with the cold, put together with my aching bones and feet and the throbbing of my previous wounds, put me at a point where I didn't care anymore. Maybe it was my brain releasing endorphins to alleviate the circumstances. My body started to go numb. The only thing I was afraid of was the possibility of waking back up. I crawled to the wall on my back and propped my head up on it.

I saw Satin hunkered down under a staircase screaming, crying in the fetal position. I pulled my cigarettes out of a grenade pouch. My shaking hand put the Lucky's in my mouth. *I wonder what smoking feels like with a sucking chest wound?* I tried to reach for my lighter, but before I could find I, everything faded to black...

6 SHOCK TRAUMA PLATOON

I woke up to the cold. I was on one of those flimsy green cots. Doc was sleeping in a chair a few feet away. I felt the stinging pressure of tears building behind my eyes.

"Doc," I groaned in a whisper. He didn't hear me. I tried to get up. My chest was in agony. I looked like a mummy with all the gauze around me. "Doc..." I looked around the floor. With great strain, I reached down to grab a pen off the ground. I tossed it to his head. My eyes started to itch.

Doc shook himself awake. Then smiled. "Morning, sunshine."

"Where are we?" I glanced around the room filled with expeditionary medical equipment.

"The shock trauma platoon station."

"Latvia?"

"Latvia."

Tears started rolling down my face, "Goddamnit."

"We're at a Latvian army FOB."

"Why am I not with other casualties?" I was on the only bed in the room.

"I wanted to see if you were going to wake up. I wasn't that worried about you. I had a pretty good feeling you were going to come out unscathed. I mean you're still pretty full of holes, but they're healing."

"I should be fucking dead."

"We both should have been dead a long time ago, man."

"How long have I been out?"

"No more than a week."

"That was quick," I thought about the dungeon in Iraq, and the Epic of Gilgamesh. "I guess that fucking book was right after all."

Doc stared at the floor, "maybe we are immortal then."

I tried not to think about the implications of that.

"Well, it's not like you had an artillery round blow you into little pieces, again."

"Yeah," I rubbed my leg and chest. They were tender and hurt from anything but the lightest touch. "Well…" I sighed. "At least when this is over I can go home to Penelope."

"Yeah if there's a world left when this is over."

"Is it that bad already?"

"Congress declared war on Russia yesterday."

I laughed, "Oh, that's fucking great. How many other places did they attack?"

"Just the Baltic states."

"I'm having a hard time believing congress declared war that quick over East Europe."

"Yeah… Putin kidnapped the First Lady."

"You're shitting me."

"Nope."

I shook my head. "Doc, do you ever think that you're in a bad SciFi movie and the director just fucking hates you?"

"I'm starting to."

I lowered my feet to the floor. "My shit around here anywhere?"

"Yeah, I'll dig it up here in a minute." Doc pulled a uniform out of a box. "But I did get you new camis." He tossed them over to me. "But there's no name tapes on them so stay away from First Sergeant."

I started putting on the uniform. "So, Putin *kidnapped* the First Lady?"

"Yeah, like him personally."

"Seriously though, that guy's a fucking James Bond villain. I mean, who the fuck else would do that? Putin is just such a hard guy to hate, I'd like to think if we captured him we'd only break eight or nine bones instead of beating him to death."

"And it doesn't look like we're going to be going home anytime soon."

"You say'n we're not getting anymore libo?"

Doc exhaled a deep breath and shook his head at me.

I hated new uniforms; they were stiff and needed to be broken in. Doc pointed me to my gear. My Alice pack was covered in blood and full of holes. I guess it's good blood stains brown. I looked at the hole the bullet went through; it wasn't more than an inch above the SAPI plate. I dug out a sweater and a pack of cigarettes. I slung my rifle and put my forty-five in my right pocket. I took a few magazines off my flack and stuck them in my cargo pockets.

I limped to the door window and peered out. It was overcast with a good two feet of snow on the ground. We were on the third or fourth floor. "This isn't much of a FOB." We were in a cluster of maybe seven buildings on the side of a mountain. There were a few dirt roads that led out. The hardest wall was made of sandbags, and there weren't many of them.

"Yeah, it's mostly just C-Wire and Claymores." Doc stood up. "We can smoke on the ladder-well."

"Awesome." We walked out. "You got a lighter?"

"I got your lighter." He handed me the lighter Penelope got me for Christmas a few years back. It's the only lighter I've used since.

"I fucking love the Marine Corps, and the Marine Corps fucking loves me." I smiled a little as I read it and thought about Penelope. I lit up and coughed. I wheezed, "It hurts to smoke."

"You *did* have a sucking chest wound."

84

"Don't remind me." I took short drags. I didn't want to waste tobacco. "What's chow here?"

"MREs."

"Great." I took another short drag, it was getting easier. "I lost my Kevlar."

"Yeah you're shit out of luck on that one, dude."

Marines were running about below us, filling sandbags, setting up more barbed wire, and cleaning their weapons, among other things. "How many did we lose?"

"About forty KIA, another hundred have been sent back to Germany. Fonzie's squad ended up taking some bad hits."

"Yeah, I found Rios' arm."

"Yeah, it was bad."

"Well, thanks for keeping me here." I said, sarcastically.

"Hank, you know full well that if I screwed you out of killing Russians you'd never forgive me."

I smiled at Doc, "Yeah." I surveyed our area again. "Are we just digging in or what's going on?"

"Three-Eight and One-Seven are supposed to be here in the next week off MEUs. There's an army division from Germany a little south of us. I heard that Blue Diamond and the Eighty Second Airborne are supposed to be here at some point, but who the fuck knows how long that's going to take."

"So fucking World War Three?"

"We'll see."

"Hey, what's the fucking deal with the giant walking tanks."

"Putinbots?"

"Is that what we're calling them?"

"That's what we're calling the Russian ones."

"Just the Russian ones?"

"Yeah, apparently we have something similar, but we haven't seen any yet."

"That's going to make things fucking peachy. You know what I think's funny though? Remember watching giant Japanese robot movies and thinking the robots were fucking invincible?"

"Yeah."

"Well those things were scary, but they were pretty easy to score mobility kills on."

"Yeah, they did seem like they needed more armor on their limbs. But those things are fast. One of the S2 Marines said there's a flying model, so it can do paratrooper shit. Like one of those could drop on us right now and probably take out the rest of the battalion out in the open like this."

"So are we hiding?"

"Kind of. But that shit's why there's Marines with javelins and Tow missiles on all the roofs and the Latvians have those antiaircraft guns out there."

"Makes sense."

We went back inside and ripped open a couple MREs.

"So that chick was the great white buffalo?"

"Yeah, how fucked up is that?"

"And you killed her husband."

"It was an accident." I tore open my main meal. "His dumb ass was going to die anyway."

"Yeah, he was kind of a dumb shit."

"So, check this out. Dude was a fucking senator."

"He looked a little young for that."

"That's why they were in town."

"Yeah, I guess that explains a few things. But seriously, that shit's fucked up."

After we ate and smoked again I hunted down the S-shops. I practically had to suck the adjutant's dick to get ahold of a satphone. I punched in Penelope's cell phone number and listened to the rings.

"Hello?" Penelope's tired voice squeaked.

"Hey, babe."

"Hank! Oh my God! Are you okay?"

"Yeah babe, I'm okay. I got a little banged up, but I'm still in the fight."

"I wish you weren't."

"I know, but getting hurt enough to leave is pretty much being crippled for life."

"That's not what I meant."

"I know, baby."

I heard Penelope sniffling.

"Hey now, hey. I'm alright. Don't worry about me, I'll be coming home to you."

"When, Hank?"

I paused for a moment. "I don't know. Probably not anytime soon. How's the baby?"

"Healthy."

"Have you thought about names yet?"

"I'm thinking Edward Thatch for a boy or Mary Reed for a girl."

"Those are good names," I lied. *What the fuck kind of names are those?*

"Is your address going to be the same?"

"It should be."

"Do you need anything?"

"Cigarettes. Lots and lots of cigarettes."

"Lucky's?"

"Please, Ma'am."

"Okay."

"Alright babe, I know you have work in the morning. I just wanted to let you know I'm still alive and kick'n."

"Thank you for calling me."

"Anytime."

"I love you."

"I love you, too."

Penelope stayed on the line for about ten seconds before hanging up. I closed my eyes and lit a cigarette. I hated not talking to her for weeks, then only calling for a few minutes, but that's the nature of the beast.

I took the phone back and found Éclair in one of the buildings they were using for barracks. "Yo." I patted him on the back.

"Hey brother, what's up?"

"Not much." Éclair looked worn out. I looked around, all the Marines did. "Hey, you got my shit by chance?"

"I grabbed your sea bag but I don't know what all I left behind."

"It's cool, man."

"So I take it you weren't shot enough for it to hurt?"

I rubbed my chest, it was still sore. "Oh no, it hurt, and my leg's all fucked up. I'm going to try to hobble along until someone kicks me back because I can't keep up."

"Yeah, well you look like shit dude. Minus the new clothes."

"Yeah, Doc grabbed'em for me."

"Cool."

"Yeah. Talk to Ginny recently?"

"A few days ago, she's flipping shit."

"Well, we did come out here to train with Latvians and ended up fighting the Russians."

"Yeah, apparently people are already protesting against the war."

"Already?"

"Yeah. They don't think East Europe is our problem."

"When *have* the American people thought that the war was their problem?"

"After Pearl Harbor."

"I guess, but what about this First Lady fuckery?"

"I really don't think anyone gives a shit."

"Hmm." I sat down on Éclair's rack, my leg was starting to sting. "Well that's American."

"Ha. You get a chance to call Penelope?"

"Yeah." I scratched the back of my head. "She sounded pretty distraught. And my kid's gonna have a stupid fucking name because I didn't want to upset her more than she already was."

"What's she wanna name it?"

"Either Edward Thatch or Mary Reed."

"I guess that's not terrible."

"Eh."

Éclair looked at his watch. "Well, hey man, I got your sea bag under my rack if you want it now. But I have to go to a brief."

"Yuck, have fun with that."

"Actually dude, you should come. The intel Marines are gonna give a brief on the giant Russian robot things."

"No shit? I'll check that out."

The sergeants and above of the battalion crammed into a makeshift auditorium. It was dirty broken concrete like every other building I'd seen in the country. But at least it had windows and was free of bullet holes. A projector illuminated a white box of light on the wall.

"Good Afternoon, gentlemen. My name is Corporal Anderson," said the Marine at the front of the room. His uniform hung around him like a tent. He was about six foot five and a hundred and six pounds. "And today, I will be briefing you on the enemy mechs." Anderson looked over at a Marine by a laptop. "Next slide, please."

The white box of light on the wall was replaced with a photo of the giant metal tank like the ones from Daugavpils. "Some of you have seen this already. Five of them were destroyed in Daugavpils last week by Marines in the battalion."

"OORAH!" yelled a few Marines from the back, probably the guys who made the kill.

"Very little is known about these. We do know that they were constructed under Operation Putinbot using Virescent technology. This mech has been designated 'Bishop.' Its arms are built to be able to utilize multiple weapons systems and its fingers are all functional so they may be used to grab or lift. The Bishop is crewed by one pilot, and is heavily armored around the cockpit, however, the armor around the limbs and joins were not manufactured well. You should be able to score mobility kills by firing missiles there. A catastrophic kill on the other hand will probably not be able to be attained without close air support or artillery. There are also multiple camera systems aboard. While taking out the 'eye' or the main camera may stunt it momentarily, there are backup systems in place. It's assumed that there is a night vision and heat signature capacity as well. Next slide."

The next photo showed a picture of a different mech. It was a lot thicker than the Bishop. The torso looked like a tank hull with the turret as the head. Instead of a barrel on the turret it had a red, eyelike camera like the Bishop did. It didn't have arms with fingers and hands, and the joints on its legs were backwards, like a bird.

"Gentlemen, this is the 'Rook.' You'll notice that unlike the Bishop, the Rook doesn't have arms. It does however have, on one side, a twenty-three millimeter Gatling gun, and for the other arm, there's a hundred and fifty-two millimeter repeating recoilless rifle. We believe it was built as a tank buster. The sides and underbelly are heavily armored. The topside however isn't as thick. Your best bet on these is going to be to hit it with a javelin missile from above. The three soldiers of its four man crew sit in the 'head' with one in the hull. Next slide."

The next picture showed a more slender mech. Like the Bishop, it was very human shaped, its head looked identical to the Bishop's, but its joints were rounded instead of square.

"This gentlemen is the last of the three, the Knight. Pay very close attention to what I'm about to say. Notice the cylinders on the back and shoulders. The Knight is capable of sustained flight for close to two miles. This allows the Knight to asymmetrically maneuver the battlefield. If at all possible, avoid contact with this piece of machinery. It is equipped with internal, one oh eight millimeter machine guns, and can utilize any of the 'hand held' weapons the Bishop uses. The suggested method of killing this is by CAS, however, if you're in a pinch and you can get it without it seeing you, any type of missile into the engines on the back *may* ground it. That said, you will still have to deal with a giant, walking tank. At this time, do I have any questions?"

"Yes," Lieutenant Toshi raised his hand. "Are there more specifics you can give us on these things? Range, fuel type, maneuvering formations, anything of that nature?"

"Uh, Sir…" Anderson said. "Unfortunately this information has been gathered by units on the ground over the last week. The three letter agencies and Headquarters Marine Corps have not felt the need to send us anything they know. However when *I* know *you* will know."

"What about information on the mechs coming here from Pendleton?" Lt Toshi asked.

"Sir, we don't know anything about them except that they exist. They should be in the AO this month and we'll hook up with their S2 then and build a brief for the staff."

"Thank you," said the lieutenant.

Éclair and I stood outside after the brief and lit cigarettes. "Jesus, dude." Éclair puffed.

"I know, right?"

"I wonder what ours look like."

"I don't know, man. But these things don't really seem much more difficult than a tank. They just pack more ass and one can fly."

"That's the one that scares me, dude. That fucker could just land here and stomp on us all."

"Dude, I'm pretty sure they have F18s flying around specifically so that doesn't happen. And you drop a JDAM on one of those and they're out."

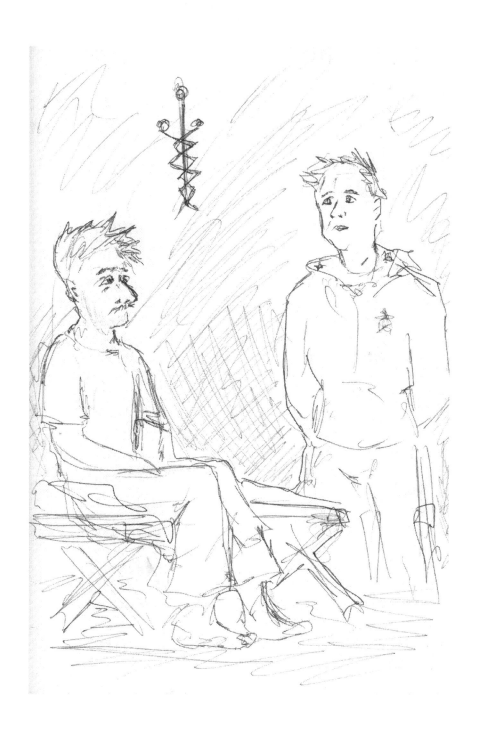

7 PANZER FOUR TO ROOK TWO

The next week was spent fortifying the FOB. Mostly filling sandbags and digging trenches. We joked around with the Latvian soldiers. They had about one guy a platoon that spoke at least broken English, so most of the conversing was hand gestures.

On an afternoon a few weeks later, Éclair and I were smoking on the side of the barracks trying to stay out of the wind.

"My toes haven't been warm since I've fucking been here," I exhaled.

"Yeah, it's pretty much bullshit," Éclair griped.

"They feel like they're going to fall off, but they won't get frostbite and turn black. I just hope they don't send us forward without giving us better socks first."

"That's why Hitler couldn't take Russia."

"No, Hitler couldn't take Russia because they didn't *change* their socks, and they didn't take Motrin."

Éclair chuckled. "At least they're letting us wear beanies instead of freezing out ears off."

"Yeah, First Sergeant DeLeon's pretty cool."

Éclair focused his eyes behind me and motioned his head. I turned around to see what he was looking at. There was a convoy of trucks driving towards the FOB.

"Ya think they're bringing mail?" Éclair asked.

When they got closer to the gate, or the opening in the C-wire we were calling a gate, I noticed the trucks weren't American and recognized the insignias on the sides. "Those are German."

"Yeah, I saw the crosses."

"It looks like they've got a lot of shit," I said. Several of the vehicles had flatbed semi trailers, and their cargo was covered with large green tarps. "I wonder what they have."

"Whatever it is, it's probably not hookers, or blow."

I lit another cigarette. "Hey dude, check it out. The guys in the back are towing Howitzers."

"That's comforting. Now we're going to have a bunch of Nazis running around the camp."

"They're not Nazi's anymore, man."

"Yeah, but their parents probably were."

"So?"

"*So?*"

"Yeah, so what if they *are* Nazis? At least we're not going to be defending a position with the French, and the Nazi's kicked ass, they were just royal douche bags."

"Eh, I guess."

"And fuck, if you think about it, besides killing Jews, what did Hitler do wrong?"

"*What!?*"

"Naw, think about it, man. All the Nazis did was murder Jews and kill the shit out of Russians. Take the Jew part away and it's just killing Russians, and I don't see a problem with that." I said.

"I know you lost a lot of blood and all, but did they give you a transfusion? And did you hit your head, and if so, how hard was it? The Nazi's did a lot more fucked up shit than just that."

"And if you *really* think about it…" I said, ignoring Éclair, "Hitler wasn't that bad of a guy, I mean he *killed* Hitler."

Éclair chuckled a little bit, I guess he figured out I was screwing with him. We smoked a few more cigarettes and watched the Germans set up camp. They set up a series of tents and positioned their canons at the east end of the FOB. A group of the soldiers took the tarps off of the semis. Their cargo was mechs, and they were a hell of a lot more elegant than the Russian ones. Their 'face' looked like an old gas mask with a cylinder and tubes, we guessed it was some sort of intake, and it was wearing something that looked like an old helmet from World War Two. The shoulders had thick metal rectangle shields that protected the arms. Unit insignias and Iron Crosses were painted in grey on sides. The mechs were painted white with green and black speckling. When they powered on, the eyes of the 'gas mask' glowed a faint orange. They sat up and stood off of the trailers. Each footstep shook the ground. The four of them grabbed weapons off of one of the other trailers and posted behind the canons.

"That's pretty sick," Éclair said, admiring the iron monsters.

"Yeah, it's cool, but it's bullshit."

"Huh?"

"Where's ours? We're supposed to be the greatest nation on the fucking planet and the fucking Germans are backing up the goddamned U.S. Marines. I mean yeah, it's better than nothing, but holy shit dude. Shouldn't there be a MEU down in the Med that could have floated up here and given us a few of these things by now?"

"No one said the Marine Corps was efficient. Remember how on Guadalcanal they dropped off the Marines and the Japanese navy sank all the ships, and Marines were just stuck on the island alone, and unafraid for a few months?"

"Eh."

"Hey, at least Comm's up."

The next few days went by smoothly. Doc, Éclair, Fonz, and I were smoking by the building closest to the German artillery line. Some soldiers were putting up IR netting over the mechs and canons. They had used the mechs to dig a thick trench around the FOB. It turns out they could be used as backhoes.

A German soldier walked up to us. "Excuse me," he said in an accent that let us know he didn't know much English, "May I, uh…" He had a confused look on his face and he motioned his hand as if he were lighting a cigarette.

"Sure, dude." Fonzie pulled out a pack and gave the German a smoke.

"Uh, thank you!" The soldier said happily. He pulled out a lighter and lit the cigarette.

"Hey, buddy," I said to him.

"Ja?"

I pointed to the mechs in the trench getting covered in snow. "What are those called?"

The soldier looked at the giant metal beasts and back as me, "Der Treten -Panzer?"

"Treten-Panzer?" I repeated.

"Ah, yas!" he said.

"What do you do?" Fonzie asked him.

The solder looked at Fonzie with a confused look on his face, "uh, mien English, ist not, uh, goot."

"Work" Fonzie said, "job?"

"Verk?" The solder said. He started speaking in German before he remembered none of us spoke it. He pointed at the Treten-Panzer then looked back at us. He said a few words and imitated working on a car with his hands.

"Mechanic?" Doc asked.

"Ah ja, mechanic." He took a deep drag from the cigarette Fonzie gave him. And stuck his hand out. "Nils."

Éclair pointed at him, "Nils?"

"Ja."

We all exchanged names. Nils put out the cigarette, waved, "Uh, thank you." And walked back towards the mechs.

I think I had been asleep for a few hours when I awoke in a dream.

I was in the aid station, where my cot was, but it wasn't the aid station. It was dreary and the walls almost seemed to move like waves in the ocean on a calm day. I was lying in my cot, but I was watching myself stand up and walk across the room. I saw myself standing next to a man with burns on his arms.

"Who are you?" The other me asked the man with the burns.

"McBland," he said. I felt like he wasn't telling the truth, but he wasn't lying either.

"Where are you from?"

"Nowhere around here." When he said that it registered to me that he wasn't from this plane of existence.

"What do you want?" I saw myself ask.

"I'm just checking things out," he said, looking around the room. Then McBland looked over to me-me. Me in the bed, "Wake up!"

I woke up sweating, my heart was racing and I felt scared. I didn't know why, it wasn't really a *bad* dream. Sure it was creepy, but it didn't have that nightmare feel. I took a swig from my canteen and went back to sleep.

I had another dream when I fell back into slumber.

It was night and I was in Hollywood. Thick red flames rose from the broken windows along the street. I was in my gear and running. I didn't know what I was running for, or from. I stopped at an intersection. I looked around me, but didn't find anyone or anything that grabbed my attention. I heard Penelope calling for me. I struggled to try to hear where her voice was coming from. She was everywhere. Someone started shooting at me from the buildings. I jumped into a burning window, I figured fire was better than bullets. Penelope was in the room. She was wearing a dress made of scales and she had snakes for hair. "Hank…" she said over the sounds of the machine guns still trying to get me, "Hank, you have to wake up."

I woke up to Doc yelling at me, "GET THE FUCK UP!"

I looked at him wondering why he was shaking me until I realized the machine guns from my dream, weren't from my dream. "Shit." I rolled off my cot and hit my leg on the floor. It was a nice reminder that it hadn't healed yet. I groaned and rubbed the sore spot on my thigh.

I haphazardly threw on my gear, still stained with my own blood, and ran as fast as my legs would let me, outside. I stopped on the balcony before heading down stairs to see what was happening. The German cannons were firing into the tree line, their barrels almost parallel to the deck. Long orange streaks flew from the barrels of the Panzers' guns. One of the ones from the western side of the FOB was moving along the south, the other kept facing west to keep watch on the rear.

The mortar men illuminated the battlefield with yellow burning balls of light that slowly drifted down from the sky. There were two Rooks coming from the east. Their hulls just barely surfaced from the top of the tree line. They had to knock down the vegetation to move through the dense forest. That's one advantage they had over a conventional tank, they could make their own way. One of the Rooks fired a round from its cannon arm. It fell just short enough of the trench to rattle the Marines.

Doc and I ran downstairs. Fonzie was leading his squad in a dead sprint towards the front. We followed after them. We ran half crouched trying not to get picked off by Russian machine guns. We jumped into the trench and threw our barrels over the edge. We didn't see anyone yet. The trees started about fifty meters away, so we would have a few seconds to shoot once Ivan came through, *if* he came through. The canons were blowing the trees into toothpicks.

One of the Panzers climbed out of his fighting hole and started advancing towards the Rooks. The Panzer from the south was circling around to flank. The gun the Panzers held fired about two rounds a second. I thought that was pretty impressive considering it was a howitzer round. A few shells hit the Rook. It jolted back and shook for a second after each impact, but it kept moving. The second Rook fired a burst from its canon and pillars of earth shot up out of the ground in a line leading up to the canons. The center two exploded in a red ball of flame.

With the mechs battling each other, and the artillery, at least momentarily silenced. A human wave of Russian soldiers came screaming through the destroyed tree line. We started picking them off. Some Marines were firing carelessly into the hoard, others were taking a second to aim and taking out a soldier per bullet.

Then we fixed bayonets.

When the Russians got to the C-wire the first wave got stuck and we supplemented the cuts in their skin from the wire with holes in the rest of their body. The men behind them didn't think twice about climbing over their dead friends' bodies and charging towards us. A good number of them ran into the claymores planted between the trench and the wire. The rest charged us, firing madly.

I was scared out of my fucking mind. I was pretty sure at that point that I couldn't die, but that didn't mean this shit wasn't going to be painful.

Fonzie changed the magazine in his weapon. "Goddamn it! This fucking piece of shit doesn't shoot fast enough!"

The Latvian soldier beside the Fonz fell back into the trench with a large gushing hole where his face used to be. Fonzie looked at him stone faced, then picked up his weapon. I don't know what model it was, but it was belt fed. The Fonz opened up on the Russians, pushing them down like toy soldiers in the wind. Another Latvian soldier next to him gazed upon him in terror for a second before turning around and grabbing boxes of ammunition. Fonzie screamed as he shot.

I aimed in on the faceless hoard charging us. They were wearing their own flack jackets and helmets, so I aimed for the crotch. Before you get mad at me for shooting people in the dick, think about how many blood vessels and muscles are down there.

The Russians kept falling, but the ones behind them kept running over them, at us. A Russian got tangled in the C-wire; he was twisting and jerking, trying to get himself free. The razors on the wire cut into his uniform and sliced his skin open, I couldn't hear him, but I saw him screaming. He half smiled though when another soldier stopped beside him and started to cut the wire to free him. I put the red chevron inside my RCO over the stuck soldier's friend's face and pulled the trigger. His friends face splattered over his and he started to wail again. I shot at the soldiers around the wire-man. I had gone through two or three magazines when the wired up Russian soldier finally got himself free. He reached down for his rifle and hopped over the death trap that had held him so painfully down for so long. When he landed I shot him in the hip and he fell back down.

McMillian and Bama were beside me firing and swearing. Bama started crying, but he never relented, defending his position.

"You'll be alright, dude!" McMillian yelled at him. "Just keep shooting!"

Fonzie ran out of ammo on his new toy and started yelling in Spanish. "McMillian!"

"Yeah, Sergeant!"

"Hold the line I'll be right back!"

"Aye, Sergeant!"

The Fonz sprinted back towards the building.

The Panzers were running around trying to kill the Rooks. Neither side looked like they were doing very well, but it kept the Rooks from shooting the trench.

Fonzie jumped back into the trench with a pack full of ammunition, "TAKE THIS SHIT!" He dropped the bag and pulled out a belt of ammo, loaded it, and started firing again. Fonzie kept Ivan at bay in our sector long enough for us to reload a few magazines. We fired until our barrels started to smoke. Fonzie jumped back out of the trench, "Hold on! I'll be right back!" He bolted back to the buildings for more ammo. We kept shooting.

The Russian infantry finally reached the trench. The first soldier got to me. He jumped down screaming, holding his weapon like a club about to smash my head with it. I lunged my bayonet up into his body between his legs and let his momentum carry him over me. The next soldier tackled me. I pulled the Ka Bar off my flack and stabbed him six or eight times quickly in the side and rolled him off. I tried to stand up but the trench was flooded with Russians. I stabbed one in the back of the kneecap. He screamed and fell and Bama smashed his face with the butt of his rifle. Bama swung his rifle around and caught a Russian neck with his bayonet. One of those communist bastards was straddled on top of Doc. He was trying to push his knife into Doc's face, but Doc was holding him back. I put the Russian in a headlock and tried to slit his throat with my Ka Bar. He jerked and grabbed at me and I accidentally stabbed myself in the bicep. I let out a yelp and Doc grabbed the Russian's knife and drove it into his belly. The Russian screamed and I kicked him to the ground. He was hollering and grabbing at his guts and Doc stomped him in the neck, finishing the job.

The machinegun fire picked back up and everyone hit the deck. The Fonz had returned with more ammo and sawed at the Russian line.

I didn't see what happened, but apparently the Panzer had won the fight with the Rook. Their twisted burning frames came crashing down before the trench. The Panzers started walking around the area in front of us. Their giant metal feet crushed Russian bodies into soup. We finished off the soldiers in the trenches. When the Panzers were done with the assaulting Russians, they fired a few volleys into the forest that was now a few hundred meters back from where it had been a few hours earlier.

A few of us climbed out of the trench to look at the killing fields before us. The rising sun illuminated the sea of dead men. We hadn't lost a huge number of Marines. I pulled my beanie off, ran my fingers through my hair, and lit a cigarette. I looked at the bodies in the trench, a few inches of blood pooled at the base.

"How many more of us are going to die before they pull us out of here?" McMillian asked.

"They won't," Fonzie said. "This war's too big. If we took these loses in Afghanistan, then maybe, but they're either going to send us replacements or merge us into a different unit."

McMillian shook his head and took off his Kevlar.

We started pulling the bodies out of the trench. What was left of Echo Company stood watch in case of a second attack. We put the fallen Marines on the backside of the trench, and tried to lay them respectfully in a line. The Russian soldiers however, we scavenged their pockets for anything pilferable and chucked them out towards the woods. We took from them anything we felt the urge to, especially their weapons and ammunition. There was enough of it that almost everyone got their own AK and a few magazines. I nabbed every cigarette that wasn't too wet from blood to smoke.

Lieutenant Wilkinson stood over the trench and watched us, "Hey, Marines."

We looked up at him.

"Don't take stuff from them, its there's..."

We stared him down. He didn't look like he spent the night in the hole with us, he was too clean.

"...And they might have booby traps hidden on them."

"Sir," Fonzie said with a cigarette in his mouth. "I highly doubt they booby trapped themselves and then ran into our machine guns."

"Hey, now Sergeant…" Wilkinson started.

"Hey now, *you* Sir. I didn't see you down here last night trying not to get yourself stabbed to death. If you're going to bitch about how we do things then you could at least get your ass down here and help us move these communist fucks!"

"I don't think I like your attitude there Sergea…"

Fonzie jumped out of the trench and stood nose to nose with the lieutenant who was easily five inches taller than him. "Sir, you fucking lost at least seven Marines last night and you weren't here with them. Do you even know who got wacked?"

"I, uh…" Wilkinson didn't know what to say.

"Get the fuck away from me before I make the number eight."

"Whoa hey, calm down there Marines," a third voice said, approaching with a group.

Fonzie looked over and saw Lieutenant Colonel Amemnon. "Good Morning, Sir."

"Now what's all this about?" The battalion commander asked.

"Sir, the platoon commander here…" Fonzie started in a belligerent manner "…skipped out on this morning's action and now he has the fucking gaul to come up and criticize us on how we're handling ourselves."

"Alright," Amemnon said. "What's your side of the story Lieutenant?"

"The Marines were clearing out the trenches Sir, and I was telling them that they shouldn't be taking things from the Russians."

"What kind of things?"

Fonzie pulled a few magazines from his cargo pocket. "Weapons and ammunition, Sir. We're running low."

"Uh, Sir," McMillian said from the trench. "Sergeant Palacios probably killed a hundred and fifty Russians last night. I don't think we'd be alive without him. He kept leaving the trench and running back with more ammo for us."

"Thanks, Marine." Amemnon looked back at Wilkinson, "and where were you this morning?"

"I was in the COC trying to…"

"Okay. Where's your platoon sergeant?"

Staff Sergeant Watson crawled out of the trench from a few yards down. His uniform was torn to shreds and he was covered in soot and blood. "I'm here, Sir."

Lieutenant Colonel Amemnon put his finger in Watson's chest. "You're the platoon commander now. Palacios, you're the new platoon sergeant." He turned to Wilkinson, "You, come with me."

The officers walked away. Watson and Fonzie smiled at each other and climbed back in the trench to help pull out bodies.

We kept taking what we desired out of the Russians' pockets. I found some more cigarettes and a few wallets. When we had the bodies all in piles the Panzers augured a whole in the ground and pushed them all into a mass grave. They then lifted what was left of the Rooks and set them down on the other side of the FOB. The Rooks' crews came out a little battered up, but alive, and surrendered without a fight.

8 DEAD IN THE WATER

We had a few hours of respite. It was only enough time to tend to minor wounds, eat an MRE, pack a ruck, and reload magazines. The cut on my arm wasn't bad. I super glued it shut and wrapped a bandage around it while Doc tended to the guys who were actually hurt. I grabbed the back up camera out of my sea bag and took pictures of the morning's aftermath.

What was left of Fox Company gathered behind the trench. It was brought up that medical supplies were running low. Doc managed to get ahold of a couple boxes of tampons and divided them around the platoons. We stepped off in a line across the trench towards the woods to see if Ivan was still out there. Two of the Panzers led us.

"You know, Doc…" I said while maneuvering through the splintered trees, "… I think it's fucked up you can't get ahold of tourniquets or gauze, but you found that many tampons on a FOB that doesn't even have any chicks on it."

"Yeah, I was pretty pissed too. But hey, it's not the craziest thing we've ever seen."

"No, no it's not."

We cleared through the killing field. What was left of the trees were covered in blood, shell casings and body parts. When we got into the trees that were still standing, we started to find more bodies. We moved slowly, the Panzers took their time to step around the trees instead of knocking them over. They were good to have, a tank wouldn't have made it through woods like that.

"How many of these fucking guys were there?" Bama asked.

"That's what the Russians do, man," Fonzie said. "They ain't smart enough to use any real tactics so their strategy is just to throw everything they got at an objective."

"And it usually works for them," McMillian added.

"There was probably a whole fucking regiment out here." Fonzie kept an eye on the woods. "But sit pretty Bama, this is the First Marine Division and not even all the communists in Hell could defeat us."

"Fucking motivator," I said as I knelt down over a body and pulled out his wallet. I also took his ammunition and weapon, he had rank insignia on a Velcro patch on his flack jacket, which also became mine. The bodies thinned out and after a certain point, there was nothing on the ground but footprints and trails of blood in the snow.

It was the afternoon, but the clouds hid the sun. The forest was thick and I imagined it was beautiful when the trees weren't viewed through the eyes of someone in kill mode.

The company line found itself at a lake. Captain Sancho called a security halt and we set up a perimeter.

"Hey, Doc," I said as we sat down beside a tree overlooking the frozen water.

"What's up, bro?"

"You know how eyes are the windows to the soul?"

"Yeah?"

"What do you think someone would see if they looked into ours?"

Doc thought for a minute. "Broken bottles, blood stained walls, knives, and bullets... and panties stuffed behind the couch."

"Hmm."

"But there'd be a perfect, untouched portrait of Chesty Puller on the back wall in a gold frame."

I smiled. "I can dig that."

Éclair came and sat next to us. "What's up, brothers?"

"Nothing, bro. You been over with Stevens' squad?" I asked

"Yeah man, shit's been *nuts*."

I patted him on the shoulder, "I'm glad you made it out of the trench."

Éclair chuckled a bit, "Yeah, and hopefully none of those commie fucks had AIDS."

"Ugh," Doc snarled, "I didn't even think of that."

"Hey, where's your Kevlar dude?" Éclair asked me.

"Dude, I lost that shit in Daugavpils."

"You gonna grab another one off someone?"

"No. I'm going to wait for the ass chewing first."

Someone on the far end of our perimeter screamed "CONTACT!" and the line fired into the woods.

"Shit! I'm supposed to be there." Éclair ran towards the fire through the forest.

Doc and I picked up and found Fonzie. He was running back and forth between his squads, directing them where to fire. Staff Sergeant Watson was knelt down behind a tree talking to the Panzers over the radio.

The Marines fired into the woods at Ivan. One of the Panzers stepped over the line of Marines and tread into the forest towards the enemy. It fired its weapon, the shells shook the earth where they fell.

McMillian pushed DeLaGarza out of the way so the hundred pound shell wouldn't crush him. Then he looked up and screamed at the Panzer, "watch where you're shooting you dumb fuck!"

Watson radioed the Panzer pilot, "If you kill any Marines I'll fucking gut you! I don't give a shit if it's an accident."

The Panzer kept firing into the woods in front of us. I pulled out my camera and snapped a few photos of it. The Panzer moved out of sight but we could still hear it moving and firing. We were all still hugging the dirt and trying to shoot Ivan on our own.

A burst of large caliber rounds raked the line the Marines were in. One round hit Flynn in the thigh and severed his leg. Flynn grabbed at his stump, wailing in pain. McMillian crawled over and put himself over Flynn's body. Using Flynn's belt, McMillian wrapped a makeshift tourniquet around the screaming Marine's thigh. Doc crawled over and started up an IV.

There was a heavy thud in front of us, a couple of trees cracked from the stress of a giant chunk of metal thrown into them. I looked closely at the iron hunk, it was one of the Panzer's arms.

"Shit." I hunkered down behind a tree showing only my face and the end of my rifle towards the enemy. There were a few more thuds and the trees to our front fell. "Fuck!" I screamed staring down the barrel of a Bishop's rifle. "Fuck! FUCK! FUCK!!!" I started trying to shoot inside the barrel. I thought maybe I could cause the ordinance inside the chamber to explode. There was a blast. The Bishop's arm exploded raining down shrapnel upon us. I stared at it in shock. "There's no way that actually worked."

There was another blast on the Bishop's hull, then a third. I looked to the left, the other Panzer was charging the Bishop while firing. The Bishop turned its body toward the Panzer and started firing its internal machine guns at it. The Panzer was unfazed and tackled the Bishop into the lake. The mechs crashed through the ice and sank into the water.

The fire from the Russian infantry stopped. Staff Sergeant Watson called in a CASIVAC via radio for Flynn. Doc and McMillian stopped the bleeding, but Flynn groaned, writhing in pain. It was hard to listen to. I looked away to the lake. There were violent waves erupting from the water. A few of the mech's rounds flew up breaking the rest of the unbroken ice. Then the water stilled and a thick pool of oil surfaced. The Panzer's head poked out of the water and moved towards the shore. A few of the Marines cheered.

Watson ran over to Captain Sancho. "Sir, fucking bird can't land here, the vegetation's too dense."

"Well where the hell can it land?"

"Not for a new miles in any direction. I don't think Flynn can hang on for that long."

"Shit." The captain stood there thinking. "Well, what the fuck are we supposed to do?"

Watson shook his head. "I don't know, Sir."

The helicopter circled above us. Lieutenant Toshi looked at bird then at the Panzer and walking out of the lake. "That Panzer pilot speaks English, right?"

"I believe so, Sir," Watson answered.

"Iron Two this is Fox Seven."

"Send your traffic." Said the German accent over the radio.

"I got a wounded Marine down here and the bird can't land because of the trees. I want to put that Marine in your hands and have the bird grab him from the lake. Can we do that?"

There was a pause. "I do not see why not."

Toshi looked over at Watson, "get Flynn to the lake."

Watson ran back to the woods and four Marines carried Flynn to the shore. The Panzer extended his hand and McMillian drug Flynn on. The Panzer very slowly lifted its hand into the air. McMillian looked scared out of his mind and the Panzer took a few steps deeper into the water.

We watched the helicopter circle around above us for a few minutes. Toshi got back on the radio. "Iron Two, Fox Seven, what the fuck is going on?"

"Fox Seven, the helicopter says that's not possible to do. I'm trying to convince him but…"

"Listen Iron Two, you have antiaircraft capability right?"

"Uh, ja."

"You tell that son of a bitch pilot that if he doesn't comply you're going to shoot his ass out of the sky."

"Uh, Fox…"

"If you don't I'm going to blast you into the pond. I have the missiles, don't fuck with me!"

"Roger."

Less than a minute later the helicopter was hovering a few feet above the Panzer's hand. The crew chief lowered a rope out of the side hatch and McMillian tied it under Flynn's arms. Flynn was raised into the door and the bird headed back west.

"Goddamn. How hard was that?" Toshi spat bitterly. "Who's bird was that?"

"It was Air Force, Sir," Watson said.

"Fucking figures," Toshi barked.

McMillian was lowered back to the ground and he rejoined the platoon.

The company got back on line and advanced towards where the Russians had been firing. We found the other Panzer. Its limbs were severed. When we got close to it the hatch on the chest hissed open and the pilot climbed out.

"Hallo!" He said, climbing down. "Goot to see friends." He said when he got down to the Marines.

Watson asked the pilot, "Do you need anything else out of the cockpit?"

"Nien." He shook his head, "No."

"Great." Watson turned looking for Marines. "Sergeant Palacios, find some C4 or Willy Pete."

Fonzie ran around to the squads looking for the explosives. Watson turned back to the pilot. "You don't have any problem with us blowing this in place do you?"

"Nien. But zee a, computer is under the seat. Make positive to get that burnt."

"Got it."

Stevens and McMillian climbed up the hull of the Panzer and dropped in a couple of incendiary grenades. Flames burst from the cockpit.

The company searched the forest for a couple more hours before turning to return to base.

"What do you think happened to the guys in the Bishop in the lake?" Bama asked.

"Hopefully the Panzer didn't kill them and the cockpit wasn't water tight, but couldn't open either." McMillian grimaced. "Fuckers."

When we got back to the FOB the C-Wire and claymores were set back and there was a platoon's worth of Russian heads on pikes facing the direction they had attacked from.

Fox Company dropped gear. Éclair, The Fonz, and I lit cigarettes by the Echo Company barracks. We were talking about the Panzer-Bishop fight earlier in the afternoon when Fowler came out of the barracks.

"DUDE!" I yelled at him.

"Hey, man!" He punched me in the shoulder. "What's been up?"

"Same old shit, traded my Hajji for an Ivan," I laughed.

"Ha, yeah, that's about right." Fowler pulled out a cigarette. "But Hajji never attacked in human waves."

"They did in Golestan," Fonzie corrected him.

"Yeah, but that was only like two hundred guys," I defended Fowler.

"Against a platoon," Fonz retorted.

"Eh, whatever." I took a drag off my Lucky's. "Hey, so you been out here all day?"

"Yeah, we're going out in a bit, but we've been planted here," Fowler said.

"What's the deal with the heads?"

"Oh, that?" Fowler laughed. "Fucking Latvians did that shit. The BC's pissed, but can't do anything about it because it's not his FOB."

"That's fucking on point," Fonzie smiled. "Fucking Ivan. You heard any other word?"

"Yeah, next week we're getting a company's worth of Marines transferred to us from Three-Seven and we should be getting American mechs soon."

"Sweet."

We shot the shit with Fowler for a few minutes and I went back to my cot. I dumped out my war trophies next to me and took inventory.

"What all'd you get man?" Doc asked.

"A bunch of cash that I have no idea what's worth, credit cards, driver's licenses I'm assuming." I fingered through the wallets. "A naked picture of some Russian slut." I handed the photo to Doc.

"Those tits aren't even bee stings."

"Yeah, but she's got enough room in that muff to hide a hive," I chuckled. "Eight magazines worth of AK rounds and two AKs." I picked up the rifles, "and they have different optics on them."

"I'm used to seeing those made of wood," Doc said as I handed him one.

"Yeah, this plastic's kind of nice, huh?"

"I just hope shit doesn't get bad enough to where we have to use these."

"I ran into Fowler outside…"

"Oh, yea? I haven't seen him weeks."

"Anyway, apparently we're getting replacements from Three-Seven next week. So they should be bringing supplies and shit."

"Killer."

"Check this *out.*" I pulled a heavy chunk of metal out of a larger wallet.

"What is it?"

"I think it's a Thor's hammer."

"That's neat. I wonder what he was doing with that."

"He was probably an Odinist. Guess he made it to Valhalla." I put the hammer on the chain my dog tags were on, next to a heavy iron cross that was already there, and put it back in my pocket.

The next few weeks were somewhat quiet. We ran into Ivan a few times while we were stomping around the woods, but he never came to visit. The Marines from Three-Seven arrived, mostly from Kilo, with a convoys worth of medical supplies, chow, ammunition, and mail. We were surprised when Two-Four showed up with them, but we weren't going to complain about more Marines. A company of engineers showed up a day or so after, and built what looked like a giant helicopter pad from heavy rubber planks.

We couldn't figure out what it was for until a platoon from the First Vertical Mechanical Assault Battalion showed up with eight of the Marine Corps' own mechs. They were intense. Apparently, we made the best deal with the Virescents when everyone kidnapped their technology to make war machines. Doc and I thought they were just new fighter jets when we saw them flying over us. They kind of looked like an F18 but with thinner swept wings and a bulkier fuselage. One by one they flew low over the FOB and stopped mid air over the runway like a Harrier would. Then half of the fuselage moved down to form legs and the hull became a torso. When they landed they looked like a metal man with a winged jetpack. What I thought was gun pods under its wings turned out to be its main weapon. Its face was unlike any of the mechs I had seen yet. Instead of trying to make it resemble a human, it looked almost like a giant video camera with a few antennas and a machine gun. The wings and its rifle, if you'd call it that, both had "MARINES" painted in big black letters.

When we got our mail Doc, Eclair, and I carried a few boxes up to the aid station where we slept. Éclair had moved up a few days prior.

I cut open a box from Penelope. "Sweet!"

"What?" Éclair asked.

"Wife sent me four cartons of Lucky's."

"Badass. What else ya get?" Doc asked.

"That's it, there's a letter in here but I'll read it later."

Éclair opened a box he got from Ginny. "Damn it this is like Christmas morning." He opened the letter in the package first. "My Dearest Richard…" He started.

"HA!" I laughed "You're her dear Dick."

"I'm worried about you, blah blah blah, work is gay…" Éclair stopped reading and looked into the box. "Penelope, Kristy and I got together and bought you these tomahawks…"

"What?" Doc asked. "I told that woman not to go spending all my fucking money."

Éclair pulled out a box from within the package that read 'Wilson' and tossed it to Doc.

Doc opened it and pulled out a steel tomahawk. It had a small cloth case that wrapped around the blade and attached to a belt. Éclair tossed me mine, and he opened his. There were engravings on the axe heads. Doc's read 'Only God can judge me.' Éclair's "Best Respect the Éclair." And mine, 'Trouble.'

"I can dig this." Éclair smiled.

"Right?" Doc followed.

I opened the letter from Penelope. Inside was a picture she had taken of herself, she was in a bikini and standing sideways in front of a mirror showing the small growing bump in her belly. "So, Penelope sent me picture of herself, her tits are already getting bigger."

"Yeah, because they weren't big enough already," Éclair chuckled.

"Yeah, yeah…" I read the letter she sent.

Hank,

Here's the cigarettes you asked for. I hope they help keep you sane. I wouldn't want you to go losing your head from nicotine withdrawal, especially in the middle of a war. Just be sure to come home to me. Our child is going to need a father and I think that you'll be a good dad. I wish I could talk to you more often, but I understand. They've been showing what's going on in the news, apparently things are pretty bad in Estonia, I'm glad it's more quiet where you are.

I love and miss you. Your Misses,

Penelope.

"So apparently things are so bad in Estonia that Latvia is quiet," I chuckled.

"Well what the fuck are we doing *here* then?" Éclair asked.

"Fighting Ivan's little brother I guess?" Doc squinted.

I put my tomahawk on my belt behind my pistol and walked outside for a cigarette. Fowler and Fonzie were out smoking in the snow. "Yo." I said walking up to them.

"Sup, dude?" Fonzie asked.

"Nothing. When are they going to promote you to staff sergeant?"

"They're probably not. They're giving me the responsibility but not the privileges or pay."

"Yeah, big, fat digital green weenie," Fowler grumbled.

One of the giant machines with 'MARINES' tattooed on its armor shook the ground as it walked past. It had 'IN THE MOOD' painted on the other side of its rifle.

"What are those things called anyway?" I asked.

"Daedalus," Fowler answered. "Their fucking exhaust reeks."

"Yeah, I can't smell it." Fonzie stated.

"How do you not smell that?" I asked.

"I can't smell anything."

"Huh?"

"When I was a kid I fell into a pool of gasoline and my mom pulled me out by my foot. It fucked up my sense of smell, but nothing really besides that."

"Well, okay," I said. "I did not know that." I watched the Daedalus tread past towards the trenches. "I still can't believe we made those things. We can take out the enemy ones with Cobras if we wanted to."

"Really?" Fowler asked. "You can't believe the organization that spent money making the F35 and the Osprey would spend money on something worthless?"

"Yeah, good point."

9 IN THE SNOW OF FAR OFF NORTHERN LANDS

Fowler, The Fonz, Éclair, Doc, Stevens and I sat around a fire looking at the stars and smoking cigarettes. We sat on rocks we found or cinderblocks to keep us out of the mud.

"How long are we just going to fucking sit on this goddamned FOB?" Fonzie asked us, knowing no one had the answer.

"I don't know but I'm glad the snow melted," I said. "And that I don't have to shit in an ammo can and fucking freeze my ball sack off."

"I think it's a good thing," Fowler said. "You may think it sucks just sitting here for months on end, but remember who we're fighting. I think we should count our stars the Pentagon didn't decide to go on the offensive and invade Russia in the fucking winter, even if they did also take Belarus, Poland and Slovakia, and the rest of Ukraine."

"Yeah, but it's almost fucking *June*," Fonzie complained. "And I haven't seen Ivan in weeks. We've just been going out there and looking for him, but I don't think he's around anymore."

"Ivan's fucking everywhere," Doc muttered. "He's just being quiet."

"I heard he's still fucking up Estonia pretty bad," Elcair said.

"Yeah, but this is bullshit," Fonzie griped. "We have more than a fucking regiment here now, we should be moving."

I tapped my tomahawk on the cinderblock where I was sitting. When the birds came at the beginning of spring I had taken a couple of feathers and tied them to the handle right under the head. I thought about the Russian soldier I had buried the axe in back in March. "It's going to suck when do start moving. Ivan digs in pretty well and he fights close." I put the axe away. "They've got a lot more balls than Hajji did." I pulled my wedding ring off and played with it between my fingers.

"Yeah, I'll give you that," Fonzie said. "Hey, what's written on your ring?"

I handed him my ring. He looked at the runes engraved in the band.

"It says, 'Always Faithful Penelope.'"

"You fucking motard." Fonzie chuckled and handed me back the golden band.

"So did you guys hear what happened to Three-One?" Éclair asked smiling.

We shook our heads.

Fowler asked, "Where are they even at?"

"Well check out this shit," Éclair started. "The fucking Marine Corps sent the battalion and some attachments to the fucking moon for some kind of low gravity space training. They were supposed to be a rotational force up there because everyone's starting to build shit up in space, and a lot of the Virescents are up there and a shit ton of scientists, and tourists and all that. Well, they got sent to the moon, and since the war kicked off, the Marine Corps doesn't have enough money to bring them back, so they're just up there chilling until either the war's over or we get enough cash to bring them home."

"Dude, that sucks!" Fonzie laughed. "Oh my god!"

"Yeah, but now First Marines can say they were the First Space Marines," Doc chuckled. "It *is* kind of neat that Space Marines aren't science fiction anymore."

"Have you guys heard about that space fold experiment?" Stevens added.

"Where they're trying to make a faster way to space travel that doesn't take decades to fly around the universe?" Fowler asked.

"Yeah."

"I heard rumors about it. Are they actually doing it, now?"

Stevens rubbed his jaw. "I was reading about it in a magazine my wife sent me and they're trying to hurry up and get it working as soon as they can so maybe we can use it for getting more materials like iron and nitrogen and shit from the asteroid belt. I think they're trying to have the first go at it in September."

"Why would they need to fold space to get to the asteroid belt?" Doc asked.

"I don't know, maybe because it turns a year long thing into a week long thing?" Stevens shrugged.

"Okay. How's your wife doing?" Doc asked Stevens.

"She's alright. She's still a little sick, but she's going to have her operation soon, so hopefully she'll be better-better by the end of the year."

Éclair looked up at the stars then down at the fire. "Hey, do you think that if you traveled into the future, that you'd be there?"

"What do you mean, dude?" Fowler asked.

"Like if you could time travel if you'd still be in the future after you left now," Éclair answered.

"Well, if you left this, like…" I circled my hands around each other. "Timeline, I guess, that you wouldn't be in the future when you showed up."

"No, as long as you came back eventually, you'd still be in the future in this time," Doc said.

"Well no, that depends," Fowler said. "Are we talking Back To The Future rules where it's all one time line, or Terminator rules where every time you time travel you actually go into an alternate universe?"

"Wait, what?" I asked. "When in Terminator did it say those were the rules?"

"They talk about it in the books. And those are the only rules it could go by, that's why the timeline's so fucked up," Fowler said.

"Okay."

"Well what if you didn't have a machine?" Stevens asked. "What if you took some drugs and they altered your reality and shot you to a different part of time. Like Clock-Acid or something?"

"Or just had the magic power to do it." Fonzie suggested.

This conversation went on for two fucking hours.

"So…" Éclair finished. "We all agree that theoretically if you went into the future with a machine, or a Delorean, or a phone booth, that you would be in the future that you traveled to because you used science to move through the time-space continuum. However, if you just magically made a way to the future you wouldn't be there because you'd have to be a god to do that and the time-space continuum would actually evolve around you versus you revolving around it."

"Yeah, I'm cool with that," Fowler said.

On the First of June, Lieutenant Colonel Amemnon gathered the battalion and outlined Operation Joker Switch, the course of action against the mighty Russians. The First Marine Division was to roll to the Latvian Capital Riga, then board ships, and on the next day, make an amphibious assault on Saint Petersburg. I remember wondering what drowning while I was on fire and being shot was going to feel like in the freezing Baltic sea. Then I wondered where and how I'd wake up. I didn't particularly like the idea of being immortal. I wanted it to wear off, but not if I had to die a thousand times first. As the First Marine Division was to hit the beach, a German Army Division reinforced by a Panzer battalion was to strike the city from the south. An hour before the first wave was to hit the beach the Eighty-Eighth Airborne Division and the British Army's Two Para were to start dropping on the other side of the city. Two-Seven's objective was a few miles away from the beach into the city, The Ilium Weapons Facility. It was the place where the Russians built their mechs. The plan was brutal. We had to sit through four straight hours of a power point presentation crammed into the bottom floor of a building that could comfortably fit two hundred people as a battalion reinforced. I had always joked about killing myself during lectures like that, but that time I was honestly considering it, except I knew it wouldn't stick. When the colonel was finally done giving us the plan of attack he stood in the middle of the room and stared us down.

He said, "Sailors and Marines, you are about to embark upon the great crusade, towards which we have striven these many months. The eyes of the world are upon us. The hopes and prayers of freedom loving people everywhere march with us. In company with our brave Allies and brothers-in-arms on other fronts, we will bring about the destruction of the Russian war machine, the elimination of Putin's tyranny over the oppressed peoples of East Europe, and security for ourselves in a free world. Our task will not be an easy one. Our enemy is well trained, well equipped, and battle hardened. He will fight savagely. The Coalition has inflicted upon the Russians great defeats, in open battle, man-to-man. Our air offensive has seriously reduced their strength in the air and their capacity to wage war on the ground. Our Home Fronts have given us an overwhelming superiority in weapons and munitions of war, and placed at our disposal great reserves of trained, fighting men. The tide has turned! The free men of the world are marching together to Victory! I have full confidence in your courage and devotion to duty and skill in battle. We will accept nothing less than full Victory! Good luck! And let us beseech the blessing of Almighty God upon this great and noble undertaking. Or my name isn't A. G. Amemnon! OORAH!"

The battalion shouted, "OORAH," and we were dismissed.

After a few cigarettes and a serious bitch session I stomped back up to my cot and staged my gear to leave, making sure to pack the captured Russian weapons and ammunition, and dropped a letter to Penelope in the outgoing mailbox.

Green girl with hair so soft

Without you would I'd be forever lost

No thing could ever replace your love

Nor a star in the heavens above

Pour your soul into my heart

Enter your light that banished the dark

Nay, even when I'm a dolt and you're scorn

Every rose on you has no thorn

Like your avocado flavored skin

Oh dear Penelope, you're my favorite sin

Peacefully not, my body's tortured by the demons of the heart

Every night dream that again I will be in your arms

Semper Fi Until I Die,

Hank Allensworth

The morning came with a Zero Four reveille. They managed to get us a good breakfast of real steak and eggs. I was happy it wasn't UGRs or MREs, but McMillian said it was cruel to give us a good meal before they sent us all off to die. We loaded into trucks and drove north to Riga.

"This place kind of reminds me of Ohio," McMillian yelled over the sound of the diesel engines.

I turned to look at him; he was staring out at the trees. They were tall and the leaves were starting to fill in. "Dude, this place ain't that bad."

McMillian looked down at me confused, "What?"

"I'd rather have been in the Waffen-SS during Stalingrad than be in Ohio right now."

"Dude Ohio ain't *that* bad," McMillian replied.

"Naw," Doc chimed in. "Ohio's better than getting killed by the Red Army, but I'd still rather sell myself into slavery than ever fucking live there."

McMillian gave us a dirty look, "That's fucked up."

"No," I said. "Canton is fucked up. Cleveland may as well be Detroit and there are places in Somalia that are nicer than CrAkron."

"So you'd rather be *here* than back home?" McMillian asked.

"*Home?* No, I'd rather be home. *But,* I'd prefer the gulag than anywhere between Pennsylvania and Indiana."

"Either way, you can say goodbye to it," Doc said.

I didn't see the city until we were closing into the port, and we weren't there very long. We were on the pier for less than an hour. We didn't have much with us, just what we were assaulting with, body armor, weapons and ammo, and a pack with a few days worth of stripped down MREs, extra socks, gortex and warming layers. I had my captured AK strapped to the side of my pack and the back pouches filled with extra ammunition. I had packs of cigarettes stuffed into every crevice I could make, all in their own zip lock bag.

They split the battalion into companies and loaded us onto different ships. We were to rendezvous on the beach. Fox and Gulf Company shuffled onto on of the ships in port. I didn't hear or see the things name. Instead of putting us up anywhere, we were led straight to the belly of the ship and staged behind the rows of amphibious assault vehicles in what they called the well deck.

We stayed there until we were under way. Then we were loaded into the back of the tracks. The AAVs seemed like they should sit about ten Marines comfortably, we had half a platoon in each. It was cramped, dark, and hot. We all either had our elbows in someone's ribs, or theirs in ours, or both. I had to flex my thighs almost constantly to keep them from falling asleep, it was a good thing they were pretty much healed by then. I have no clue how long we were back there. I fell asleep a few times, maybe for ten minutes at a time, maybe a few hours.

When the U.S. Sardines of Fox Company Two-Seven had been in their can until a day from expiration, the motor flared on. It wasn't deafening, but it drowned out what little other noise there was to hear. Hot, nauseating exhaust flooded the back of the track. After two hours of sitting there cramped, sweaty, disoriented, and now with poison gas filling my lungs, we started to move. There was a quick jerk forward, then a yank to the side. Then the engines roared and we raced ahead at full speed. The engine stayed loud, but the feeling of movement was gone. Water started pouring from the seals in the hatches. Not enough to sink us, but more than was needed to remove any shred of comfort there was left.

At first the rocking of the ocean waves weren't terrible, they were almost soothing until we hit what I guessed were higher swells. They AAV started to twist and turn. My guts felt like a blender making a milk shake inside of a Dodge Challenger that was doing donuts on pea gravel during an earthquake. The heat and fumes and shaking got to be too much for me. I emptied my stomach on the floor. I tried to miss my boots, but my head was too fucked to tell. I rested my head back on the bulkhead and was glad that the fumes drowned out the smell of the puke so I had a better chance of not doing it again.

The rocking became more violent. The rumbles of explosions started rocking the track and we heard the pings of bullets hitting the vehicle. There was a large swell and gravity seemed to dissipate. Everyone started yelling and we all crashed into the roof. The track was pounded by the waves and flipped back right sending us flying back towards the floor. Fonzie was yelling something, but the AAV's engine drowned out his voice.

The rolling and rocking stopped and the back of the vehicle dropped letting in the early morning's sunlight.

Fonzie, who was closest to the back screamed, "GET THE FUCK OUT!" and led the half platoon out of the track. I jumped out. My right foot hit water and my left foot hit sand, and I ran through the machine gun fire to the short wall at the end of the beach. There were already Marines curled up at the base of the wall, holding onto their rifles, shaking, and hoping to God that none of the little metal Russian hate mail had their names on it.

Fonzie looked over at the Marines huddled up behind the wall, "HEAD COUNT!"

The Marines, that weren't lying facedown on the beach behind us counted off, all twelve of the seventeen that had been in the track.

"Shit," Fonzie swore looking back at the fallen Marines on the beach. "Anyone seen Watson?" Fonzie swiveled his head.

I looked around, Éclair was taking photos, Doc was pinning an IV into someone, McMillian was patting down Bama and DeLaGarza. Stevens and Hano were popping up intermittently and firing at Ivan, Greer and Becker were hunkered down.

Jets were ripping through the sky, sending their ordinance screaming down onto Ivan's head. I could hear the artillery blasting the area between the beaches and buildings and the screeching of the mechs' moving joints.

The next wave of AAVs came weaving through the lead rain. One hit the beach behind us. The ramp dropped and the Marines came scurrying out. I didn't see what hit it, but the track exploded into a ball of fire, the Marines who had just departed we no more than twenty feet away. The one's who weren't swallowed by the flame were ripped to shreds by shrapnel. I watched one Marine keep charging the wall. Half his face was gone and his arm was a bloody stump. He was screaming, but it wasn't from pain. I think his brain refused to acknowledge what happened to him and he charged the wall like the soldiers of the Light Brigade.

A Daedalus came screaming down from the sky towards the city. It switched from flight to walking mode as it fell towards us. The wings were chewed up and thick black smoke left a trail behind it. The pilot managed to slow it down and he landed it between the wall, and the buildings firing at us. The Daedalus let out a quick burst of hot led into the glassless windows and fell over. I peered over the bulkhead, the Daedalus was lying on its side on the ground. The cockpit opened and the pilot slid out to the dirt.

Fonzie yelled, "GET OFF THE BEACH!" and climbed the wall. The Marines behind, his platoon or not, got up and followed the Fonz past the downed Mech and into the buildings ahead.

The sand crunched under my boots. I hurtled over the fallen Marines from the previous wave and swerved around the barbed wire, most of it had been trampled by the Daedalus. I saw Fonzie grab the pilot and drag him along to the first row of bullet riddled, concrete slab, Swiss cheese excuses for buildings.

We flooded into the first floor via a large hole in the wall. It looked like a hotel lobby. It was painted red with Russian blood from the mech's canon. I didn't waste time taking in the view. There was fire coming from the second floor. The establishment was only a few stories tall and Ivan had rented out the rooms for night.

"Who are you guys?" Fonzie demanded of the Marines not from Fox.

"Echo Two-Seven," one of them replied.

"Hold down this floor, we're going up," Fonzie ordered.

"Got it." The Echo Marine whistled to his troops and barked orders at his men.

Fonzie pointed his rifle up the stairs and charged up, squad in tow. We systematically kicked down the doors of the second and third floor, but only found body parts. I guessed the fire I heard was coming from adjacent buildings. We moved to the side of the building facing the city on the roof and hunkered down. We took shots at muzzle flashes we saw from nearby structures. Most of the city was still standing on one piece. Fonzie started barking into the radio looking for the rest of Fox Company.

"Hank," Éclair grabbed my attention. I turned my head and he snapped a photo of me. "Welcome to Saint Petersburg."

I shook my head. "Yeah, welcome to fucking Stalingrad."

"Listen up!" Everyone turned an ear to the Fonz. "The rest of the company's three buildings north. Get down stairs, stay on the beach front, and keep down." Fonzie slapped the Marines' backs, counting them as they ran down the stairwell off the roof. We filed downstairs, ran through the rubble and up the street to link up with the rest of the company. "Wait out here." Fonzie told the Marines as he headed into the building to link up with the CO and find the rest of the platoon.

A few Marines pointed their barrels down the side of the building in case Ivan decided to come give us a housewarming present.

I looked back at the beach. There were Marines in the water, some still moving in, some floating facedown. I looked away. I'd seen enough dead people that it didn't bother me, unless it was a Marine. That pain never dulled.

With Fox Company consolidated; we started kicking in the doors of the beach block buildings. No skyscrapers, mostly hotels and restaurants. Glass and bits of concrete littered the streets. Every second of action for at least the next week was done dancing to the machine gunner's soundtrack.

The company was dispersed throughout the block. We were in our third building of the assault into Saint Petersburg. An intersection decorated with burning cars marked the no-man's-land border between newly acquired American soil and the remnants of the Soviet Union. It was starting to get dark. Ivan was making us pay in blood for every foot we took.

Fox's Weapons attachments were on the roof setting up their missiles and heavy machine guns. First platoon was spread throughout the building, roughly a squad per floor. Things had been relatively quiet for about fifteen minutes. And by that I mean no one else was wounded.

There was a massive scream from deep in the city. The war cry of thousands of vengeful lungs, the spirit of Saint Petersburg roared against us. Then there was absolute silence, barring the wind, and the ocean.

I shot Doc a concerned look, "Another wall?"

"I don't know man," Doc said.

"That's what it sounds like," Éclair said, as he gripped his rifle, wide-eyed.

I pulled out the first cigarette I'd had since the FOB in Latvia and flicked open my lighter.

Fonzie looked over at me, "Really?"

"We're probably all about to die anyway man," Stevens said, lighting his.

"Fuck it," Fonzie grumbled, lighting his own. Doc, Éclair and a few other Marines followed suit.

A ways down, a Russian mech climbed to the top of a building, it was too far off to identify with the naked eye. The sun was still on its path to the top of the sky, which made silhouettes of everything east of us.

The human wall of screaming Russian soldiers ran down the streets towards us, running over and destroying everything in their path.

Fonzie turned back towards the Marines on the roof, "YOU!" He pointed at the Marines behind the Mk19, "They get in range you turn them to hamburger!" The Fonz turned to the Fifty Cal, "Don't cut down anyone further away than the intersection!"

The Marines on the heavy machine guns adjusted their weapons.

"Everyone else…" The Fonz looked over the Marines on the roof, then winked at Doc and me, "Fix bayonets." Fonzie flicked his cigarette over the roof.

Ivan's ocean splashed its human waves through the buildings. The Marines opened fire. The forty-millimeter grenades blew the soldiers into little pieces. Those pieces though were the water droplets that bounce off a small rock when a tsunami crashes down on a city. The wall kept coming, I could almost imagine Stalin surfing the wave with his gloriously groomed mustache and matching AK47.

The buildings smoked from the amount of bullets hitting their face. The Russian mech was hopping the rooftops toward us. A couple of missiles from Marines on other roofs screamed at the mech but missed. A rocket from the second wave hit the mech in the chest and it disappeared in a thick cloud of smoke, a few seconds later, it reemerged. It was close enough to tell what it was.

Fonzie started barking into the radio for close air support.

Ivan ran over his fallen brothers in the street. Their blood pooled enough to stream into a storm drain. The Russians came right in the front door. We had given up firing any direction but straight down the sides of the building.

I looked up while I was changing my magazine. The Bishop was just a few buildings away. Its gleaming red eye locked onto our rooftop and the giant iron beast leaped towards us.

"SHIT!" Everyone leaped and hugged the deck in an effort to not get trampled.

The Bishop was only a few yards above us.

CRACK!

I looked up and a Daedalus foot was crammed in the Bishop's chest. The mechs fell into the buildings across from us. The stone and mortar collapsed over them.

Our guns started again ablaze. The fifty cal didn't join the choir of death.

"The fuck dudes?" Fonzie grabbed the Marine behind the fifty cal's shoulder, the Marine fell over, blood spilled from the hole where his chest used to be. "God Damnit!" Fonzie yelled. "Hold this position!" *like we had a choice*, and ran down the stairs.

The Marines that had grenades dropped them off the side of the building. Ivan was still trying to force himself in. The Daedalus and the Bishop were wrestling in the rubble. When they tossed and turned, they both stomped on Russian soldiers. The Daedalus had the Bishop on its back. The Bishop reached for the rifle it dropped when it was kicked. The Daedalus, with *In The Mood* painted on its chest, ripped open the Bishop's cockpit and stuck in its fist. When the robotic hand reemerged it was soaked in red liquid.

A squad's worth of Marines busted through the ladder well. Fonzie came up last, carrying Staff Sergeant Watson. The Marines kicked a few grenades into the doorway. Fonzie dropped Watson by the ledge. "Doc!"

"Yeah?"

Fonzie pointed at the bleeding Staff Sergeant, then ran to the fifty cal and pointed it back towards the ladder well. The first few Russians stomped up and Fonzie cut them in half.

Doc ripped open Watson's flack jacket and started shoving gauze into a hole in his side. Watson held onto the ledge of the roof while trying to suppress the pain enough to stay on the radio with command.

I leaned over the rooftop and fired a few more rounds at the Russians in the street. There were less of them, at least less of them that didn't take cover. Bang, bang, click…

I canted my rifle to the side to check for a jam. *Nope, out of ammo.* I reached for another magazine, then another. I looked down and all my mags were empty. *Fucking great.*

I dropped my pack and pulled out the AK and ammo I had taken from Ivan in the trenches. I broke down my M4 and stuffed it in the pack and threw it back on. I racked back the bolt on the AK and started firing at muzzle flashes. I hadn't had a chance to adjust the sights on it, so only God knew where those rounds went.

"First Platoon!" Watson screamed.

We offered him our ears but only had eyes for Ivan.

"We're moving!"

I looked at Watson because I had no idea what the hell he was talking about. *Where the fuck do you plan on taking us?* The Daedalus had put its rifle across the building tops.

Doc helped Watson to the bridge. "Let's fucking go!" He screamed at his platoon. One by one the Marines scurried across the rifle until we were all on the other building. When we were over Ivan made his way up the staircase. The Daedalus picked back up his rifle and leveled the building, Ivan and all.

I watched the mech pound the building into nothing. Russian blood glued dirt and debris to *In The Mood*'s hull. The Daedalus scanned the immediate area. When it found nothing worth killing, it boosted itself into the air a few hundred meters, transformed back into a jet, and soared into the sky.

"Hey, Fonzie," Doc said.

"What's up, man?" The Fonz replied.

"Hey, I gotta get Watson back to the beach and out of here before he bleeds out."

Fonzie looked at Watson, his head was limp and his eyes were shut. "Alright Doc, get him out of here. McMillian, Bama, and Becker go with him."

They disappeared off the roof. I watched them come out of the back of the building and drag Watson to a track. We were still only on the first block of Saint Petersburg.

10 TAKE MY HAND

We survived to the middle of July. The lines were blurred into a mess. Ivan and the resistance took turns owning property in the beaten down jagged structures that was now Saint Petersburg.

The Ilium military complex was the only real estate we hadn't tenanted. Every time we got close, Ivan brought out the big guns. The base had thick concrete walls. Rooks and T90s patrolled the perimeter in packs.

The few civilians we saw looked at us in horror, and ran the other way. We had run out of American cigarettes, luckily Ivan smoked more than I did. We took whatever we desired from the bodies we found. We got supplied enough that we weren't terribly in want, except for showers, sleep, and food. Most of us though still thought it safe to use Russian ammo in case we ran short.

Stevens, McMillian, and I stood on the hull of a Knight that Athena (CAAT) had taken down. We pointed the AKs we "adopted" at the cockpit hatch. Marcsky, one of the engineers, was grinding away at the door with a very large electric saw. The Machine was dead in the water, but we weren't going to take chances with the pilot.

Marcsky sawed off the last hinge of the hatch and tied a tow strap to one of the edges. The other end of the line was attached to a truck that pulled the heavy metal door off the mech.

A set of hands raised out of the hull to the tune of indistinguishable blabbering. McMillian pulled the pilot out by his collar, and threw him down on the hull. Stevens tied the pilot's hands together.

Marcsky disappeared into the cockpit. "What do we have here?" He lifted out a stuffed backpack.

"Cookies, vodka, cigarettes, and porno," Stevens joked.

"I wish," I grumbled, looking down into the cockpit.

"You want to take pictures of this shit?" Marcsky asked, pointing at the Knight's control panels.

"Not really, I got some of that shit for the S2 a few weeks ago after that assault on Ilium."

"Ugh," McMillian shook his head. "Don't remind me of that shit."

The pilot said something to us in Russian.

"Shut up, fucker!" Stevens kicked him in the ribs.

We climbed down off the wreckage of the mech where first platoon was waiting for us. We lowered the pilot with a rope.

We stood the pilot up on his feet and Fonzie grabbed his face, "You speak English, Ivan?"

The pilot blubbered in Russian.

"So, no?" Fonzie displayed a hand signal and McMillian put earmuffs and a blindfold on the pilot. "What's in his bag?"

Marcsky dropped the pack and started rummaging through it.

"I doubt Ivan here's gonna tell us anything," Fonzie said.

"Oh hey, here we go!" Marcsky pulled a Russian flag out of the pack. He rummaged around some more. "Pistol magazines, half a bottle of Vodka..."

Fonzie grabbed the vodka. "Score. That's about half a shot for each of us, right?"

Marcsky continued. "Flash light, maps..." Marcsky stared into the pack quietly.

"What's up?" I asked noticing the silence.

Marcsky's fist rose from the bag clenching a tattered American flag. No one spoke as he extended the battered colors. The edges were singed; a stain marked where someone had bled out onto the stripes. Marines had written their names into the stars.

"Those guys are One-Seven," Fonzie whispered somberly. "Put that away."

Marcsky and Doc folded the colors the best they could into a triangle and put it in Marcsky's pack.

Fonzie turned to the Russian pilot. He calmly pulled off the Russian's blindfold and earmuffs. The rest of stared down the pilot. "You like killing Marines?"

The pilot's speech sounded confused.

"You take that flag yourself or did one of your bitch ass cronies grab it for you?"

The pilot stared at The Fonz, not knowing what he was saying.

"Either way, it's not like we should take it personally, right?" The Fonz smiled and dropped his Kevlar to the ground.

The pilot smiled back.

Fonz chuckled, "I mean you're just defending your motherland, right?" Fonzie's voice grew in volume but not in anger. "It's not like you fuckers started this war or anything!" He brandished the bottle of vodka. "Cut this dude's flexi cuffs."

"Uh, sergeant…"

"Do it McMillian." Fonz chuckled.

With his hands unbound the Russian started to smile.

"Yeah, we're going to have a good time, you *should* laugh!" Fonzie laughed and playfully punched the pilot in the shoulder as if they were friends. The rest of us only stared.

The pilot grinned and started to say something, but Fonzie broke the bottle on the Russian's forehead. The clear watery liquid mixed with the Russian's blood. Fonzie grabbed his hair and repeatedly stabbed him in the neck with broken glass. The Fonz let go of the pilot, who fell limp to the concrete.

Fonzie picked up his helmet and gave Marcsky a stern look, "Torch the cockpit."

Charges were set under the computer in the mech. The platoon huddled together in front of the collapsed Knight and held up the Russian colors we took from the pilot. Éclair put his camera on a brick and set the timer. When we looked at the photo on the camera's display the dead Russian's legs were in the foreground and no one was smiling.

"I didn't want to do the paperwork on that fuck anyway," Fonzie muttered as we moved on.

We patrolled back to the company's command post. Our sleeping area was in a warehouse next to an overpass. The floor was cold concrete. Crates full of machine parts filled the rooms. We slept between the wooden boxes. When there was a storm, rain dripped through the windows in the ceiling. It wasn't all bad, there wasn't any traffic to keep us up, not that we weren't all half deaf from constant gunfire that it would keep us up anyway.

"Why wasn't this fucking place leveled before we even got here?" McMillian asked.

"Because there's civilians here and even if they did start the war, Uncle Sam wants to be the good guy," Doc said.

"Fucking Congress and the god damned bleeding heart mothers of America would rather have all of *us* face down dead in the dirt than have America fight a war correctly. It's a bunch of honkey-dory Mickey Mouse bullshit." Stevens bitched, lighting a cigarette. "Nobody wants to do what it takes to win a war, they just keep throwing people into the meat grinder when, if they let us do what needed to be done we could break the grinder. War is *supposed* to be terrible, but they're making us play nice with Ivan. No excessive damage, no flamethrowers, nothing bigger than a JDAM, bullshit rules of engagement. We're going to lose this war because the people of America won't let us tear this bitch down brick-by-brick and spatter everything that fucking moves."

"We're not going to lose this war," I noted. "Congress will, but kill for kill the Marines *are* winning."

"Yeah, live and learn right?" Bama said.

"No. Not live and learn," Éclair shot back at Bama. "Fuck, two fucking weeks ago they tried to helo insert into Ilium and we fucking lost most of Echo Company."

"We technically lost *all* of Echo Company," McMillian corrected him. "The guys that made it back were reassigned to Gulf so that at least one of the companies was at T.O."

"Yup, see!" Stevens pointed to the Ilium Military Complex on the horizon. "If they'd just napalm or nuke or gas that shit there'd be a hundred less Marines in Arlington National Cemetery right now."

"Oh but that's *inhumane*," Doc said sarcastically.

"Is there a humane way to kill someone, Doc?" I asked.

"Good point." Doc snuffed a cigarette out with the bottom of his boot. "But everyone always wants to talk about this meaning of life bullshit, and their philosophy of how a war should be fought, but I still have to go to work tomorrow, I have a war to fight. Congress or not, we're all still here eating the same shit soup sandwich with a butter knife."

An hour or so later I was digging at an MRE and watching the sun set over the ocean with Stevens, Doc, and Éclair. We were sitting on top of the overpass looking over the little territory we could claim was ours. McMillian walked up to us with a sack on his back.

"What's that?" Éclair asked.

"Mail, dude," McMillian dropped the sack at out feet and rummaged through it.

We all eye balled the burlap bag like children waiting for a present from Santa Claus. McMillian handed Éclair and I each a box and Doc and Stevens letters.

"Sick dude, thanks," Éclair said.

"Don't thank me man, I didn't send it to ya," McMillian smiled.

"Alright well then, fuck off," Éclair chuckled.

McMillian patted Éclair's head and disappeared.

I opened my box. There was a letter and a carton of Lucky's. "Oh fuck yes," I showed off my smokes. "I'm getting tired of Ivan's shit tobacco."

"It's not *that* bad," Éclair said, smoking a Russian brand. "It's not like they're *Pines*."

"Bleq." I opened the letter. Penelope sent me more or less the same letter she's been sending me, full of 'I love miss and am worrying about yous.' She enclosed a picture of her in a nightgown that used to extend to the middle of her thighs. It now barely covered her panties because of the big round belly our child grew in. I put the photo in my wallet next to the others. I fantasized about one day when I was an old man, someone looking through a scrapbook I had on a shelf, full of pictures of Penelope pregnant, Marines in Saint Petersburg, and dead Russian soldiers. I got a kick out of the disgust on an imaginary person's face. *Fuck, that's if I grow old. This immortality shit better just be for wounds.* "Whatchew get?" I asked Éclair, peering over at his box.

"Ginny sent me a playboy, but she glued photos of herself, in the same poses as the models, over all the pictures."

I looked into the magazine. "I never got the whole shaved pussy thing. Why do people want to pretend they're banging twelve year olds?"

Éclair closed the book. "Come on dude, that's my wife."

"Sorry, bro." I started opening my Lucky's. "Curiosity got to me."

Éclair shook his head.

"But seriously though, when you get back you should get a pin up tattoo of her on your arm or something." I offered him a Lucky's. Éclair pulled a cigarette out of the pack. I offered one to Doc but he waved me off, he was too deep in his letter. "Stevens."

He didn't respond.

"John!" Éclair nudged him.

Stevens shook his head. "Huh?" He looked at us.

"Lucky's?" I offered him the pack.

"No, I'm good."

"Ya alright dude?" Éclair asked.

"Suzie, had her surgery."

"Oh shit, is she good now?" Doc asked.

"Yep, everything turned out well, she's good and fucking healthy now," he said in a flat tone.

"Well, that's good." I said, finally lighting a cigarette for myself.

"Yup. Suzie's recovered, no more illnesses, all hunky-dory, and moving to San Francisco with some guy named Jody."

"Wait, what?" Éclair snapped his head to Stevens.

"Yup. Fucking bitch said, 'Hey Johnny, thanks for taking care of me when I was sick and probably going to die, but now that I'm better and you're gone. I found this really awesome dude and we're going to Frisco.' Cunt."

"Dude, I'm *sorry* man," I said not puffing my cigarette out of respect.

"I don't fucking give a fucking shit." Stevens made a paper airplane out of the letter and flicked it towards the ocean. "I'll go back to Cali and fuck hotter, younger chicks. They're all over the place down there."

"No dude, that's like seriously fucked up," Éclair said.

Stevens shook his head. "It's alright. That situation's no worse than being stuck in Russia. And all cats feel the same in the dark."

"Sure you don't want a cigarette man?" I asked.

Stevens took a cig.

"Yeah, sometimes you just have to chain smoke your problems away," Éclair told him.

We sat there silently for about half an hour. Our only music was distant gunfire and lighter clinks.

"I thought there'd be more big city here," Doc said.

"Huh?" I asked.

"There's like three skyscrapers here," Doc said. "Besides that nothing's more than five or six stories tall. I always thought Saint Petersburg would have that big city feel, with skyscrapers and shit."

"I guess not." I lit another cigarette.

"But the architecture here is pretty cool," Éclair observed. "It's actually really fucking beautiful, even if half of it *is* destroyed right now."

"I think it's beautiful even with the holes and grit," Doc confessed.

"I don't know," Stevens started, "it's gives me a weird feeling. Like all the columns and art that's built into everything, reminds me of photos from World War Two where all these guys with guns were running around and fighting in the old world."

"You do know this place used to be called Leningrad back in World War Two, right?" I asked.

"Did the Nazis come through?" Stevens asked.

"I think so," I wondered aloud. "But I don't know how they did."

"They probably got their asses kicked like in Stalingrad. You really *do* have to be fucking stupid to invade Russia," Stevens stated as fact. "But hey, now I can point Saint Pete out on a map. War *is* how Americans learn geography."

The sun disappeared over the water in the distance. We climbed down to our packs and hit the rack.

I laid there staring at the concrete lines in the over pass. It was dark. The power was out in most of the city and we were exercising strict light discipline. I hadn't had a hard time sleeping since we got to Russia. I was usually too exhausted to stay awake longer than a minute while I was lying down, and much too tired to dream.

I thought about being home in my room with Penelope and a bottle of wine, red wine, not the Virescent stuff. I thought about Penelope lying naked on her stomach with her head resting on crossed arms on the bed with the olive tree posts. *That was a bitch to build.* I thought about massaging Penelope's back with olive oil, I never figured out why, but she loved it. I fantasized about rubbing the cool liquid into the muscles in her back and tracing the outlines of her rose tattoos with my fingers. She would have her hair flipped over her head exposing her neck. After I'd made my way down her back I'd walk my hands up to her shoulders then around to her breasts. She's turn to me, and when our lips touched I'd breathe in what she exhaled. I'd start rubbing my shaft on the slick skin the oil produced. I'd position myself to where I could get the head of my penis to kiss her little downstairs lips. And then I'd...I'd...

...I'd be off to Never Never Land

I was in a church kneeling in the pews. There were dark figures in the benches around me. Fear boiled in my belly. The church was on fire, but the with every flicker of the growing flames the chapel grew darker. The dark cloaked figure beside me whispered into my ear. His words terrified me. I couldn't understand what he was saying, but I knew whatever it was... was a sinister lie. The fires of the burning church engulfed the walls and they crumbled to the ground. The church was in Saint Petersburg. There were Marines and Russians in flack and Kevlar fighting with swords and shields in the burning city. A great red dragon spread his wings and soared above the skyline spewing down his napalm breath. The dark cloaked figure beside me pulled down his hood. It was Satin! I sighed in relief. I pointed at her and half laughed. "This is a..."

I woke up in a cold sweat.

11 The Gods Of The Garden Shout At The Devil

August came. Leaves hadn't started to litter the ground, but some of the trees were now orange, red, and yellow, the ones that weren't blown into toothpicks anyway. It was night, and we were in our warehouse bivouac. Water leaked onto the crates and the concrete floor. Lightning from the storm offered us brief moments of light. We didn't have power, but even if we did, we didn't want to advertise our location.

Fonzie and McMillian sat on two MRE boxes. A chessboard sat on the third between them. The pawns and kings and queens were illuminated by the red light from their headlamps. The game seemed to dance with the storm. Both the Marines had their headphones on and were rocking to the beat of whatever they were listening to, to get their minds away from Russia, however briefly. Everyone and everything else, except in flashes of lightning, were but shadows.

"I want to go home," I whispered to Doc over the sound of thunder and thick raindrops slamming the ceiling's cracked windows.

"We all do man," Doc replied as we sat on a crate filled with packing peanuts and large cogged metal gears.

"No, I mean like I *really* want to go home. I'm tired of this shit. I don't care about this fucking war."

Doc's silhouette gave me a look. I didn't have to strain my eyes to understand what it meant.

"I don't have any qualms with fucking slugging it out with Ivan, but they're not letting us fight this fucking war the way we need to. It's one thing to do this cat and mouse bullshit with piss ant countries or insurgents, but Russia's not fucking around and they're killing the shit out of us and we can't call in fucking airstrikes that pack any ass. We were doing the same shit in Afghanistan, and when we left there was no 'So What' because the fucking Afghans weren't going to come to America. If we leave, Ivan's gonna come to us, but Washington won't let us do what we need to do to win. They'd rather us all die here than give the Russian's a painful death."

"I hear you, man."

"Shit the Russian's are destroying the city more than we are. We've been here since *June* and haven't really made much more than a beach head. No one at home is fucking supporting the war, there are too many casualties. They're protesting and fucking everything. And who the *fuck* cares if Vladimir Putin kidnapped the First Lady? Why do we have to deal with this shit? Why can't they just send in SEAL Team Six or some CIA dudes?"

"Yeah, but we kicked Russia out of the Baltic states."

"Yeah, because the fucking host nations and the Germans aren't afraid of leveling shit. This fucking city should have been rubble before we left Latvia."

Doc sighed, "Yeah. We should just cut our losses and leave this place to rot."

"And fuck politics, we need to do what's right."

"That's not how shit works."

"Eh." I pulled out a cigarette. The people with too much of their time spent sticking their noses in other people's business always said these things will kill me, *maybe this one would be the one,* I laughed to myself. Usually we weren't allowed to smoke inside, but since Fonzie was the acting platoon commander and this was his area, he let us do pretty much whatever we wanted, just so long as our weapon was never more than an arm's length away. I watched the chess game for a moment and looked up to light my cigarette. I saw a shadow pass over the ceiling windows over a lightning crack. "Doc, is someone supposed to be up there?"

"The sentries and some snipers should be."

"Okay," I took in a deep drag. "I think I might drag myself through a minefield. I'll miss another year, but fuck it I'll be in Balboa and have Penelope with me when I wake up."

"I don't think that's a good idea, man."

"Why, not? It'd be quick and painless. Sure I'd have to start back at the gym from zero, but it's not really like I've been working out since I got here. Besides I'm pretty confident we're both immortal. We shouldn't have eaten those berries in Iraq. We'd have been happy and dead a long time ago."

"Yeah, but you can't just leave everyone. We're already undermanned as fuck. Shit the fucking platoon only has twenty fucking Marines in it."

"Eh. Well then maybe I should start doing more heroic shit. Like running through fire and grabbing people and standing in the street while I gun down Ivan."

"You've already been doing that Hank, we all have. They haven't awarded anyone anything, but we've *all* done medal worthy shit here. Everyone here's thinking the same things you are, except I don't think anyone else is thinking about stomping on a landmine."

"No one else is in the position we are though."

"True, but you know if you left you'd hate yourself for the rest of your fucking life."

I took a deep breath. "I know. Maybe I'm just talking out of my ass."

McMillian took a bishop and Fonzie stared down the board.

"Doc…"

"Yeah, dude."

"Are we aging?"

"I don't know. I think so. If not we're in for a shit load of pain in the future."

"If we're still alive by the time the technology and our wallets allow it we should shoot ourselves into the sun," I chuckled.

"Ya think that would work?" Doc joked. "What if we just hung out at a nuclear weapons test site?"

"That could work." I laughed, elbowing Doc.

I looked up to watch the streams of rain collect and run away in the lightning and wind. The windows shattered into a million little diamonds and fell into the room with the rain. For an instant I thought lightning had struck the roof, then I saw ropes fall into the room and dark figures fall from the new broken windows.

Doc and I grabbed our AKs and started firing at the ceiling.

"CONTACT!"

The Marines grabbed their weapons and fired at the intruders, except Fonzie and McMillian, who in the heat of their game were oblivious to the assault.

A rope was dangling a foot away from me, I opened fire on whatever was descending. The body fell from the rope and slammed down, knocking me from the crates to the hard concrete floor. I grunted, rolled over and put a few more bullets into the body, just to be sure.

The area between the crates was lit brilliantly from the combination of muzzle flashes and the battle Thor and Zeus were having in the clouds. Light bounced off the thick rain then fell into the warehouse in columns under the broken windows.

Fonzie and McMillian were dry and engulfed in their own war on the board.

In the darkness it was hard to see who our friends were. I shot anyone with a flack and Kevlar. The Marine's wouldn't take the time to put them on with Ivan in their bedroom. I had my AK on single fire, trying to be careful not to shoot Marines.

"Hank! Get back here!" Éclair called from behind a crate.

I jumped over the splintering wood and landed next to Stevens, Doc, and Éclair. The machinery parts inside the crate halted most of Ivan's lead.

The four of us took turns popping up and letting out a few rounds.

"Let's go, we gotta circle around," Stevens shouted.

We moved in a counter clockwise course around the stacks of boxes and chests. Stevens led us. Five fingers held his rifle ready to fire. The other five ran down the wall to keep straight, the muzzle rested on the back of his wrist. We were blind. Éclair walked backwards behind us making sure we weren't gunned down from the rear.

POP POP POP Stevens let out a burst, a dark clad figure fell onto the floor.

POP Doc put another round in the shape's face as he stepped over it. We turned the corner of the crates and looked into the opening in the main area. Flashes lit across the room, but they all were the same, almost all of the Marines were using Russian weapons.

"How the fuck are those two just sitting there?" Éclair barked looking at Fonzie and McMillian, still playing chess.

"How the fuck are they not shot yet?" Stevens followed.

"Fuck it, keep moving," Doc hollered.

We kept creeping around the crates until Stevens stopped. He poked his head around a corner, then said as quietly as he could but loud enough to hear over the guns, "There's like twenty dudes there."

"Us or them?" Éclair asked.

"I don't know," Stevens said.

"Do they have Kevlar's on?" I inquired.

"What difference does that make?" Éclair said gripping his weapon.

"Do you really think there's even one Marine in here that took the time to grab his shit? Plus there's barely twenty Marines left in the platoon, four of us are here and two are fucking playing chess," I responded.

Stevens' shadow shrugged and peeked back around the corner, then rolled back to us. "It's defiantly Ivan. You guys got ammo?"

We checked our magazines and gave him a thumbs up.

"Okay, they don't know we're right here. If we all start spraying them at the same time I think we can get them." Stevens pointed at Doc, "You shoot from the crate, I'll hit the wall." Stevens looked at Éclair and me, "You two in the middle. We'll go in like we're clearing a hallway."

Stevens put himself at the edge of the corner of the crate, then me, Éclair, and Doc. We passed the kick from Doc to Stevens, letting him know we were ready and Stevens jumped to the wall muzzle first towards Ivan. No longer than half a second later Doc was hooked around the crate and Éclair and I were between them unloading our AKs on full auto into the Russian troops.

One hundred and twenty rounds later the room was silent again but for the rain. When the last empty shell casing made its ting on the floor we reached for new magazines. Mine were in a cargo pocket. We crept up the line of Russians bleeding on the deck. If they were still gasping for air we put a short burst in their face. If they didn't seem to still be among the living we poked them in the eye with our muzzles to see if they flinched, if they did, their helmets became a bowl for brain matter soup, served at a perfect ninety-eight degrees.

"Who's still over there?" Becker shouted from the other side of the room.

"Stevens, Éclair, Doc Evans, and Allensworth!" Stevens shouted back, "It's clear on this side!"

"This side's clear too!" Becker shouted.

We stepped an uneasy creep back between the crates. After a few seconds of nothing I stomped over to the two chess players and kicked over the board sending the little wooden players across the floor.

"The fuck, dude?" Fonzie protested, pulling out his headphones.

"Good game?" I bit at him.

Fonzie and McMillian looked at the Marines around them, all bearing their weapons, some bleeding.

"The fuck?" McMillian asked confused.

Stevens pointed to the holes where windows used to be. "Ivan made a house call."

"How the fuck did we miss that?" McMillian asked in shock.

"I thought that was the storm dude," Fonzie said.

"The thunder and lightning wasn't that bad," I shot back.

"Well fuck, I take it we won?" Fonzie looked around the darkness of the room. He grabbed the AK that was resting on his boot. "Anyone get hurt?"

The Marines all looked at each other for someone missing. There were a few cuts and grazes, but no one was seriously injured.

"Doc, patch these guys up," Fonzie told him. "Stevens, take your Marines and check on the other platoons. McMillian's squad and I are gonna go check on firewatch."

Éclair bounced with Stevens and I went with Fonzie. We climbed the rusted steel ladder well up the wall to the roof. The two Marines overlooking the complex laid over their sandbag citadel with their throats slit. The rain washed their blood down the building.

Fonzie shook his head and whispered, "Mother fuckers."

"We couldn't have helped that one man," McMillian whispered.

We pulled the fallen Marines off the roof and posted two more to the watch. When we got back downstairs we started looting the Russian soldiers. They were wearing all black and had no identifying information. No insignia, no dog tags, no wallets, cigarettes or anything.

"I gotta go talk to the CO," Fonzie told Stevens as he and his squad returned.

I reached for a cigarette and my pack was empty. I found my Alice pack. "God *DAMN* it!" I gritted. My pack and sleeping system were fucking soaked. I unrolled my sleeping bag and threw it over a crate, hoping it would dry out. I grabbed a pack of cigarettes, stowed away in a waterproof bag, and walked back to Doc, Stevens, and Éclair.

I opened the pack and offered the three smokes, they all took one.

"Third Platoon got hit pretty bad," Stevens lit up.

"How bad's bad?" Éclair asked.

"Half," Stevens whispered. "Doc, you better go help them out."

Wordlessly, Doc disappeared into the darkness towards Third Platoon's hooch.

"Who the fuck were these dudes?" I asked.

"Who knows," Stevens said. "Probably Spetznas or some other GRU dicks."

"There weren't a lot of them whoever they were." Éclair looked around in the darkness. "Why didn't they use grenades?"

"Yeah, even flash-bangs?" I followed.

"I don't know," Stevens said slowly. "Did they have any on them?"

"Not that I saw." I took in nicotine. "But Ivan's getting ballsy."

Fonzie came back into the room. "Hey everyone, listen up." The squad and a half sized platoon circled around the Fonz. "Before we hit the sack tonight there's a few things that are going to happen. First off, all these Russian fucks; their bodies are going to be soaked in fuel, thrown in the street and set on fire."

"CO's cool with that?" Stevens asked.

"Captain Sancho's on fire watch at the pearly gates," Fonzie informed us.

Mutters of 'Fuck' and 'Damn' came from the crowd.

"Lieutenant Toshi want's these guy's heads on pikes and posted around the roof."

"Shit's that fucking bad?" I asked.

"Yeah. Ivan hit us pretty hard. Half of Third Platoons gone, so are some of the S2 Marines that were here. Ivan ran off with a bunch of secret hard drives."

"Jesus, fuck," Éclair whispered.

"Yeah, Fox Company is almost combat ineffective. We're still waiting on word, but plan to leave here at zero four to link up with Gulf."

We pulled apart the crates to use as pikes. We sawed off the Russian's heads and posted them in a perimeter around the warehouse complex. The bodies were soaked in fuel and burnt in the street, in full view of any Russians who may have been watching.

I left the contents of my pack out to try to dry. I was soaked. It wasn't cold out, but being wet in the warmth isn't much better than wet in the cold when you're trying to sleep. I tried to sleep through the sweat and the shivers. I had no nightmares, no dreams.

We woke up a few hours later to move out. The little sleep I got wasn't restful. I was still wet and it was still raining. I stuffed my gear into my Alice pack. "This shit's still soaked," I muttered to no one in particular.

"Yeah, but there's no Morning Prayer," Éclair said, putting his flack jacket on.

"How thoughtful of Ivan," I grumbled.

"You gonna shave?" Éclair asked.

"No, I'm skipping that shit."

The company mustered in the rain between the buildings. Doc was still sitting with the casualties by the trucks. I shook my head. "That guy's one caring son of a bitch."

"Dude, that's his job," Éclair said.

"No, he only *had* to patch those dudes up. He sat with them because he cares about'em. We probably should have been there too."

Éclair let out something somewhere between a sigh and a yawn, "It doesn't matter, man. We're all going to die out here." With no dread or concern. "It's just a matter of time."

First Sergeant DeLeon and Lieutenant Toshi formed us into a column and we marched out into the city towards Gulf Company's location. Ivan's dead eyes watched us move past the charred skeletons in the street. Their still burning flames cast our shadows on the bullet-peppered walls.

When we left the industrial area and started into the town gardens, our Daedalus escort morphed into its human looking form and walked beside us.

I doubt anyone wasn't on edge. McMillian hummed the tune to 'The Rooster' to keep himself cool. Doc did the same thing with 'Shout at the Devil.' The garden we were in gave me a terrible feeling. The walkways were lined with marble statues of Grecian gods. From under the trees they stared us down in the darkness. Dawn wouldn't be for another hour or two. The maidens holding a cloth over their stone bodies seemed as if they were running in fear. They were probably quite a sight in the sun, lifelessly lightening the mood of the park, watching families picnic in the shade, lending their smiles to traveling observers. But now their carved, curved bodies, that no doubt the sculptor lusted after as he fashioned them perfectly with a chisel, scowled at us with hate-filled eyes. Svetlana welcomed us no more than Ivan.

There was a screeching roar through the air. The Daedalus' legs exploded throwing shrapnel in all directions. The Marines that weren't thrown to the ground from the blast volunteered to meet it. I looked back at the collapsing mech. Doc was still falling to the ground. He hit the dirt ten meters from where he was standing with a thud.

Enemy machineguns kept us pinned to the deck. Most Marines fired back. I said to hell with it and ran after Doc. Before I could get to him he started crawling towards a statue of Zeus brandishing a lightning bolt. A few feet from the safety of cover I grabbed the back of Doc's flack and started dragging him as he crawled. We slammed into the base of the statue.

"I'm good, dude. It just knocked the wind out of me," He wheezed.

I peered beyond the edge of the statue. I saw Ivan shooting from the hedgerow. I aimed in and squeezed off a few rounds. "Come on dude, we gotta get back to the platoon."

"Give me a minute," he gasped and held his eyes open wide.

Bullets zipped over our head and shot fragments of Zeus' body onto us.

"FUCK!" Doc screamed.

"What?" I looked back at him.

"Fucking shit's in my fucking eyes."

"Quit being a pussy, Doc."

"Fuck you!"

"Doc, I can hear Marine's screaming over there."

Doc tried to blink the rocks out of his eyes.

"Be strong."

Doc got himself to a knee "and shout at the devil."

"STEVENS!" I yelled.

"YO!"

"WE'RE COMING TO YOU!"

"GOT IT!"

Stevens' Marines let out as much fire as they could. Doc and I were lightning from Zeus to Stevens and slid into the trail. Doc scrawled over to a Marine bleeding in the path.

"FUCK!" McMillian screamed.

I snapped my head towards his voice.

He was firing in a rage. "ENEMY AMROR IN THE OPEN!"

I looked back at the hedgerow. There was a gap in it, the tank that was now heading towards us, left.

The Daedalus came back to life. Its legs were missing, but it balanced itself and pointed its weapon towards Ivan and turned the hedgerows into shredded lettuce and ketchup. The mech crawled to the front of our file and then laid back on the other side between the Marines and Ivan. The Daedalus emptied its ammunition in the direction the Russians were. One round punctured the tank. It stopped dead in its tracks, but didn't burn. The enemy guns silenced and someone yelled, "Cease Fire!"

The Daedalus pilot opened the hatch and jumped out, pistol in hand. Lieutenant Toshi grabbed the pilot and pulled him down.

Stevens' squad jumped behind the wrecked mech for cover. When Doc was done bandaging up the wounded Marines and loading them into a truck, we took cover with the squad.

"I left a charge in the cockpit!" The Daedalus pilot told Toshi.

"When's it gonna blow?"

"Five minutes."

"Sergeant Palacios!" Toshi yelled.

"Yes, Sir?" Fonzie scurried over to the lieutenant.

"This mech's gonna explode in about four minutes. Take that squad and go make sure there ain't nothing left of that tank crew besides ground beef."

"Aye, Sir." Fonzie ran over to us, "Y'all year that?"

"Yeah," Stevens growled. He gave the squad the hand and arm signals to follow him and hopped over the Daedalus' scraps. The squad, if you'd still call it that, crept behind Stevens and Fonzie.

There was a thin, translucent stream of smoke rising from the hole the Daedalus left in the tank's hull. Stevens and Marcsky climbed the sides of the tank. The rest of us found what cover we could and waited for Ivan to return. Stevens pointed his rifle at the hatch and Marcsky started laying a charge that would open it.

Stevens and Marcsky slid off the tank. "Everyone hold on," Marcsky said, holding the detonator. "SHIT!"

I looked over at Marcsky. He was gawking at the sky. I looked to see what he was worried about. I expected to see a Knight falling on us but it was worse. Straight in our line of sight an A10 was bearing down on the tank.

"GET THE FUCK OUT OF HERE!" Fonzie yelled.

We got up to run…

The A10's front burst into fire.

BBRRRRRRRRRRRRRRRRRRRRRRRR!!!

The tank popped like a tin can full of confetti and dynamite.

Marcsky and Stevens were vaporized. The rest of the squad was thrown from the explosion in every which direction.

I didn't land as much as I slammed into a tree.

Gunfire erupted again over my head. The curtain in the theater behind my eyes closed.

I woke up cold and wet.

I couldn't see anything.

How long was I out? Where are the lights? My whole body ached. I went to rub my chest, but my hand was stuck. *What the...* I moved my head around, there was something over it. I jerked my hands, they were tied together. *Fuck fuck FUCK!*

12 Born To Die In A Dark Paradise

Damnit this is bad. Is anything broken? Maybe a few ribs. How the hell did I get captured? Fucking Air Force.

My chest was an agonizing amalgamation of broken glass. I sat there on my ass with something over my head, my hands bound. I could feel I wasn't wearing my body armor. *Well-played Ivan.* My body shook from being cold and damp, or maybe it was the shock of getting blown through the tree. I had to figure out where I was, and who was with me.

I coughed and immediately got a swift kick to the thigh, "Shut up!" a heavily accented voice barked. *Fucking Great.* I don't know how long I sat there. My best guess would be hours, maybe a day. At first they had me next to a few other people they captured. The only one I knew for sure that was there was DeLaGarza. I heard him say he had to piss, he got kicked and told to be quiet. After coming in and out of consciousness a few times I was hoisted up and dragged somewhere else. I heard a heavy clank and guessed I was in a cell. I didn't move though. I was bound and blind. *How could I get... where? Now I wish I had gone to SERE.*

After a while I heard a tapping coming from the other side of the wall. I listened, wondering what it was. It didn't sound mechanical. When I put it together I said, "Sorry, I don't know Morse Code." Even if I did know it I wouldn't be able to tell if they were friendly or not with that sack over my head. The tapping stopped.

After a while the metal door clanked again and hands grabbed my arms. "Get up," said the accented voice.

They walked me for a while and sat me down in a cold metal chair. The sack was pulled from over my head, everything got bright and blurry. I winced so the light wouldn't burn a hole to my brain. The ropes around my hands were untied. I rubbed my wrists and looked up.

There were two men in Russian uniforms sitting across a table from me, two more men behind them stood with rifles. I assumed there were more behind me.

The one on my left gave me a faint smile. "Good Morning," he said in a thick, Russian tone. The one on the right mean mugged me.

"Hey."

"Mister Allensworth, if I am not mistaken?"

"Yup."

I put my hands on the table. There were three steaming Styrofoam cups.

"I am Captain Michaelovna and this is my comrade Senior Lieutenant Ludmila. We are with the Western Operational Strategic Command. You may call me Hector and the Lieutenant, Paris."

"Cool." I shifted my gaze between the Russians, "Name's Hank."

"Would you like coffee?" Hector offered.

"Yeah, thanks. Which one?"

Hector slid one of the cups towards me. I thought for a second that it may be spiked, but when I realized I was in a gulag and immediately hoped it was poison. I thought about throwing the steaming hot coffee in their face and jumping the guards. Realizing I wasn't Chuck Norris, and that it wouldn't work, I took a sip.

"We have much to discuss Hank." Hector pulled out a notepad and a pen.

"Yeah? 'Bout what? I haven't seen the new James Bond movie, so please don't ruin it for me." I faked a smile. *Don't tell them anything important Hank, think OPSEC.*

"Hank, what is your business in Russian Federation?" Hector asked.

"What do you think, man?" *Bravado, don't let them know you're scared. Wait, what do I have to be scared about? Maybe I can get them to shoot me and I'll crawl out of the grave a few days later and get away. Eh, on second thought, getting shot fucking hurts. Fuck it.*

"I think you are here to kill us," Paris Sneered.

"Or am I here for you to kill?"

They gave me a confused look.

"I mean shit..." I took a sip of the coffee. It was bitter and tasted like instant bullshit, but it was hot and took my mind off of what I was sure was a broken rib. "We've been here three months and haven't taken the city yet. You guys are giving us a run for our money."

Hector smiled but didn't show his teeth. "Yes, but what are *you* doing in Russia? You are infantryman?"

"Nooo, I'm the camera guy. I just take pictures."

Paris reached under the table and produced my camera. "We know about pictures Mister Allensworth."

"Oh cool! You guys get to take a look at them yet?"

"How do you feel about us looking at photos together?" Hector asked.

"Yeah dude, I'm down." *Fuck, there's at least twenty pictures of dead Russians on there. Thank God I didn't take photos of the severed heads.*

Paris turned on the camera and positioned it so that the three of us could all see the display screen on the back. The first few photos were of destroyed buildings.

"You know," I started, "This city is beautiful. It's a damn shame what we're doing to it. I might have to visit after the war and everything's cleaned up."

"It is marvelous city." Hector said.

"Yeah? Ya from here?" I asked

"No, I am from Volgograd."

"Never heard of it. There good beer there?"

"Mostly Vodka."

"I guess that makes sense."

Paris scanned through more pictures. The screen showed Marines firing stolen AKs at the Russians. "So where did Marines get Kalashnikovs?"

Uh... "We took them from you guys."

"After you murdered them?" Paris accused.

"Well, they shot at us first. I've seen some of those dudes with M16s," I lied. "Have you shot those things? God, the M16 is such a piece of *shit*."

The Russians kept their cool. "No, I have not shot M16," Hector said.

"Let me tell you about *those* fucking things." *Good maybe I can feed them information they can find on Google and they'll eat it up.* "The round is smaller, if the thing doesn't stay clean it jams. The damn weapon had this thing called a forward assist..."

"Forward assist?"

"Yeah, man. It's on the right side of it. If the bolt gets stuck back, you press the forward assist and it makes the bolt go forward for you. You guys have our guns somewhere, right? Check it out."

Paris flipped to another photo. This one was of Marines chilling out in the warehouse we vacated earlier.

"That's our house," I said.

"*Your* house?" Paris asked.

"Well we're renting it. It stays pretty warm at night and it doesn't leak when it rains. It's not too bad," I lied.

"How long have you been there?" Hector asked.

I pretended to think for a second. "I wanna say, June," I lied.

"Hmm."

"Hey, so how long have I been here?" I asked.

"Not so long," Hector answered.

"Well, where can I get some chow?"

"What is chow?" Paris asked.

"Food?" I shrugged. "Whatchew guys got to eat around here? You have a restaurant or are you eating rats like we are?"

"You're eating rats?" Hector was pretty good at sounding sympathetic.

"That or we catch a cat every once in awhile." *I wonder if they know how much smoke I'm blowing up their ass.*

"You will get food soon." Hector kept the smile on his face. He nodded at whoever was standing behind me. The faceless set of hands put me in steel bracelets and stood me up. I didn't see the man behind me. Hector rose and walked with me back to the cells. "If you could wait, we can have dinner together."

"I'd like that." I nodded my head and faked a smile.

The hallway outside of the interrogation room was windowless and blank. Hector produced a key and unlocked a metal door, "After you."

I stepped into another hallway. This one was lined with thick bars. Red bricks divided the cells. I tried looking around to see if I knew anyone else there, but it was hard with the size of the cells and how quickly we were moving. I thought I saw a few people, but I couldn't be sure. At the open, barred door a quarter of the way down the hallway Hector held his hand out, as if he were an usher.

"Hank, I look forward to discussing more with you later. However, I have to meet your friends." Hector closed the cell's door. "Give me your hands." I raised them and he removed the cuffs. "Have a good rest of afternoon."

I bet that guy's goal is Stockholm syndrome. Fucker.

"You too, dude." I said as he walked to the cell across from mine. The Soldier that had been behind us grabbed a Marine with a sack over his head and the three of them disappeared.

I looked around the cell. I must have been sitting on the short end of the bed before our chat. It was half the size of a single bed, if I was going to use it I'd be sleeping on my side. At the other end of the bed was a metal toilet, *No shit paper,* I could touch both ends of the cell with my elbows. I tried to look into the other cells, but things were situated so I couldn't.

"Hey! Anyone else here?" I said loudly, but didn't scream.

"Yes," Doc's voice said through the wall. "And be quiet. They're listening."

"Well no shit they're listening," I griped back "Was that you trying Morse Code earlier?"

"Yes," he said, just above a whisper.

"So what's the difference between talking and tapping?" I asked, trying to keep my voice low.

"Anyway we can make it harder for the Russians, we should."

"Well, why aren't there any guards here?"

"Why, does there need to be?"

"I don't know." I sat down on the hard sheet they were trying to pawn off as a bed. I smiled a little. I didn't think we'd be able to get us out of this, nor did I think anyone was coming for us. I lay down on my side on the bed. *FUCK!* My ribs pinched together. *Guess lying on my side is out of the question.* I laid with my back flat on the floor. I had to muscle up my shoulder blade on the toilet to keep my back at an angle that didn't make it feel like it was being stabbed. *For as much as I've been broken I should be able to take this kind of pain.* I closed my eyes and tried to go to sleep. I told myself that there's no point in trying to escape right then and I should get some rest. If the Russians started up with the water torture and scorpions any time soon... *Might as well sleep while you can, Hank.*

Hector woke me up with a tap on the foot from his boot. I squinted up at him. "Good Evening, Hank."

"Hey," I said, not remembering exactly where I was for a few seconds.

"Would you care to join me for dinner?"

I pressed my eyes shut and rubbed the back of my neck. "Sure." I stood up slowly.

"Your hands?" Hector said as if he were asking for a second bowl of soup.

"Yeah, sorry dude." I put my palms together and our escort slapped the cuffs on me. I rubbed the inside of my arms on my body. *Good, I dried off.*

We strolled out of the cellblock without a word. I was released from my cuffs when Hector and I were seated at the table with Paris. My rib was sore, but it didn't hurt too much if I leaned forward in the chair.

"How are you enjoying accommodations Hank?" Hector asked.

"It's not too bad. The bed could be better." I cracked a smile. *I wonder how long I can pretend to be okay with this shit.*

"Well, you are in prison," Paris needlessly reminded me.

This ain't prison. Being a lance corporal in Twentynine Stumps is prison. Fuck, I might be alright for a while here. "Yeah, well we all fuck up. At least I haven't been traded for a cigarette yet."

"What is traded for cigarette?" Hector asked.

"It's, uh, a prison thing. Like the boss prisoner dude will let other dudes fuck the smallest guy there if they pay with cigarettes." I nodded my head.

"That is in American prison?" Hector asked showing shock. I don't know if it was real or not.

"Yup," I lied, I've never even seen the outside walls of a prison before.

"And you were there?" Hector inferred.

"That's where the Marine Corps gets their troops. The Army, Navy and Air Force have dudes that enlist. Marines are all taken from prisons, that's why we don't care if we get killed." *I wondered if they believe a word of my bullshit.*

"Interesting." Hector pulled a pack of cigarettes out of his pocket. "Would you like one?"

"Are you serious?"

"Why would I not be?" He offered me the pack.

"I mean you're allowed to smoke inside?" I took a cigarette.

"Yes?" Hector looked genuinely confused as he held up a burning lighter.

I stuck the cigarette into the flame and took a puff. "Can't do that in America."

"Yes you can," Hector said.

"Where?"

Hector was silent.

"Nowhere I've ever been. Everyone's such a pussy about that. I understand restaurants and stores, but I should be allowed to smoke in a fucking bar," I exhaled. "Thanks for the smoke by the way."

The door opened behind me, a soldier walked in and a plate with small potatoes and a pathetic piece of chicken appeared on the table alongside a fork.

"Eat, is good," Hector assured me.

I picked up the fork and started eating the chicken between puffs from the cigarette.

"So one can't smoke in America?" Hector continued.

"No dude, you can smoke outside, that's it. Most of the time you can't even smoke inside your own house."

"What about in winter or in rain?"

"Gotta go outside."

"Well now I have no desire to ever visit your country."

"Hell, I'm starting to like Russia," I lied again.

Hector smiled. "Hank, you like Vodka?"

"Like it?" I tried to look like I was more desperate for food than I actually was. "I'm all about it. You guys ever mix it with milk and Kahlua?"

"No, we drink straight."

"That's cool, too. Hell, if you grab a bottle and a pack of cigarettes I'll stay here and chat with you all night."

"Good."

Hector produced a bottle of Russian Vodka and a few tumblers.

"Damn man, I didn't we were doing all that. Can I get another one of those cigarettes?" I wolfed down the rest of the meal.

Hector placed the cigarettes on the table and poured our drinks.

I grabbed mine and held it up, "Cheers."

The interrogators tapped their glasses to mine. *These guys are trying to get me drunk to talk about shit I wouldn't say sober. Good thinking Ivan, you poor bastard. I'll drink you fuckers under the table and you won't get shit out of me.*

Hector kept the conversation light until we needed a second bottle. Mostly just talking about different kinds of alcohol, cigarettes and a few movies. When the time came for a second bottle Hector asked me "So Hank, what do you think about Russian soldiers?" as he poured another round.

"Well you're all fucking *ugly!*" I laughed pretending the alcohol was affecting me a lot more than it was.

The interrogators laughed with me.

"No, but seriously, you guys are good shit. You're tougher than nails and fight colder than a witch's tit." I was still faking a giggle.

"This is motherland, of course we fight hard," Paris said. The vodka was lightening up his bad cop routine.

165

"Well, Afghanistan was Hajji's homeland and we kicked his ass."

"Wait, you were in Afghanistan?" Hector waved his hand over the table.

"Yeah, man. Two deployments."

"My uncles were all in Afghanistan."

"Yeah? What'd they say about it?"

"Almost nothing. They said it was very hot and the people were nice when they weren't trying to kill us."

"*Dude.* I tell people that all the time!"

"No!"

"Yeah! I don't want to talk about that shit, but people ask and ya gotta tell 'em somethin' right?"

"I suppose."

Hector downed his glass.

I followed suit.

"But between you and me, those Afghan chicks are fucking beautiful."

"What?"

"You know, when they're not covered in that rag shit and crusty from the sand." I hid my eyes with my hands then peeked through my fingers and laughed.

Hector laughed back, "I can only imagine."

"And that Helen chick you guys nabbed. Woo, she's a beaut ain't she?"

"Yes." Hector smiled. "How did Menelaus catch woman like that?"

"Ah who the hell knows, probably because he's the president. I'd bet old Vlad Putin's got some hotties he keeps around."

166

"Probably, I know if I were him *I* would." Hector laughed and poured us another drink. "You have wife, yes?"

"Uh, yeah. I have some pictures of her in my wallet if you guys still have that."

"We have *all* of your things in other room." Hector looked at one of the guards and said something in Russian.

"Hey, can I get my wedding ring back while you're at it?" I asked.

Hector yelled something at soldier as he was leaving the room. "I have wife. Her name is Natalia."

"That's a pretty name. Where's she?"

"Volgograd."

"Got a picture of her?"

Hector leaned over, pulled his wallet out of his back pocket and flipped it open to show me the picture of the woman whose name was Natalia, but looked like an Olga.

I wonder if he's with this chick so he can use her as a heat source in the winter. How many chins does she have? "She's got pretty eyes." *And that's about it.*

"Yes, we've been together for some time." He put the wallet away. "How about you, Hank?"

"I actually married a Virescent."

Hector's eyebrows raised, "Really?"

"Yeah, she's green and pretty."

The soldier returned with my wallet and ring and dropped them on the table. I put on my ring and opened my wallet. I showed Hector and Paris the photo of Penelope in her bikini on the hood of my GTO. "She's my little emerald."

"She is very beautiful." Hector complimented her.

"How does she feel about war?" Paris asked.

"Oh she hates it. She doesn't care about the war one-way or the other. She ain't from Earth and don't care about the countries." I tried to sound drunker than I was so that my rambling seemed honest. "She hates the Marine Corps almost as much as I do."

"Why do you hate Marine Corps?" Paris asked.

"Oh man, don't get me started." *Get ready for a metric shit ton of useless information you're going to think is relevant.* "So I've been in for like nine years, right. And if I wasn't married I'd have to live in the barracks, but now two queer privates can get married and live on the beach."

"What is queer?" Paris asked.

"Homos."

They shook their heads not understanding.

"The guys that have sex with other guys."

Both men grimaced and turned their heads. "America lets *them* in the military?" Hector asked.

"Yeah. Pissed me off too! Fucking faggots. The god damned government is just giving those cock suckers anything they want!" I personally didn't care one way or the other what people did in their bedroom, but if it kept these guys friendly, and I wasn't giving up real information, I'll pretend to hate someone. "And before they let the gays in, the general went to all the units and asked if the troops thought it was cool. Everyone told the general 'no' but Fucking General Amos let in all those homos anyway. Can you believe that?"

"So you're saying the officers treat you poorly?" Hector tried to sound sympathetic.

"Poorly? They shit on us every chance they get. Check this out, the sergeant major in charge of the whole Marine Corps told congress that it was okay to cut our paychecks!" *That one was true.*

"They want you to have no *morale*?" Paris asked.

"Nope, none, nobody in the Marine Corps has morale anymore!" I lied "They're pushing us to our deaths out here just so that we can go back to the states and get kicked!"

That seemed like something the interrogators liked to hear. They leaned in and let me rattle off my gripes against the Marine Corps. I continued my rant through another bottle of Vodka and a pack of cigarettes. But I was very careful to not show them that I was pretending to be drunker than I was and extremely careful not to tell them anything they couldn't find on a disgruntled Marines' social media page.

I don't know why they went the wine and dine route instead of the bamboo under the fingernails trail, but I appreciated it, and to be honest, I had a little fun feeding them bullshit.

13 If That Railroad Train was Mine

I don't know how many people can say they know from experience that being hungover in a prison cell is only slightly better than being hungover in a firefight. But I was now one of the few.

I hadn't seen Hector and Paris for days. I tried to sleep to pass the time, when the guards weren't amusing themselves by kicking my ass. They'd come in intervals. One would hold me, and the other would punch me until he was tired, then they'd leave. Luckily all the fractures in my ribs were on my back side.

I talked to Doc when we had something to talk about. I saw DeLaGarza and Fonzie come and go from Hector's little talks. I don't know if they saw me in my cell, but I'm sure they'd seen me going to the interrogators in the days prior.

After an absolutely joyful meeting between a guard's boot and my ass, I laid on the floor looking at the bricks that divided the walls. I was holding onto my sanity, I had no doubt that I could keep it up, however much I didn't want to. I crossed my arms and propped my shoulder up on the base of the toilet to make my ribs feel better. My face hurt, but not as much as my stomach. I told myself that I'd been through worse. Then I wished that the drill instructors were allowed to beat you senseless in boot camp to help people get prepared for this kind of shit. *I guess SERE's for that, too bad I didn't go.*

I closed my eyes and tried to imagine myself somewhere else. Before I could get too far away from my own mind, I heard a scratching noise. I unsheathed my eyes and looked at the wall. One of the bricks was moving away. There had become a small hole in the bottom of the wall, just big enough to see Doc's mouth.

"I don't think they're done with you, Hank."

"Oh yeah?" I creaked.

"They do the same thing to everyone. Hector and Paris make you feel at home. Then you don't see them for a while and the guards rough you up. In a few more days Hector and Paris will *rescue* you from the evil guards and you'll be prompted to talk more."

"That'll be fun. I haven't been telling them anything."

"You're always gone for a long time to not be talking."

"Oh I talk. But I tell them bullshit information they could find on the internet. I talked to them for about an hour about the forward assist on the M16 and how useless of a weapon it was. Stuff that isn't classified, but they think's important just because they don't know. Like, for a while I just bitched about the Commandant and the Sergeant Major of the Marine Corps."

"You'd be surprised what that tells them."

"What do you mean?"

"If you're complaining about the chain of command, that tells them that your morale is low and they may find a way to use that against you."

"How would they do that?"

"They could put out a broadcast via loudspeaker or drop leaflets with messages that chip away at your morale and confidence and make it easier for them to kill you."

"Somehow I doubt that *anyone* is *ever* going to be less efficient just because they read a message from the enemy. How do you even know this shit, Doc?"

"Just be careful what you tell them."

"You dug a hole to my cell just to tell me that?"

"No. I think I can work these bricks so that I can take the wall apart and we can jump the guards."

"Really?"

"Yeah, but it's going to take a few weeks. I've been working that one brick since we've been here."

"How do you know how to do that?"

"Don't worry about it."

"Alright."

The next few days, or weeks, or hell, maybe it was only hours, Doc and I worked the wall. I couldn't keep track of the time. The kickings weren't on a schedule and the rare meals weren't regimented. There were no windows and the lights never dulled their glow. One by one, brick by brick. One of us always kept look out for the guards and we never had more than one brick out of the wall at a time. We'd rush to put the bricks back when it was time for the beatings or while the guards were entertaining themselves with the other prisoners.

We finally got enough of the bricks loose that we thought while I was getting hammered Doc could push the wall down. I was just supposed to yell 'Ultra violence' when I was pinned to the floor and a guard was on top of me. That way most of the bricks would hit the guard, and my face might be spared more bruises.

"Hey, guys." I cheered sarcastically as the two guards stopped in front of my cell. *I'm about to smash your fucking skulls.*

One of the guards barked something at me in Russian and motioned me to move away from the door.

I put my hands in the air, "Okay Ivan, I know the drill."

One guard grabbed my collar and pushed me back to the wall above the toilet. The second one took a step into the cell. An arm in a Marine's camouflaged sleeve reached from behind the second guard. I looked behind the guy with his hand around my throat and he smiled saying something in Russian. The arm grabbed the other guard's pistol and wacked him in the head. When his body made a thud, my guy turned his head to investigate.

Fonzie jolted through into the cell and shoved the pistol into the guard's mouth. The guard fell to his knees and started to plead. I snatched a brick out of the wall and turned the Russian's head into red jello.

"Fonz, how the fuck did you…"

"Not now." He bent down and took the keys from the guard's belt.

I took the pistol from the other guard who was lying on the floor. On the way out of the cell I stomped on the first guard's neck until his chest stopped rising. "Who else is here?"

"Let's find out."

"Alright." I stopped at the door. "Hey Doc, Ultra violence."

"You have the keys don't you?" Doc said.

"Let's get Doc first, Fonzie."

Fonzie slid the key into the lock on Doc's door. When they made eye contact Fonzie looked back at me.

We opened the other cells. DeLaGarza sprang to the door when we arrived.

All of us had had the shit kicked out of us. There were Marines in the other cells.

"Who are you guys?" Fonzie asked, releasing them.

"Echo Two-Seven." One of the twelve other Marines responded.

"Shit, you survivors of the air raid?"

"Yup."

"Are we in Ilium?"

"I think so."

"Alright, let's get out of here."

We left the cellblock. Fonzie and I led, we were the only ones armed. We knew the interrogation room was to the left, so we went right. We stopped at the first intersecting hallway. Fonzie peaked his head around the corner. "There's a guard at the desk by the door." He whispered back, "he's reading a magazine or something. Hank you come with me, rest of you stay here."

Fonzie and I crept down the hall towards the man reading at the desk. His nose was stuck in a Russian porno mag. When we got to the desk the soldier looked up as if he was expecting to see someone passing by. His eyes grew wide. Fonzie grabbed a pen from the desk and stabbed him in the neck. The soldier tried to yell but he had a hole in his windpipe, only gurgles were released from his throat. He fell on the ground and the two of us stomped him until the blood stopped pumping. I grabbed his gun and Fonzie grabbed the keys.

There was a room behind the desk. I peeked in. There were shelves of all sorts of random things. Mostly Boxes for files, but on the far end I saw our gear.

"Hey, Fonz," I said, looking back. "Our shit's in here."

Our little group entered the room. We brought in the dead guard and stashed him in a janitor closet. We got to the desk with our packs.

"They have our weapons somewhere else," Fonzie observed.

"Yeah, but they didn't take everything." Doc pulled his tomahawk out of his pack.

My axe was in my pack. "Why did they leave these?"

The other Marines had their gear there too and were digging for anything useful.

"Hey, just take what you need. Fuck bringing the pack, fuck the flack and Kevlar. We have almost no ammo and that shit'll just slow us down."

"Those mother fuckers took my cigarettes." I growled, looking through my pack. I was a little happier when I found my lighter. *I fucking love the Marine Corps, and the Marine Corps fucking loves me.* My Alice pack had sentimental value, I brought it along.

We went back out to the hall, all with knives, guns, or axes.

The Fonz stood by the next door ready to shoot anyone who entered and I signaled for the others to come. When they got near I handed an unarmed Echo Company Marine the extra pistol. We lined up on the wall behind Fonzie as much as we could and he eased open the door. Before we could go through, a Russian passed behind the line of Marines. The last man in line punched the soldier in the face and before he could land the Marine put him in a headlock and stabbed the soldier's eyes out. The Marine's arm was too tight around the soldier's neck for him to scream. He kept tightening it until there was a crunch and the body went limp. Another Marine helped him carry the body into the storage room.

Fonzie looked back at us, "There's a couple of buildings across the street. I think we can all fit in between them if we rush. There's a spotlight that passes by a couple times a minute. Next time it passes we're going to book it." Fonzie looked back through the crack in the door. "Shit." Fonzie flung open the door, but instead of running out he brought in a Russian soldier by the hair and flung him on the ground.

The soldier pointed his AK at Fonzie and the Marine I gave the pistol to shot him in the face. He passed his pistol to the next Marine and took the Russian's rifle.

Fonzie barked, "Okay, let's go!" and bolted across the street. The rest of us followed. We landed in the alley between the buildings and crept to the other side. It was night, but well lit. Ilium still had power. We left the alleyway in favor of a storage area lined with big metal shipping containers. We snuck through them without being noticed.

"Gentlemen," An Echo Company Marine said.

"What's up?" I asked.

"I can see the wall."

Fonz swung his head around, "Which direction?!"

He pointed to the seven story steel and concrete ramparts of the fortress in the distance.

"How fucking big is this place?" DeLaGarza asked.

"That's only five hundred meters away," Fonzie estimated. "We can make that."

The sirens blared alarm.

"Shit!" Fonzie barked. "Anyone not okay with running that far?"

No one rejected the idea and we took off in a single file line towards the wall. Before we got halfway, Fonzie stopped. There was nothing else between the wall and us except open ground and scrambling Russian soldiers. Fonzie ducked us behind the last building we could use as cover.

"What do we do?" DeLaGarza asked.

"I don't know," Fonzie said. "Running for it is suicide."

"There was a manhole." I pointed out.

"Where?" Fonzie asked.

"Thirty meters back. This place's got its own electricity, but I doubt it has it's own plumbing."

"Well there's only one way to find out."

I got up, and trying to keep my cool, went as fast as I could to the manhole while keeping my eye out for Ivan. We got there without being noticed and Doc helped me pull up the cover. I heard troops running somewhere near us.

"Marine's without weapons go first," I said, and they started pouring in. The four of us with guns pointed them in different directions waiting to get spotted and gunned down by the Russians.

I heard barking and screaming, then bullets. Attack dogs and soldiers were rushing towards us, firing. Everyone was down the hole besides Fonzie, Doc, and me. Doc emptied his magazine at the Russians. When the first of the dogs reached us he beat its head in with his AK, then threw it at the next animal. He jumped in the hole without grabbing the ladder. Fonzie pushed me in.

I fell fifteen or twenty feet and landed on DeLaGarza. *Fuck my ribs.*

He pushed me off, "Come on!" DeLaGarza crawled up the tunnel in front of me. Fonzie slid down the ladder. Our little group slithered through the concrete pipes. I was glad it ended up being a drain and not a sewer. It wasn't much wider than my shoulders and turning around wasn't an option. After we had gotten a little ways down, pops came from behind. It sounded like grenades, but the route had turned enough that they didn't affect us. The tunnel wasn't lined with shit or anything that could have been flushed, but it was plenty filthy. Mostly run off mud and roaches. Lots and lots of roaches. Their guts were displayed on the walls from the people in front of me. When live ones made it my way I tried not to crush them, but I couldn't help for the ones that crawled up my sleeve. It was pitch black, none of us had flashlights. I kept touching DeLaGarza's foot to make sure I didn't get lost, Fonzie kept hitting mine. Since the head of the train had no light we slugged through the drain.

We snaked through for hours.

Finally there came a little light. I waited my turn and pulled myself out of the concrete tube. We were on a riverbed. The city's silhouettes blocked the starlight. Ilium's sirens were still blaring in the distance, but there was gunfire closer.

We peered over the sidewalk by the river. There were a couple of dead Russians lying on the street. The windows of one of buildings lit up for an instant every time a bullet cracked.

Fonzie turned to us. He gave one of the Echo Company Marines his pistol. "Hank," he nodded at mine. "Give that to someone."

I tossed the pistol to an unarmed Marine.

"DeLaGarza, Doc, Hank, and I are going to grab these guy's guns and scout this shit. Everybody else stay here." Fonzie whispered.

We slid up over the ledge, covered in dirt, mud, and bug guts. I gripped my tomahawk tight. We got to the dead Russians. Each of the four of us took a rifle and as many full magazines as they had left and crept up to the building with the guns. There was only one house firing from the side we were on. Across a courtyard were several other structures raining lead onto the one we were about to enter.

Fonzie went through the door first. We cleared the first floor without seeing a soul. We crept up the stairs. As we paced down the hallway someone opened a door. It was dark, but from the silhouette of his helmet we could tell he was Russian. Fonzie beat him in the face with the muzzle of his newly acquired AK. The Russian staggered back and Fonzie crushed his face with the buttstock.

A second soldier came out to check on his buddy. I pulled the trigger on the AK. CLICK! The fucking thing was jammed. *How the fuck does an AK jam?* The soldier raised his weapon towards me. I chucked the rifle at him, as he swatted it away I lunged at him with my tomahawk over my head. My first strike hit his helmet and slid off. The soldier clawed at me, I swung again into his neck.

While Fonzie and I beat down the soldier who came out of the door, Doc and DeLaGarza stuck the ends of their rifle into the room and turned the other soldiers into Swiss cheese.

Then the only fire we heard was coming at us from the other buildings. We pulled the ammo and weapons off the dead troops and hurried back outside.

Whoever was shooting at Ivan realized there was no fire coming back and ceased theirs.

"Stay here," Fonzie said. He headed towards the courtyard the bullets had flown over. He held his rifle over his head in a surrendering stance. When he made it to the center of the yard, he threw his weapon to the ground.

A few moments later a group of men appeared from one of the buildings with their rifles pointed at the Fonz. Then tackled him. There was some shouting, but I didn't catch any of what was said. I couldn't tell who the people were, it was too dark. One of the men pulled Fonzie up, shook his hand and handed him back the weapon.

Fonzie led the men towards the other three of us. "Marines, they're on our side," he said walking down the alley.

"Kind of figured that Sergeant," DeLaGarza replied.

"Hallo," said one of the men with him in a German accent.

We went and picked up the Marines from the riverbank. The German soldiers took us on their patrol back to their FOB. Their condition wasn't any better than ours. We told their commanding officer our story. He spoke enough English to get the point across. He put us up in a shot up church and gave us some of their MREs and some thick wool blankets.

"We will radio your command and get you back in za morning," the soldier told us. "If you need anyzing, we are in ze building across from the street."

"Hey man," I said, "you got any cigarettes?"

The soldier threw me a pack of Marlbs and waved goodbye.

"Danke!"

We sat in the pews eating the food the Germans gave us.

"You know, this shit's probably not actually good." I ate what could only be identified as *something* with a plastic spoon.

"But you're so hungry is doesn't even matter?" Doc asked.

"Yup." I smiled for the first time in God knows how long. "And it's better than that shit the Russians were feeding us."

"Those mother fuckers," Fonzie spat. "They were trying to be all nice and shit, buttering us up, then POW! Kicked in the dick."

"Yeah I just bitched about Amos to them," I said.

"Really?" Fonzie asked. "That's kind of funny. I told them about El Chupacabra."

"I thought you weren't Mexican."

"Yeah, but they didn't know that."

Doc grabbed the smokes and pulled out his lighter. "Yeah, and explaining that shit to command is going to be fun."

"It's not our fault though," I said.

DeLaGarza mumbled, "Goddamned Air Force."

His eyes were sad. I would say he was just a kid, but he survived this long and that would be insulting to call anyone what he... what we'd been through, a child.

Fonzie put his hand on DeLaGarza's shoulder. "Shit happens man. The Air Force has almost killed me as many times as the enemy has. Ask Sergeant Allensworth and Doc."

"Yeah, when we were in Afghanistan they dropped JDAMs, more than once, on the wrong side of the fight," Doc said.

"Yeah," I backed them up. "Like one time in Now Zad they dropped a JDAM behind us. We were like 'Bad guys are over there dipshits.'"

None of that seemed to help DeLaGarza's mood. I offered him a cigarette. He and Fonzie took one. I flipped the pack back towards me.

"I swear to God through," Fonzie started. "If I ever see Hector or Paris again, I'm going to stab them in the fucking neck."

Doc winced at the Fonz, "Really, dude?"

"Why not?"

"No, I mean, that's the best you can come up with? No butchering to ground beef and butt-fucking their corpses while you make a necklace from their dicks? You're better than that, Fonz."

We all chuckled, even the Marines trying to sleep in the pews eavesdropping on our conversation.

"I'm sure you'll think of something better when you get there." I took a deep relaxing fill of nicotine. I leaned back on the pew. A lightning bolt of pain shot up my back. "Doc."

"Yeah, dude?"

"I think I broke a rib."

"When?"

"When that fucking A10 blew me into a tree."

"Does it hurt?"

"Only when I touch or lean on it."

"Take off your shirt and turn around."

Doc ran his fingers up my spine. "Does this hurt?"

"No."

He moved his hands, "Does *this* hurt?"

"No."

"How about this?" He tried a different spot on my back.

"Uh, no."

"How about…"

I jumped forward in my seat and grunted. "Yup. That one."

Doc went and sat back at his pew. "It's not hindering your breathing or anything?"

"No."

"You'll be alright. All you can really do for that is deal with it."

"Lame." I took another puff.

14 Song of Ilium

Two-Seven had been pulled back to Division. The coalition held most of the city, except for Ilium… that damned fortress. We were taken to the Battalion's command post, in care of the German army. We got debriefed before we got a chance to shower, shave, or eat.

I told an interrogator, this time a Marine, about what happened since the garden. I told him everything I could remember, and he asked me every question three or four times. It got old quick.

When we were finished I smoked a cigarette outside of the command post. Headquarters was almost at the beach. I thought, *it must be nice to be this far away from combat*. When Doc, DeLaGarza and Fonzie were done getting debriefed we were taken to the Battalion Commander's office in a shredded up apartment.

Lieutenant Colonel Amemnon walked into his office. When he saw us standing at attention he told us, "Relax gents."

We stood at a loose parade rest.

"So, you men have seen some shit this week," he started.

"Yes, Sir," we said almost in unison.

"I was listening to the debriefs, so I already know your stories. But are you all alright? Do you need anything?"

"We lost all of our gear and weapons, Sir," The Fonz said.

"*All* of it?"

"Yes, Sir," Doc said. "We're wearing everything we have."

"Well that's some shit luck." The colonel leaned back in his chair. "Talk to the S4, get what they can give you. I don't know about a full issue, but they should be at least able to get you flaks." He looked at Fonzie, "Sergeant Palacios, you were an acting platoon commander in Fox Company right?"

"Yes, Sir."

"Well, in your absence I gave the platoon back to Wilkonson."

Fonzie mean mugged Lieutenant Colonel Amemnon. "Sir, that lieutenant will get Marines killed."

"That's why he's going to have you as a platoon sergeant, at least until we get combat replacements."

"Sir?"

"We should be getting enough Marines to put us at T.O. in about a week. There's a few staff sergeants fresh out of the academy that I'm putting in place for the missing Staff NCOs."

Fonzie's blood boiled. I thought he was going to jump over the desk and strangle the battalion commander.

"You shameless fuck!"

"Excuse me?"

"How the fuck is anyone willing to follow your orders, garrison or in the field? When I got to Latvia, I didn't give a fuck one-way or the other, they ain't never done nothing to me!" Fonz started barking like he was yelling at a junior Marine who fucked up. "There's too many rivers, oceans, and forests between Moscow and L.A. I don't care about them. I came here for the Marines! I'm fighting for America. I'm fighting to avenge Menelaus, I'm fighting for my junior Marines, my brothers. I'm fighting for you too, you dogface motherfucker! You're robbing me of my position for some boot staff sergeant that ain't set foot in Russia yet? You're taking my billet for keeping the Marines I could alive?"

Amemnon shot back "Sergeant, I'm not bowing to you. You better stay in your fucking lane. The only reason I'm not going to take a stripe away from you right the fuck now is because of your reputation around the battalion. Now shut your mouth and get out of my office."

"Sir," Fonzie barked. "I would rather be a fucking company clerk than fight under Wilkonson after you stripped me of my billet."

"Okay," Amemnon retorted. "And so you shall. Now all of you get out of my office."

We left and searched for Fox Company.

"That bitch eyed mother fucker," Fonzie steamed. "He ain't never out on the line. He doesn't go on raids with the motherfuckers who actually fight. That fuck!"

I put my hand on the Fonz's shoulder. "I'm sorry man, that sucks."

We found Fox company, Fonzie reported into Lieutenant Toshi. The rest of us found first platoon. There was a block of abandoned houses, DeLaGarza found his squad and Doc went to go find the Medical Officer. Éclair was standing outside smoking a cigarette, looking at the small river behind the neighborhood.

"Dude!" I called to him.

"What the fuck?" He pulled me in for a hug.

"I spent some time in Folsom."

"Yeah, we didn't know what the fuck happened."

"What?"

"Well that fucking A10 sawed most of you guys up, and we saw Ivan carrying people away, but they weren't budging and we weren't going to call in artillery with Marines over there."

"Yeah…" I sighed. "You got a cigarette?"

Éclair handed me the pack, I took out a smoke and handed it back.

"You keep it, man."

"You sure?"

"Yeah, dude."

"So where are we? Are we off the line?"

"Kind of," Éclair winced. "We're just chilling out here until we get replacements."

"Yeah, that's going to suck."

"Hmm?" He hummed through a cigarette.

"They aren't going to know anything and they're all going to get whacked."

Éclair took in a deep breath. "Yeah, that might happen."

I looked around the half destroyed houses. "Do we have an extra camera? Ivan took mine."

"Yeah, somewhere, I'll dig it out for you."

"Score."

"So…" Éclair smiled. "Now that you've been to prison, are you only gonna listen to Johnny Cash and David Allan Coe?"

I chuckled a little, "No, fuck I don't even know where my phone is. I think it's in my main pack or my sea bag."

"Yeah, those are all in the back of a truck at battalion."

"That'll be fun to find."

Éclair gave me his spare camera and helped me dig out my extra bags from the vehicle at battalion. Luck would have it they were in the back. It took an hour and a half to unload all the seabags and packs, put mine aside and reload them all. I didn't have anything much of value in them, just another fleece, my phone, a canteen, and a couple pairs of socks and shirts. It didn't bother me too much; I had my ring, my lighter, and my tomahawk. The rest of the bags were packed with gear that everyone had but no one used. I went to supply and got a new flack and Kevlar, beanie, and gloves. They didn't have any more uniforms, so I was stuck wearing my sweaty, blood and bug gut stained woodlands. I didn't have anyone to impress, I didn't care. My shirts were cleanish… I went to the armory, there weren't any more M16s. I said, "fuck it, we're all using AKs anyway."

A week later, I was sitting on a bench, in front of a house, smoking a cigarette, writing a letter to Penelope. My letters to her stayed about the same. I didn't tell her about the fight or about casualties, and definitely not about being captured. I didn't want her to worry more than she already was. I just sent love, hugs, kisses, and my longing for her, and a cold beer. She wouldn't understand my affection for gunpowder and CLP.

The replacements had already trickled in, they were all still at battalion awaiting assignment.

I tried to write Penelope that we were actually staying in houses. I caught myself writing about the living conditions. I wrote about sleeping on the floor trying not to freeze at night, even though it wasn't cold, *yet.* I wrote about the holes in the walls from the fire fight that had to have happened before we got there, the eating MREs that tasted like bricks, the pills we had to take that would probably lead to me calling a number I saw on TV because someone twenty years from now will say 'Were you a veteran of *this* war? Were you exposed to medicine *X*? You may be entitled to money from the government's fuck up.' I lit the corner of the paper on fire, and watched it burn. Then I wrote a longer version of 'I love you, be strong, don't name the kid something stupid.' Even though, if memory served right he was due sometime the next month. We hadn't gotten mail in a while. I had no idea what Penelope was up to.

I looked over at Doc. He was dropping a deuce in a doorless wooden outhouse. The seat was positioned over a barrel of diesel fuel and once a day someone had to burn the shit. Usually with a gas mask and a metal pole. It was a gruesome affair.

"Doc, don't you think it's fucked up that we're staying in houses and we still have to shit outside?"

"Don't you think it's fucked up we're making eye contact while I'm squeezing out a turd?"

I shrugged, "Eh."

"There's no electricity or plumbing here, man. What the fuck else do you think would happen?"

"I don't know."

Doc lit a cigarette. I gave him a judgmental look.

"What dude? Diesel doesn't burn like gas does."

I shook my head and returned to my letter.

"Hey, Doc!" I heard First Sergeant DeLeon's voice call.

"Yes, First Sergeant," Doc answered.

"You really think that's safe? Put out that goddamned cigarette!"

"First Sergeant, diesel doesn't burn like that. It needs pressure to ignite."

"I don't give a shit put it out."

Doc gave first sergeant an unentertained look and smudged the cigarette on the plywood wall.

"Good. I catch you doing that again and you're going to be burning shitters for a month."

"Aye, First Sergeant."

When DeLeon left I pointed at Doc, "Ha ha."

"Shut up, Hank."

That night Fox got replacements. Éclair, Doc, and I watched McMillian bark at the new Marines from the benches.

"God, they look like they're fucking twelve," Éclair observed.

"Most of them are straight out of SOI," Doc added. "They piled them up in Twentynine Palms until there was enough of them and shipped them over."

"Most of them are going to go home in boxes." I lit a cigarette.

"That's a little grim," Éclair mumbled.

"Dude," I exhaled a thick plume of smoke, "we got a long fucking war ahead of us. Even if all we do is go to Moscow. Think of how long it's taking us to take just *one* fucking city."

"I guess." Éclair watched McMillian instruct the new guys.

"And it's not even winter yet." I shook my head. "We're going to be fighting a ground war in *Russia* in the winter," I sighed and said, "you're all going to die."

Éclair winced at me, "*You?*"

"Huh?"

"Don't you mean, *we?*"

"Oh, yeah. What'd I say?"

"You said, 'You're all going to die.' As if you think you're not."

Doc gave me a worried look. "Well everyone's gotta die. I just hope I don't get frostbite on my dick."

McMillian broke the formation and the Marines went to their respective bivouac with their new squads. Doc raised his head, staring into the cluster. "Oh fuck no."

"What, dude?" Éclair said, looking at the Marines.

"Hey!" Doc barked.

The Marines, all with scared looks on their faces, like sheep that know they're slaughterhouse, stopped and looked at Doc.

"Corpsmen, get up here!"

Two young sailors in Marine uniforms ran up to Doc and stuck themselves at parade rest. "Aye, HM2."

Doc scowled at them.

I wondered why Doc was so mad, then I saw their name tapes. Both of their blouses read, 'Evans.'

"Awe dude, that is *fucked* up," Éclair smiled.

"You two fresh out of Field Med?" Doc asked.

"Yes HM2," They responded.

"What are your first names?" Doc's cigarette hung from his lips.

"Wilson," the first one said.

Doc had a vexed look on his face, "…and you?"

The second corpsmen sheepishly whispered, "Wilson."

"Goddamnit!" Doc shouted. "Okay." Doc put his finger in the first corpsman's chest. "You're Doc red, and you're Doc Small, because you're a skinny bitch. I don't care if your squad calls you whatever they want, but if mother fuckers start confusing me with your boot asses there's going to be trouble. Got it?"

"Yes, HM2," they said in unison.

"Alright. I'm Fox Company's senior line corpsman. We're short on docs so I've been hanging out with first platoon. I want Red with third platoon, and Small, I want you with me in first. Let's go talk to Chief and put you where you need to be." Doc took the other Doc Evans to the medical area.

Éclair watched them leave, "That's fucking weird."

"Yeah." I lit another cigarette and turned towards the river behind the houses. The river wasn't wide; it was just technically big enough to call a river. "We're going to be here for a long time, man."

"What makes you think that? You know, besides that we're making no headway."

"They fortified the river. It's like a fucking moat around a castle. The battalion wouldn't have dug in like this unless they expected to stay here for a while. The river is full of barbed wire, the only way across is the bridge." I took a drag from the cigarette. "I just hope that our command is smart enough to stay here through the winter."

"Huh?"

"Because the Russians are probably going to withdraw when it gets cold, hoping that we'll chase them and they won't have to fight us because everyone's just going to freeze to death."

"I wrote Ginny and told her to send me more socks. I wouldn't expect to get happy suits."

"Yeah, and MREs are going to fucking suck when it's negative forty outside."

"Ugh. Yeah, we might as well eat the bricks."

"We had better just batten down the hatches when it starts to snow." I flicked my butt into the barbed wired river. The sun was setting over the ocean in the west. There were a few trees that hadn't been completely torn to shreds, but none were spared completely. I watched a snake climb one of the trees. I thought it was odd, I didn't know there were snakes this far north. I watched the serpent climb the trunk and slither over a branch. There was a bird's nest with eight chicks chirping for their mother. The snake started eating them. When he had gobbled up the eighth chick the mother bird came back screaming. The snake grabbed the mother bird by the wing and ate her too. As soon as he was done eating he crawled down and disappeared into the stones below the tree.

I lit another cigarette.

15 Don't Shoot Unless You See Them

A few days later, Fox Company went across the river looking for Ivan. Lieutenant Toshi led the patrol. Lieutenant Wilkonson and Staff Sergeant Ronyon were the new heads of First Platoon. Ronyon was fresh out of the Staff Academy and had spent approximately thirty-six hours in Russia. Doc and I tagged behind Toshi. Éclair disappeared into second platoon.

The company made it halfway to the Ilium Fortress before we made contact. We hadn't walked into an ambush, but we were stepping on an unwelcome doormat. As Russian metal pounded the buildings of the industrial center around us, we all broke for cover.

An RPG came screaming by us. Toshi grabbed Sergeant Correa, his radio operator, by the collar and threw him into a door and dove on top of him. Toshi caught shrapnel in his flack, but nothing got through to his skin.

I was in the adjacent building. I fired a few rounds from my AK and grabbed my camera.

Lieutenant Toshi leaned out from the building, balanced his rifle, and fired at Ivan. One of the Russian soldiers took a hit to the waist and spun to the ground. He managed to crawl away before he was killed.

The enemy hailed fire upon us, they threw smoke grenades and charged. When they got to our line Correa swung his Ka Bar at an enemy soldier and struck him on the helmet. Correa's knife snapped into three or four splinters. Toshi grabbed that Russian soldier by the helmet and dragged him into the building through the window. He pulled on the

193

helmet to choke the soldier with the neck strap. The strap broke and Toshi flung the helmet away. The lieutenant leapt back towards the Russian with his rifle to club him, but he managed to get away into the smoke. Toshi glared into the thick plumes like a lion searching for prey. He turned back and grabbed the radio and called in a contact report.

We fought the Russians close. Some Marines managed to shoot, but most of us were using our fists. Doc and I had fallen into the street and were fighting Ivan with our tomahawks. Men from both sides shouted as they killed, and groaned as they were slain. I swung my axe hard enough to crack through a soldier's helmet. The axe head stuck in the man's skull, blood poured over his eyes. I had to kick him to get the blade free. When the soldier was on the ground, his comrades pulled him by the feet, away from the battle.

Doc swung his tomahawk and hit a soldier to the right of his chest, the momentum carried the blade all the way up to his shoulder. Another soldier charged Doc, he was screaming at the top of his lungs. Doc moved to the side and the soldier missed. Instead, he drove his bayonet into a Marine that was carrying off a wounded man.

That pissed me off. I screamed and threw my tomahawk at the Russian with the bayonet. My axe found its mark in the soldier's temple, right under the helmet. I pulled my weapon out of his skull and swung three or four more times until the concrete below him was stained with his blood.

Lieutenant Toshi screamed through the radio to advance. I helped Doc carry the wounded Marines in the street to a truck to be evacuated. Walking back towards the advancing company, I picked up the AK with the bayonet that the Russian soldier had carried, as well as more magazines from the troops. There was one Russian lying on the ground, screaming. It looked like a grenade had taken off most of his right shin and ankle. I could see the bones, sinew and gore. He reached out his hands to his friends that had left him behind, gasping his last breaths, I buried my new bayonet into his chest and drug it down to his groin. His guts spewed onto the ground and the life left his eyes.

Fox Company took another few buildings and dug in. Lieutenant Toshi told us we were to hold the position until the rest of the battalion got to us. "We're not going to let Ivan sucker us in and surround us," Toshi told the platoon commanders.

We spent an hour defending our position before the battalion arrived. Toshi ran to the platoons, telling us, "Don't shoot at Ivan unless you see

194

him. Conserve your ammo so we don't get overrun waiting for the rest of the battalion to get here. Last thing we need is to be alone out here without ammo." Russian bullets chipped away at our cover, but we didn't fire back unless we saw a soldier.

When the battalion came to the line, Lieutenant Colonel Amemnon led the assault forward. Our Daedalus support gave several tons of fire and brimstone to Ivan for his birthday and we charged into the fury.

Amemnon fired at a Russian and blew out the inner part of his chest above his flack jacket. Another Marine shot a Russian soldier in the face and his teeth and tongue flew out of his mouth.

Mortar fire fell on us as we charged through the streets. I looked for cover but found none. I curled up in a ball as close to a wall as I could while thunderous shrapnel and flame hailed from the sky. I saw a dud mortar shell hit a Marine in the shoulder and sever his arm. Small Doc Evans ran out to the screaming Marine and dragged him into a building.

"Looks like you got good boots!" I yelled at Doc.

"Yeah, I'm glad they're not shitting their pants!" He shouted back.

The mortars stopped falling. I could hear a Russian soldier yelling, rallying his troops to battle in the distance. Machine gun fire started peppering the street. Doc and I crawled to the closest door we could find. McMillian's squad came in after us.

The Russian Army came to us like a storm.

"How many of these fuckers are there?" McMillian barked, shooting his rifle out the window.

When the Russians reached us, Toshi stabbed a soldier in the collarbone and Correa chucked a grenade into the crowd. Correa grabbed a soldier and dug a bayonet into his temple, then kicked him down. Apparently Correa didn't stab him deeply enough. The soldier was buckled over on the ground and groaning. He stayed there until more Russian troops trampled over him in the dust.

Two Marines in the street were wounded and helping each other crawl to safety. Both of them were bleeding profusely.

"I can't leave them there!" Doc barked.

"Doc, wait!" I yelled but he was already out the door. "McMillian! Cover Doc!" The squad and I started firing over Doc to hold back Ivan.

A Russian met Doc over the two bleeding Marines. Doc shot him in the gut and he fell over dying. Doc tried to grab the soldier's weapon but was turned around by the sheer volume of machine gun fire. He grabbed the two bleeding Marines, pulled them to cover and started administering aid.

A blast hit our building and knocked us to our feet. Sharpton, one of McMillian's Marines, had a spear of wooden shrapnel sticking out of his throat.

"Help me!" McMillian shouted, grabbing under Sharpton's arms. Another Marine grabbed his legs. "We gotta get him over to Doc. Give me a fire team, the rest of you wait here and cover us!"

The Marines ran out of the building, dragging Sharpton's body over to Doc. Sharpton cried, "Don't let Ivan get me… don't let Ivan get me…"

We opened fire down the street at the enemy's muzzle flashes. I shot seven of them in the span of a minute.

McMillian called the squad over and we hauled six or eight Marines back to the trucks to be evacuated. Ivan shot one of McMillian's Marines in the neck under the backside of his helmet. He was dead before he hit the deck. Doc and I loaded him into the truck with the other casualties and closed the door. The truck sped back to the aid station.

A Knight flew out of the sky and landed on a building at the end of the block. It started pumping lead into the street, tearing bodies apart, staining the pavement red.

A Daedalus screamed through the air towards the Knight. The Knight fired at the Daedalus but missed. The Daedalus fired a missile and hit above the cockpit. The explosion was terrible. The Knight's armor crumpled and burned. The Mech fell forward, into the street. A whirlwind of black smoke rose from the metal monster up to the sky.

We ran back to a building and fired back at Ivan. Doc punched a wall and yelled, "Motherfuckers!" He was angry. Doc's eyes were bloodshot and his uniform was stained red. I couldn't think of anything to console him, I was also enraged.

The sidewalk had trees planted every twenty feet. Most were splintered as if struck by lightning. One of the trees, although leafless, still held a branch. Upon it sat two vultures watching the carnage. I hadn't ever seen a vulture that looked happy, but those two had watering beaks, waiting for the feast they were about to receive. The gumption those two birds had, made me see red. I aligned my sights on the center of one of the vultures and pulled the trigger. The bullet missed the mark, but it rattled the birds and they flew away.

Lieutenant Toshi was firing at the enemy. They seemed to be dwindling. Toshi yelled at the Marines around him, "Keep Moving Marines! If we don't we'll rot in this shit! If we die, no one will be able to have called us feeble minded pussies!" With that the Lieutenant jumped into the street and charged up the road. His company stayed hot on his heels. We rushed into the buildings the Russians occupied and blood spilled on both sides.

"I'm fucking scared, Doc!" I yelled to my friend.

"Me too, bro! But fortune favors the bold!"

"That doesn't mean shit isn't going to hurt!"

Doc and I ran down the street with McMillian's squad. Our rifles shook from firing. We kicked in a door and found ourselves in a room full of Russian soldiers.

One of the soldiers tried to bayonet Doc, but Doc's flack jacket stopped it. Doc tried to bayonet him back. His knife went into the Ivan's shirt but only scraped his skin. Doc jumped on the Russian and they fought like wolves over meat. The Russian stabbed at Doc's belly with a dagger but his flack shielded him. Doc pulled out his tomahawk and hacked at Ivan's neck. The soldier jerked and Doc's blade hit the Russian's helmet and slid off, just barely slicing his flesh. Ivan staggered back, grabbed a brick and threw it at Doc. Doc smacked it away with his Kevlar. He picked up a larger brick and threw it at the soldier hitting him in the head. Ivan fell down for a moment. Doc charged him, not wanting him to get away. The soldier found the strength to stand up and jump out of the window.

While Doc was fighting the Russian, the rest of us, Americans and Russians, fired madly at each other. By the time Doc's scuff was over the entire Russian platoon and half of McMillian's squad laid entangled together in a mess of blood, guts, and bile on the dusty floor.

My flack jacket stopped a round from cutting through my chest and I had three or four nicks in my arms and legs. The wounds stung and bled, but weren't more than flesh wounds.

"Let me see your arm, Hank," Doc said.

"No, I'll take care of it," I grunted. "Fix up the guys worse off than me."

"If you're not hurt, you're holding security!" McMillian screamed at his men.

Doc and McMillian tended to the wounded. Bama had a bullet rip off half his ear. He was holding his hand to his head. Tears streamed from his eyes, but he wasn't verbalizing it.

"Take off your Kevlar dude," I told him. He did and I opened his aid kit. I took out some thick gauze. "Put this on it." I handed it to him. "Alright. This is gonna hurt a little, but you'll be alright."

Bama nodded. I took a long green stretch of cloth and fixed the gauze to Bama's head. He winced and gnashed his teeth. I tied it off and slapped his shoulder, "You're gonna be alright dude."

"Thanks."

"Let's loot these guys for smokes and ammo."

Bama and I dug through the dead enemy's pockets and pouches and kept the cigarettes, magazines, daggers, and anything else of interest we found. One of the Russians had a Nineteen eleven. I pulled it from his belt and spit on his dead face. I kept the pistol, I didn't have a pouch so I put it in my front pocket. Bama and I distributed the ammo to the Marines that were going to be around. McMillian and Doc bandaged up the rest. McMillian radioed in that he needed help from another squad to carry off the wounded and dead.

16 Shades of Death

We sat in the building waiting for either Ivan to make a house call or for Amemnon to evict us. We'd been there for hours. The Russians were fighting down the block, but we held our position silently. Doc and I were in a room with no view to the street, smoking cigarettes and sitting on the ground.

PFC Boyce was bitching about the day. "This sucks. What are we doing here? Why are we fighting for the president's wife?" He grumbled. "Who cares? Russia didn't attack us. And why is the battalion commander pushing us so hard? When is he going to have enough? We're all going to die here."

"Hey," I growled.

"Yeah?" Boyce answered.

"*Yes, Sergeant,*" McMillian corrected him.

"I'm sorry, Sergeant," Boyce said.

"You're new, right?" I asked him.

"Yes, Sergeant."

"Then shut the fuck up. We don't know if we're going to make it home or if Ivan's going to gut us. Sure, I'll give you that. Yes, this shit hole is brutal and you might go home with nightmares about this place because you're disgusted with it. But you fucks haven't even been away from your

200

fucking girlfriends for a month and you're getting impatient. But most of us left the States in January and we're keeping cool. Shut the fuck up, and quit being a bitch!"

Boyce didn't say anything else.

We sat there through the night. No one slept. We kept our eyes open for Ivan trying to snake his way into us. Dawn spread its saffron robe over Saint Petersburg. Ivan let out a massive war cry and hit us like Mike Tyson's punching bag. Fire erupted on both sides of the streets. Ivan stopped caring about casualties and flooded us with men. Mechs walked over the rooftops, smashing buildings the Marines were shooting from.

The battalion slung every ounce of lead we had. I usually had my weapon on semi, but the wave of men rushing us was so great we all put out guns on full auto. We were running out of ammo. I, we, would shoot a soldier, he would fall to the ground and, like a hydra, three more would run over him.

"We're falling back to the bivouac!" McMillian shouted.

"What?" I barked back.

"Colonel called it over radio. We're getting our asses kicked." McMillian stood by the back door. "Come on, let's go!"

I looked at Doc and shook my head. He could see the hate in my eyes.

"It's better than getting stabbed until they think you're dead man," Doc yelled, following the squad.

I emptied my magazine out the window and reloaded the AK, running after them. One of McMillian's Marines took a round to the back of his shoulder. A fountain of blood gushed from his chest. We didn't have time to pick him up. Doc and I each grabbed one of the shoulder straps on his flack and started dragging him. He left a trail of scarlet behind us.

A Daedalus landed on the rooftops, its feet straddled the buildings over the street. It fired its cannon and machine guns behind us to give us cover. Ivan ran right through the lead rain. Soldiers fell, but their comrades ran right over them, chasing us like wolves after prey.

Doc and I kept dragging the moaning Marine. Other Marines had bleeding men on their shoulders, rushing as fast as they could. Platoons of Marines would stop and fire at Ivan long enough for men to get by with the wounded, then turn into the retreat. Another platoon would take their place.

We shuffled over the bridge and river that moated our buildings. Doc and I packed the man we drug from the front into the aid station and ran back to the bridge. Marines with heavy machine guns sat on the tops of the houses. Fire spat from their muzzles, cutting the advancing Russians down. The mortarmen dropped the bombs in their tubes and shrapnel rained on the enemy. When Ivan got to the bridge there wasn't enough of a break in the metal we sent for them to funnel into our gates.

Lance Corporal Tune was taking cover by the bridge. He popped up and shot a Russian, then fell back for cover. A couple of soldiers made it past the machinegun fire onto the bridge. Tune shot one of them in the chest. The other soldier lobbed a grenade at the gate and dragged the wounded Russian away. The grenade punched Tune in the chest as he popped back up to fire. It exploded before Tune had a chance to look down. Two Marines from another squad dragged what was left of him off.

I ran from position to position, taking photos of what I could and shooting when I saw Ivan.

We eventually halted them at the bridge.

The smoke cleared, but there were still pop shots until early the next day. Division passed down that there had to be a company on watch at all times. We got put into eight hour shifts of looking over the river for Ivan. We could hear him over there, but he was careful not to let us see him.

"This is bullshit," McMillian grumbled.

I sighed and looked over the river. We were huddled in a house. Bama had a machine gun propped up as he slowly scanned left to right and back. If Ivan showed his face Bama would end him.

"I know man," I told McMillian while lighting a cigarette.

"I mean Marines *retreating? Marines!*" McMillian barked, "Fucking disgraceful."

"We didn't *retreat* retreat," I said. "We just fell back to a defensive position."

"Eh."

"It's not like we own property here."

"It's still bullshit."

A squad of Marines from Gulf Company walked into the room. We nodded at them and left. McMillian told his squad, "Hey, get some chow and sleep. Make sure you're good on ammo and all that good shit."

The squad said, "Aye, Corporal," and walked to their sleeping area.

"Wanna go see what Fonzie's up to?" I asked.

"Sure."

We found the Fonz outside the company's command post playing a metal song on a guitar. It had a silver bridge and a deep tone.

"Where'd you find that?" I asked him.

"Some dude's house," Fonzie said softly. "Spoils of war." Fonzie stood up and hugged us, guitar in hand. "It's good to see you guys! Let's go inside." Fonzie led us into the house where the headquarters Marines slept. There wasn't enough left of the walls to keep the wind out, but the couch was comfortable.

"That's an interesting rug," I said, staring at the bright purple carpet.

"Yeah, it really ties the room together. Whoever lived here seems like they were interesting. I found the guitar in a closet," Fonzie said, putting the six-string in a case.

"Cool."

"So how you guy's doin?" Fonzie asked.

"Eh. This place is a fucking disaster." I pulled out a couple of cigarettes and gave one to Fonzie. "Everybody's afraid and starting to question if they're going to live or die. I'm afraid we're going to get pushed back into the fucking ocean. The Russians are fucking madmen." I sunk back into the couch and lit my cigarette. "When are you going to get over what Amemnon said and come back to the company?"

"Let me tell you how I feel about that," Fonzie started. "I fucking hate that man. I'd rather be at the Gates of Hell than apologize to that fuck and go work for Wilkonson. I get no recognition for the blood, sweat, and tears, I put into that platoon, for the battalion. I could stay back here and get the same pay as I would up at the front. There's no benefit in me going out, suffering in pain, risking my life, and watching Marines die in every single firefight. I'm like a mama bird that gives all the worms I catch to the babies and Amemnon kicks me around. I've been lying in my rack having nightmares about being soaked in blood in combat. I earned my position as platoon commander and that stupid, ungrateful fuck just takes it away from me. And this whole war is bullshit. At least there was something to pretend Iraq was about. Who the fuck cares if Helen VonTroy Menelaus got kidnapped by Vladimir Putin? Send in SEAL Team Six to pull her out. There doesn't need to be a war over one fucking woman, I don't care *how* hot she is. The President isn't the only man on Earth that loves a woman that much. I'm not helping Amemnon anymore than I have to. I'm sure he's gotten a lot done without me. Fuck he put all that C-Wire in the river, but that ain't gonna keep Ivan out for long."

McMillian and I were silent after Fonzie's rant. We sat quietly and finished our cigarettes.

"I know you're angry, man, but calm your damn temper. The Marines need you and you're sulking. No one doubts you earned that shit."

McMillian told Fonzie, "Come on, man. We know you're pissed, but think about us. Aren't we your best friends in the damned battalion, if not the Corps?"

"I'm just too mad, man." Fonzie shook his head. "He treated me like I was a fucking boot and made me a disgrace to the battalion. You guys get going. I'm sure you can hold off Ivan."

With that McMillian and I left. Lieutenant Toshi found us on the way back to our bivouac and told McMillian to come with him to the CP. I went and laid down. I was worn out and fell asleep as soon as I closed my eyes.

I woke up to Doc shaking me. Swung at him out of instinct. Doc Dodged the punch, "Chill out dude, it's me."

I rubbed my eyes. "Sorry, man. What's up?" The sun was setting and it was starting to get cool out. The rest of the squad was packing their rucks.

"We're going out."

"What?" I shook my head, I wasn't fully awake yet. "For what?"

"Patrol, man."

"Damnit," I muttered. "When?"

"An hour. Get some chow and make sure your shit's ready."

An hour later First Platoon stood under the outpost by the bridge. The Marines on watch were wide-awake. They watched for Ivan with falcon's eyes, armed to the teeth. Their faces were white stone from the strain of battle. The air in the night was stale, awful, and tense.

We passed over the bridge into the darkness of the city. As we patrolled the streets I heard a heron honking in the distance, I don't know why but it comforted me. I thought *Dear God, you saw us through this much, please still be gracious. Bring us back safe.*

After we had been out for a while, stalking through the night, we heard someone running towards us. We hunkered down. It was only one person running down the street.

Lieutenant Toshi whispered to McMillian. "Grab that guy, but be quiet about it."

McMillian nodded and the company hid in the buildings around us. When the runner passed us, McMillian and I sprinted after him. He stopped in the road when he heard us. He turned back, saw us and ran to escape. We chased him for a few blocks before McMillian shouted. "Stop or I'll fucking kill you!" McMillian shot at the man and he froze in his tracks.

We got up to him, his teeth were chattering with fear and pale with terror. The rest of the squad caught up and grabbed the man by the arms. He was wearing a Russian Army uniform. He started crying and pleaded in a heavy accent, "Don't kill! Please let go! I have money, I pay you!"

I told him, "Woah, calm down dude, we're not going to kill you. Where are you going? Why are you alone? You gathering war trophies or are you out here spying on us?"

The soldier was trembling, "I'm here to look for you. See what Americans are doing."

"Why are you alone? Where are the rest of your men?" I demanded.

"Guard is patrolling. Soldiers are by Ilium." The soldier was shaking. "Many soldier sleep in houses."

I pulled my tomahawk out and brandished it to the soldier. He started whimpering. "Are they all asleep? Where are the sentries?"

"Two Kilometer north. Soldiers there." He looked us all in the face. "Take me prisoner, or tie up me and see if I tell you truth."

McMillian frowned at the soldier and said to the squad. "If we let this guy go he's going to go rat us out or try to kill us on the way out."

"So…" Bama asked.

"So kill him," McMillian ordered.

The soldier wept bitterly and started begging for mercy. Bama didn't give him the time. He silenced the soldiers cries with a knife to the windpipe. The soldier fell into the dust. The Marines looted his pockets for cigarettes or ammo. McMillian snapped a chemlight and dropped it near the body.

We moved further into the city. Russian bodies still littered the streets. *Why don't they gather their dead?* The pavement was slick with blood and shell casings. I almost fell a few times when the tread on my boots wasn't thicker than the blood on the ground. Patrolling through the streets I looked down an alleyway and stopped. I put up the hand signal for halt.

McMillian and Lieutenant Toshi jogged to me. "What's going on?" Toshi demanded.

I pointed down the alleyway, "Look." There were three rows of sleeping Russians with their gear staged next to them in the alley.

Toshi signaled for the rest of the company to hold still. "You two ready?" He asked.

"For what sir?" McMillian inquired.

Lieutenant Toshi fixed his bayonet and crept down the alleyway. McMillian and I followed. One by one, we slit the Russians' throats. Toshi bayonetted them, McMillian stuck them with his Ka Bar and I hacked open their necks with my tomahawk. Before we were done they drowned, headless, in a pool of their own blood.

Toshi muttered, "We're heading back to base before we have to run for it."

Correa radioed it in to the company. There was a break in the silence. The Russian sentries started screaming and firing their weapons. The Marines dove for cover. Toshi raised his rifle and shot the couple. "Let's get out of here."

We made it back past the river without incident. But when we crossed the bridge Russian artillery started raining on our camp.

Someone yelled, "INCOMING!" and we jumped to the ground. We answered Ivan's steel shower with our own rain dance. I was balled up next to a wall. Shells blew the dirt out of the Earth a few meters away from me. I started crawling to one of the concrete bunkers across the road. When I was close Doc, McMillian, and Éclair grabbed my flack and pulled me in.

"Got those fuckers good, huh!" I shouted over the explosions.

"It was like kill'n hogs dude!" McMillian yelled. He smiled and slapped me on the shoulder.

"I didn't see it, what happened?" Éclair screamed.

"Ivan's firewatch wasn't doing their job and me, Hank, and the XO put down a whole platoon in their sleep." McMillian hollered.

"Dude, epic," Éclair smiled. "Fuck Ivan, man."

Lieutenant Wilkonson called McMillian over the radio. "Send your traffic!" McMillian answered.

"Ivan's running up the street in force. We think they're going to charge the bridge   when the arty's up."

"Roger that." McMillian barked into the radio. He looked up at us. The bunker was filled mostly with his squad. "Fix bayonets!"

The sky stopped raining Russian steel. Ours kept firing away. Troops poured over the bridge, our machine guns cut most of them down before they even made it to the middle.

The Marines scurried to wherever we could see Ivan to send him hate mail. Our group ran up to the second floor of a house three or four down from the bridge. We didn't fire at the bridge, there were enough soldiers in the adjacent buildings. I shot one soldier through the helmet. When he hit the deck his brains oozed out. We fought them for about thirty minutes before the Daedaluses slammed into the ground across the river. They stomped on the Russians they could, and shot at the ones they couldn't.

Amemnon ordered the Battalion to cross the river and hunt down Ivan. The Russians were still firing at us. A Russian Knight tackled one of our Daedaluses and they fought with their mechanical fists. I ran with Fox Company's First Platoon under the iron boxing match.

As soon as we were across the river the fire intensified. McMillian saw a soldier in the street. He shot the Russian in the helmet, he fell to the ground, dazed, then shook it off and ran out of the line of fire. "God Damnit!" McMillian shouted. "He fucking got away."

"Yeah, God must love that guy." Doc muttered, taking cover behind a wall with the rest of our squad. The eastern sky turned from black to light purple. A Daedalus fired in intervals down the street next to us.

McMillian peaked around the wall. "After the mech's next burst, we're moving into that next building!"

The Daedalus fired a burst and we ran over the street. Russian fire flew at us as we dived into the house.

"Corporal!" Bama screamed.

"What, dude?" McMillian answered.

"Dimes got hit!"

We looked out the door. Dimes was on the ground screaming. He had only gotten shot in the foot, but he was in pain. He pulled himself into a crater in the road. Ivan wasn't letting him move any further in any direction. He was screaming at the enemy, his voice was wet with anguish. "Come on Ivan! Fucking shoot me from far away, you pussy! Why don't you come here and put a knife in my gut like a damn man would! You fucking faggots!"

Dimes kept shouting at Ivan. Doc bolted out into the street.

"Damnit, Doc!" I shouted and took off behind him. We slid into the crater. I peeped over the top with my rifle and started firing at the Russian muzzle flashes.

"SHUT UP, DIMES!" Doc shouted. He patted the bleeding Marine down for other injuries.

"I'm alright Doc, it's just the foot," Dimes groaned.

"Well you could have at least fucking crawled to the building instead of staying in the damned street."

"Crater was closer."

Doc and Dimes rustled around in the hole behind me. I aligned the sites on my AK at the soldiers trying to kill us. The adrenaline in my blood put nitromethane in my engine. The world passed in slow motion. My eardrums ruptured a little more every time I pulled the trigger.

"Ivan ain't fucking around today is he, Doc?" I shouted back at them.

There was no response. *Great they got hit.* I looked behind me and I was alone in the crater. *The fuck?* I shot my head around and saw Doc carrying Dimes into the building with McMillian. "JESUS FUCK, DOC!" *This is bad news Hank! Last time I was separated Ivan wasn't around.* I fired a few more rounds and sank back into the crater and reloaded my magazine. *Shit, do I make a run for it? I don't give a shit about medals. If I run I'm probably going to get shot. That's going to fucking hurt. If I stay here I'm going to risk someone else running in after me and I don't want a Marine's blood on my hands.* I looked up, Russian troops were closing in on me like dogs. Four of them charged apart and dove into the trench with me. I smashed one of their face's with the AK's butt. I pulled out my nineteen-eleven, the only American made weapon I had on me besides my tomahawk, and shot the other three. One of them lived through the bullet. He clutched at the dust and gasped for air. I caved his face in with the pistol grip and grabbed the AK. Another three Russians charged my fighting hole, shooting. I shot back at them. One of them fell to the dirt. The second shot and his bullet nicked my neck. I screamed but held the trigger down. I shot the second one in the chest. The last one turned his back and ran away. I put a bullet in his back, he fell with a thud.

I clamped my hand over my bleeding neck. "That was too quick a death for you bitch!" I screamed, "You can't escape the reaper! I hope Satan's making your parents gang fuck you in Hell right now!" The pain in my neck, pun intended, was sharp and throbbing. The bullet didn't hit anything important, but I was still bleeding pretty bad. "I hope crows eat your face and you get a closed casket funeral!" The blood loss started to worry me. I loaded my last magazine. "Doc!" I shouted. I fired off the rest of my AK rounds and slung the weapon. "McMillian!" I held my pistol in one hand and my axe in the other. The squad was shooting towards the Russians that were closing in on me. "ANY OF YOU FUCKERS!"

Doc ran out to the crater. The Russians were closing in on me like jackals. He sprayed out a full magazine and laid down the first rank of Russians around us. "Why am I always saving your ass?" He shouted while reloading.

"DOC! ALLENSWORTH!" McMillian screamed from his position, "I'M THROWING FRAGS!"

I half gave McMillian a thumbs up. Another group of Russians ran up to the trench. Doc fired into them. I shot one with my pistol. Another one got close, I dug my axe into his thigh and pulled him into the makeshift fighting hole. I holstered my pistol, grabbed the dead Russian's rifle, and started shooting.

"FRAGS OUT!" McMillian screamed. Doc and I sank into the crater. My head was throbbing.

POP POP POP!

The grenades shot shrapnel into the Russians around them. The sound sent shockwaves through my brain and I couldn't quite see straight.

Doc was picking up one of the soldiers in the hole. "Help me with this Hank."

I grabbed the soldier's legs and we flung him outside of the trench towards the enemy and used him for cover. We fired at the Russians.

Another Knight fell out of the sky at the end of the street and started sweeping the buildings. It leveled a few structures before a few more Knights showed up behind it, a couple of Rooks backed them up.

"We gotta get the fuck out of here now!" Doc screamed.

We looked over at McMillian. He was pointing behind us, "FUCKING RUN!"

We got up and ran, McMillian's squad in tow.

My head was splitting in half. There were daggers behind my eyes.

The company ran back across the river. When we were safe, and I use that term very loosely, Doc put ointment and gauze on my neck. McMillian counted his Marines.

"We're fucked, Doc. They're going to stomp us out and push us back to the ocean. Then when we load in the AAVs they're going to pick us off like it's fucking Duck Hunt. I don't want to fucking drown while I don't have enough blood to know what's going on." I rattled, as Doc finished mending my wounds.

"Yeah, but there's nothing we can do about it," McMillian grumbled. We were outside the first bunker behind the bridge. He was standing over us, firing at Ivan.

"You know, you really need to quit bitching," Doc said, lighting a cigarette.

"Doc, we're fucking fucked," I growled.

"And your complaining isn't helping anyone else."

"Fuck off, Doc." I rubbed the area around the cut in my neck.

Doc pulled the sleeve up on my arm and put his cigarette out on my skin.

"Fuck, dude!"

"Snap out of it Hank!" He shoved my AK into my chest and ran to help a Marine who was dragging his bleeding friend.

I knelt up and looked at the bridge next to McMillian. "There's too much shit in the river. The C-wire won't let Ivan over it." McMillian said, reassuring himself.

"Yeah," I said sarcastically.

Our end of the bridge had two bunkers on the end, each with fifty caliber machine guns. They had been keeping Ivan off the bridge, striking soldiers down like lambs to the slaughter. The enemy mechs were being held back by Daedaluses. One of the Rooks bore down on our position only to get peeled in half by an F18's five hundred pound bomb, but before it fell it let out one of its hundred and twenty-five millimeter rounds. It obliterated one of the gun nests.

McMillian and I were behind the other nest. The force of the round blew us back a few feet. Metal shrapnel, rocks, clumps of dirt and body parts flew at us. McMillian and I hit half a destroyed wall with a thud and a crack.

I laid on the ground moaning.

"You alright, man?" McMillian asked.

"Yeah." I coughed up a speckle of blood. There was a cloud around us, blinding our vision. The ringing in my ears was louder. I tried to rub my eyes. "It feels like God just bitchslapped me." There weren't any big holes, but all of my exposed skin stung and I was bleeding from millions of tiny cuts. My vision cleared. McMillian wasn't looking any better. "Are *you* alright?"

McMillian pushed himself to his feet, and held the wall. "I think so," he wheezed. "Oh fuck." His eyes widened.

Ivan was storming the bridge. Soldiers ran up to the other machinegun nest. They sprayed it down and stuck their bullets and bayonets into the Marines in the hole, spilling their brains and innards in the dirt.

"FALL BACK! FALL BACK!" McMillian shouted to the Marines. We ran to the next line of buildings behind us as fast as our legs would take us. Bullets danced in the dirt around our feet. We dove into a building and immediately started throwing everything we had at Ivan, bullets, grenades, fucking rocks, everything.

Our building didn't have a complete wall to protect us. There was a gaping hole in the side. Ivan tossed in a grenade, Doc Little hit it with his rifle like it was a baseball and it went flying back to the Russians. The grenade hit a soldier in the face before it exploded and turned he and his friend into hamburger meat.

My Doc was firing at Ivan when he took a round to the flack jacket. He fell to the ground, and coughed and wheezed. I crawled over to him, took hold of his flack and drug him to the backside of the house.

"You good?" I asked.

"Yeah, just got the wind knocked out of me," he winced, trying to breath.

I gave Doc my canteen and he took a sip. "I wouldn't be too worried if I thought I would just die and the pain would be over."

Doc looked up at me with fear in his eyes.

I put my hand on his shoulder. "This shit's going to fucking hurt."

Doc shook his head. "Yeah, death would be easier."

17 Blood Soaked Rain

Things went from bad to the part of Hell where demons in clown costumes cut your dick in half long ways and gang fuck you with razor blades. The sun had only been up for an hour.

Tears swelled from the windows of McMillian's soul. What was left of his squad was hunkered down in half dug fighting holes. "This is bad, man," he said.

"No shit it's bad," Bama screamed.

"Ivan's a fucking fire and he's burning us alive," he moaned.

Lieutenant Wilkonson tried to comfort his men. "You just have to keep faith Marines."

"*Sir,*" McMillian spat, "I can smell the ocean. We're four blocks away from the fucking thing. The First Marine Division is about to get pushed back into the fucking sea!"

"No we're not McMillian," Wilkonson argued back.

"Dude," I said with no regard to customs and courtesies, "The only reason the Division ain't getting pushed into the ocean is because half of the fucking Blue Diamond is laying face down in the street. There ain't enough of us to push any further. There are fucking battalions that have been wiped out since last night. I'm pretty sure you're the only platoon commander in Two-Seven right now."

"Yeah, the company Gunny was split in half," McMillian added, "but that doesn't matter because there aren't enough Marines left in Fox to need a Gunnery Sergeant. We're barely a platoon and a half right now."

The lieutenant sulked and quit his rhetoric. The Marines' eyes were all bloodshot cue balls, staring down Death. There were a few days worth of beard on every face and all skin was black from dirt, gunpowder, and smoke.

We were wedged into a position where going further back was just as out of the question as moving forward. We hunkered down in craters left over from artillery shells. Ivan decided it was worth destroying the city to evict us. There was barely a story to the building in front of us. The Russian's leveled everything, and they did it in a night. Over the rubble, blood and carnage, Ilium's walls stood in defiance.

Daedaluses, F18s and A10s ripped chunks of earth into the sky. Russian Mechs sent trails of fire after the bird. Some erupted into balls of fire and left black trails of death as they fell from the sky. MiGs and Hornets chased after each other.

"I'm going to pull that place apart brick by brick," I grumbled.

"Dude, we're not going two feet closer to that place ever again," Éclair said.

"Yeah, we will," Boyce complained. "When we're captured and put in the fucking place's gulag."

"Boyce," McMillian barked. "If you don't shut the fuck up I'm going to let Allensworth chop you into little pieces and throw you in the ocean."

Éclair lit a cigarette. "Well since we're all about to die anyway I have something I want to get off my chest."

"What?" McMillian asked. "Did you frag Staff Sergeant Ronyon? Because I'd be okay with that."

"No.," Éclair said as calmly as someone who thought they were about to die could. "A couple years ago I killed my wife's best friend then chopped her up and threw her into an impact range."

The crater stared at him.

"What?" Boyce asked in disbelief.

"True story, man," I backed Éclair up. "I helped chop her up."

"That's fucked up," McMillian said. "You didn't do it at the barracks did you?"

Éclair and I looked at McMillian stone faced, "Yup."

The Marines cracked half a smile and chuckled nervously.

"Remember those Motor T guys in the news a few years ago that the media though gang raped that chick and murdered her?" Éclair asked.

"No," Boyce answered.

"I do," Bama said. "I was at SOI."

"It was us and we let them take the fall," Éclair confessed.

"Huh," McMillian hummed. "Well I guess that doesn't matter anymore because at the rate Ivan's going, we're all going to be dead in about half an hour."

Éclair sighed, "But it feels good to get that off my chest."

I patted Éclair's shoulder. Another barrage of mortars huddled us in the bottom of the hole. My hands gripped my rifle and I shook. My heart was punching my ribcage. Tears of fear and hate filled the Marine's eyes. The dirt shook beneath us, and the metal and stones that were blown out of the ground buried us in the gravel.

The artillery stopped and there was a great cry. Another human wave came to push us back into the sea. We emptied our weapons until the wave broke over the Marine filled craters. Bama grabbed a soldier and drove his dagger behind the Russian's ear. Another soldier jumped into our hole with his bayonet aimed at Bama's heart. As he came screaming through the air Bama dodged him, but the blade fell into Boyce' chest above the flack and they hit the ground with a thud. McMillian lunged at the soldier but only cut his sleeve. The soldier hit McMillian's Kevlar with his butt stock. I drew my pistol and turned the soldier's head into lasagna.

"You alright Mc?" I shouted.

"Yeah," McMillian knelt up, "just dazed." He looked down at Boyce. "Goddamn it." McMillian grabbed Ivan's weapon and emptied its magazine into the soldiers around us.

Across the line by the ocean, the First Marine Division fought the Russian Army like starved lions over meat. We held a room in Ivan's house, and Ivan wanted it back. Most of the guns were silent. The Americans and Russians were almost too close for knives.

Doc Little and my Doc took advantage of the lead-less air to grab the wounded and carry them on their shoulders to a safer spot.

Another group of soldiers jumped into our hole. One of them stabbed at McMillian with his bayonet, but McMillian grabbed the rifle and pulled it away. He took the Russian's rifle, stuck it in his stomach, and pulled the trigger. The Russian screamed and his bowels fell out of his body to into the dirt. McMillian hammered his face into a cave.

Another one of the soldiers fired into the crater. Éclair took a bullet through the arm and the rest of the burst went into Bama. Éclair grabbed the soldier by the foot and pulled him into the crater. He took his Ka Bar, drove it halfway into the soldier's windpipe. Then grabbed his arms and hacked off his hands. The soldier tried to scream through the blood running down his throat, clawing at his neck with the stumps that used to hold fingers. We let him suffer.

McMillian looked at Bama's lifeless body and started to cry. His tears didn't dull his ability to fight.

Doc was running back to the fight after pulling more wounded Marines out. He was covered in other people's blood. His body was black from gunpowder, covered in dirt. A bullet struck him in the front plate of his flack where the strap for his weapon was and he tumbled to the ground. The rifle fell off his body. Doc grabbed his weapon and rolled into a ditch. He pulled out a grenade, screamed, "FRAG OUT!" and launched it towards Ivan. The grenade hit a soldier in the head and sent him spinning like a top. The grenade rolled into a crater. Five or six Russians jumped out and the grenade blew the dirt out of the hole. The Russians that jumped out grabbed the man that was hit in the head and dragged him into the safety of the crater.

Doc jumped into our hole panting, wide-eyed.

"You okay, bro?" I asked.

"It's like a day at the beach," he tried to laugh.

"If the beach was fucking Pellilu," Éclair grumbled.

"Naw dude," Doc shook his head, "Oakland."

Doc Little came running towards us.

"Goddamn dude," Éclair screamed. "Your little buddy can fucking sprint."

Doc peaked over the edge of the crater. "Yeah, fast little fucker."

Doc Little was booking it. A soldier tried to tackle him, but Little dodged and shot the soldier in the shoulder. He kept running and dove into the crater.

McMillian laid Boyce and Bama face up in the crater. The rest of us started taking ammo from the Russians.

"All Stations, All Stations, Fox Six." Lieutenant Toshi's voice buzzed through the radios. "If you have grenades still, throw them to the next crater up. After they blow, assault the position. Signal will be red flare. Break. This is the moment gentlemen. Pray to your deities. At the very least they won't be able to say that the First Marine Division didn't die standing... Fox Six out."

McMillian produced a grenade he pulled off one of the dead Russians in our fighting position. We made sure we had a full magazine in our rifles. I strangled my AKs pistol grip and shook. I was sure the other Marines thought death was near. I thought about getting shot in the leg, then stabbed to death, then waking up in a mass grave under a hundred other rotting Marine corpses, and shuttered.

The red flare burst into the sky. McMillian threw the grenade, it rolled into the next Russian filled crater with a POP. Before the dust settled, McMillian, Éclair, My Doc, Doc Little, and I were jumping into the hole. It was a bowl of body parts with blood stained walls.

"One step at a time, Fox." Toshi's voice filled the crater via radio. By dusk we had butchered our way back to the river. Most of the Russians we killed with our bare hands. If their corpses had weapons, ammo, food, or smokes we took them and moved forward, inch by bloody inch.

We pushed Ivan over the river. The lucky ones made it over the bridge. Many of them tried to ford the river only to get stuck in the mess of C-wire under the waves. During the day, the spiked death traps, running bank to bank, could be seen clearly under the blue. But when it was dark, the barbed wire was invisible. The Russians that got tangled in the mess screamed when the prongs dug into their legs. Streams of blood flowed down the river when we killed them mercilessly with their own weapons.

The Russians on the other side used the river to their advantage and hailed fire over the choke point bridge. They used the natural barrier to halt our advance.

The dark sky glowed with lightning. Thunder opened the doors to the rain. The artillery, machine guns, and bombs had turned all the buildings anywhere near the river into splinters and pebbles. Either lightning or bombs had set what little of the buildings were left into fire in the pouring rain.

There was still about a platoon worth of Russians on our side of the water by the bridge. Lieutenant Toshi led the charge, firing at the Russians, shooting at least one above the waist. We flew at them like wasps from a rattled nest.

McMillian screamed and fired his rifle. He shot one Russian in the shoulder and bayoneted another in the neck, driving him to the ground. McMillian shot another soldier in the thigh and buried his bayonet in his belly.

The yard, that still had benches and splintered tree stubs, was filled with smoke. My eyes stung and my lungs grew tight as I breathed in the burning mess. I pulled the trigger, charging at the Russians. The bolt locked back over an empty magazine. I threw the gun to the ground and pulled out my tomahawk. A soldier thrust his weapon at me. I grabbed his hand and drove my axe into his shoulder. His bones cracked and his sinew tore. I yanked his hand and his arm fell free from his body.

Doc tackled another soldier and hacked away at his throat. His tomahawk was hot with the red fluid from the Russian's neck. He grabbed another soldier and swung the axe so the blade went into the soldier's mouth. It stopped with a squish. The soldier's eyes turned red, his body convulsed and his mouth, ears, eyes, and nose let loose streams of crimson.

McMillian screamed, "KILL!" every time he pulled the trigger.

BANG

"KILL!"

BANG

"KILL!"

BANG

"KILL!"

McMillian ran out of ammo and chased after Ivan. Somehow he made it to the riverbed. He stabbed a soldier in the mouth, his teeth flew to the dirt. McMillian swung again, slitting the soldier's throat. He picked up a cinder block and smashed it on another soldier's head. Blood and chunks of bone sprayed down his neck.

With the Russians still on our side of the bridge, their artillery rained back down on us. Explosions rocked the earth. Russian soldiers and Marines, locked in each other's arms in a battle for death rolled down and continued their battles in the craters. I tackled Éclair into a rut and we huddled down for cover. There was an equal amount of steel, rubble, and bits of body parts flying through the air. Blood rained from the heavens under the lightning and storm. The artillery stopped, but the bloodshed continued.

McMillian picked up an AK with a bayonet and threw it a soldier. The blade stuck into the soldier's heart and he fell. McMillian put his foot on the Russian and jerked out the weapon. A soldier charged McMillian from behind and drove his shoulder into McMillian's back. McMillian's helmet flew off and rolled in the dirt. McMillian turned around and shot the shoulder. A bust of blood, from a bullet, shot from McMillian's back, and he stumbled forward. McMillian snapped out of his bloodlust and looked at Éclair and me in the trench in the ground. He started running towards us. A couple of Russians chased after him. Éclair and I shot at the men chasing down our friend. One of the soldiers fell into the dirt. The other one tackled McMillian and drove his knife into his gut. Éclair and I fired madly at the Russian, he rolled into a nearby crater.

Lieutenant Toshi appeared out of the smoke and rain, which was half blood, and straddled himself over McMillian's body. He was screaming and shooting at everything that had a shadow, "DOC!" Toshi slung his rifle and drew his pistol. "DOC, GET YOUR ASS OVER HERE!"

Doc ran up to the lieutenant and the two of them drug McMillian's body to cover. The bullets tore through the rain around them.

"You think Ivan got him?" Éclair asked.

"Even if McMillian's alive, with a wound like that he'll be dead soon." I tried not to start crying, "Doc can't fix that. He'd need to be evacuated to a ship, that's a three hour wait at *least*."

Éclair's eyes started to water. He growled and fired at the Russians at the bridge. I had a lump in my throat for McMillian. I joined Éclair in giving Ivan one-way tickets to hell. The artillery fell again. I grabbed Éclair and pulled him back into our rut.

Many good men died on those days; there wasn't an instant of peace.

Over the hours, the fire smoldered and the rain stopped falling red. The Russians had their side of the river and we had ours. The storm let up throughout the night.

Doc, Éclair, and I huddled under a fallen wall. The wind was blowing the rain over us. We were wet, but water wasn't dropping directly on top of us. McMillian's body laid beside us, covered with a poncho.

"I haven't slept in three days." Éclair shook, there was very little life in his voice.

"None of us have," Doc grumbled after him, "but I've still slept more recently than I've eaten."

"I'd eat three veggie omelet MREs right now," I muttered.

"When was the last time anyone talked to the wives?" Doc asked.

"A couple of weeks," Éclair droned.

"I got a letter a while back, but it was from two months ago. The mail here is shit." I flicked my butt and lit another cigarette. I was careful with my fingers not to get the paper wet. "Fuck, I'm pretty sure I have a kid right now. But there's no way to know it." I thought about Penelope in a hospital gown, holding a light green baby and being torn between if she should be happy or sad. "This whole situation is fucked."

"It could be worse," Éclair said.

"How?" I asked.

"We could be in Ohio."

Doc and I half smirked.

Fonzie came sprinting around the corner. He didn't have a flack or Kevlar, just his rifle. His eyes were wide and startled. I'd never seen the Fonz in distress before, no matter what shit we've been thrown into. He looked at us, then at the body under the poncho on the ground. "Is that…"

"Yeah," Doc whispered.

Hot salty beads of water streamed from the Fonz's eyes. He knelt down beside McMillian and pulled back the sheet covering his face. Fonzie started sobbing. He punched McMillian's chest and wailed.

I stared at Fonzie with pity and fear. I had been convinced The Fonz was made of Iron and hate. I've seen him bleed before, but only literally.

"I'm so fucking stupid!" Fonzie shouted, "If I'd have swallowed my pride and taken a squad you'd still be alive," he told the dead man on the ground.

"Whoa dude," I tried to comfort him. "It's not your fault," I said to the Fonz. Doc, Éclair, and I put our hands on his back.

Fonzie ignored us and kept talking to McMillian. "You died before we got home. What am I going to tell them? I swear to God in heaven, I'll slit every fucking throat in Russia."

Fonzie stroked McMillian's face and cried. He opened McMillian's breast pocket, probably looking for his Kill Cards, but instead pulled out a sheet of paper.

"What's that?" Éclair asked.

"I don't know," Fonzie whimpered.

"What's it say?"

Fonzie read the paper:

"A war fought for nothing, we're afraid and alone
For a woman not even from our home
Rip the souls from our hearts
Bathe in the blood of body parts
Our best years spent in a foreign Hell
Sulfur the only thing we smell
Do your drugs and have your party
You're safe from the wrath of artillery

'Get out of Russia' you say on TV
You have your protest but care not for we
Your war's objection I don't understand
You don't care for the men fighting for this land
Draw cartoons of the Red Star make fun
You're a coward who refuses to wield a gun
When you die I hope you come here
And witness my life, the one you fear
Besides my brothers, the only ones I love great
In my veins there is only hate
No cares you give for the fires of war I'm in
You just think talking shit makes you cool and fit in
Well I'm the one in a sea of blood
Who fights the Ivan in the mud
We're the ones who in war cries
But you don't give a fuck when a Marine dies."

Fonzie folded up the paper and put his hand in his pocket. His hand came back out with two coins. He put them on McMillian's eyes and rubbed his face. "Good Bye, cousin." He put the poncho back over McMillian's face. "Make sure that he gets where he needs to," Fonzie said as he walked away.

"Where you going man?" Doc asked.

"I'm going to get my job back."

18 Sing Goddess, The Wrath of the Fonz

The battalion commander gave Fonzie his position back as platoon sergeant. First platoon only had twenty Marines. Éclair and I made it an unofficial twenty-two. Fonzie was looking over them, learning the new guys' names and telling them what he expected out of them.

"What do you think he said to Amemnon?" I asked Doc.

"No fucking clue," he watched.

"You think he apologized?"

"I don't think so. I think he just told the Colonel that he needs as many people fighting as he can get, and he knows that Fonzie's a good leader."

That night Fox Company huddled behind the bridge. Other companies hid behind their own structures. Other battalions, I'm sure, prepared for whatever they were going to assault. An hour before dusk F18s soared over the city, fought with the MiGs and dropped an ungodly amount of firepower on the opposite side of the river.

Daedaluses left their black trails and razed the first hundred yards after the river. One Daedalus positioned himself over the bridge and Lieutenant Toshi led Fox Company's charge across.

Ivan sent his troops to meet us. Steel rained on us from the sky, but at least the actual rain had stopped. First platoon turned left after the bridge, The Fonz in the lead. Lieutenant Wilkonson was still a sheep.

Fonzie's rage escaped him, "Come on you pussies!" He screamed at the Russians. He ran down the street, the platoon struggled to keep up with him. Fonzie stopped at a blown out intersection and barked at the squad leaders where to put their Marines. Ivan opened up on us. The

Marines hit the deck. Fonzie stood in the road, fearlessly firing back at them. Unlike the other platoon sergeant and squad leaders, Fonzie returned to his roots and carried his M240. Our backs were now to the river.

Ivan's terrible war cry shook the air.

"Goddamnit!" I shouted. "Doc! How many fucking people does Russia have to throw at us?"

"I don't know, man, but we can only be so lucky. We're definitely getting stabbed this time."

Instead of a human wave that washed down the streets, the Russians rose out of the rubble around us. There were just as many of them as there had always been.

Fonzie let out a burst and cracked a soldier's face in half. "TAKE THAT FUCK BITCH!" He opened fire on Ivan and charged towards them. He was possessed by the demons of rage. He sawed off another soldier's head with bullets. When his friends tried to carry him off, Fonzie cut them open.

The platoon didn't have deliberate orders, so we took our time to aim and shot the soldiers around Fonzie. One of them turned to run and was shot in the back, his guts spilled to the dirt. Writhing and screaming on the ground, one hand gripped the Earth; the other tried to shove his guts back inside his belly. Fonzie let a burst of rounds escape into the wailing Russian's guts. He was still crying when Fonzie walked away from him.

Fonzie turned his head back to us. "Come on!" The platoon got up and ran after the Fonz. We charged the Russians. Fonzie held his weapon at the hip and fired madly into the ranks. When he reached their position he held his gun by the barrel and clubbed a soldier's head sideways. He raised the weapon to strike again, but an explosion rocked the earth from a Russian mech. Fonzie flailed and dropped the gun. The Fonz screamed, grabbed his Ka Bar and stabbed a Russian in the throat. He stabbed another soldier in the liver and twisted the blade around his torso, bathing Fonzie in blood. He grabbed another soldier's hand and ran his dagger through his elbow, severing the arm under it. Fonzie beat the armless soldier to death with his own limb.

The rest of first platoon fought the enemy, but nowhere as fiercely as The Fonz. He went on, devouring the enemy, burning a valley through the mountains of Russia, the platoon trailed behind him.

The fog of war thickened. Smoke grenades, fire, and flame turned the sky dark. We found ourselves out of Russians in front of us to kill. "Where the fuck are they!" Fonzie demanded.

We scanned around the blood soaked rubble and shells.

"They're behind us!" Éclair shouted.

"What?" Fonzie swung around. We had somehow pushed through the Russian line. Ivan was between the river and us. Fonzie leveled his machine gun and fired into the Russian ranks. "CONTACT REAR!" First platoon moved on line with Fonzie. We charged them and started beating them with our weapons. Some of the Russians jumped to the river in an effort to escape. Fonzie ran through who stood and fought, and opened his machinegun up on the Russians in the water. Most of them were already hung up and bleeding on the barbed wire that laid under the waves. The river started to turn purple, then red. Fonzie fired until his arms were sore from lugging the heavy weapon.

Fonzie dropped the weapon and pulled out his pistol and his Ka Bar. When he turned to face us, there was a soldier behind him. Fonzie shoved his pistol in the man's mouth. The soldier dropped his rifle and trembled. The soldier, on his knees, hugged Fonzie's legs begging for mercy. "No one escapes the death God put in my hands. Not one of you Russian fucks!" Fonzie's pistol was still in the man's mouth, when he stabbed him in the throat. The soldier fell, blood burst from his wound and soaked the shattered concrete. Fonzie grabbed the man by the legs and hurled him into the river. "Fish food!" Another soldier rushed Fonzie, firing. Fonzie shot back, both of them missed each other. When he reached Fonzie, the Fonz drove his shoulder in the man's chest and his Ka Bar into his gut. Fonzie grabbed his falling intestines and yanked them out. The soldier screamed in pain and Fonzie kicked him into the water.

Fonzie kept up with his slaughter. The rest of us beat, shot, and stabbed the remaining enemy. When there was no one left to kill, we threw the bodies in the river. They piled up, caught by the barbed wire underneath. On one side of the stream was an almost clear cobalt. The only exception was from a downed Russian mech fifty yards upstream leaking a brown and green stream of fuel into the water. The other side of the human damn was scarlet. The red water washed away, exposing the bed, the Russian corpses dammed the river.

I lit a cigarette in the respite of chaos and stared at the mangled flesh, "That's not the *most* fucked up thing I've ever seen."

"What was?" Fonzie panted.

"Right now, I don't know, but I'm sure there was something else." I offered Fonzie a cigarette.

"Yo, Hank," Éclair called from behind.

"What's up, bro?"

Éclair lifted his arm. His camera was broken. The lens was shattered and body was cracked.

"What happened to that?" I raised an eyebrow.

"I was out of ammo and Ivan punched me in the face..."

"Yeah, you got a shiner."

"When the guy hit me I dropped my knife. This was the only thing I had to beat him with."

"You beat a guy to death with your camera?"

Éclair smiled, "Yeah."

"Remind me when we get home to write you up a NAM," I chuckled.

Éclair laughed, "HA! That's funny." He shook his head. "We ain't ever going home."

"Alight," Fonzie said, "Let's get moving. We got a long night in front of us." Fonzie flicked his cigarette into the dam. The fuel from the mech upstream ignited and the bodies burned until the water covered them again. First platoon followed Fonzie back into the jaws of Death and Hell.

We were at the walls of Ilium when the sun broke over the horizon. Ivan was putting up a fierce fight at the gates. Doc, Éclair, and I followed Fonzie in front of the platoon through what was left of alleyways, towards Ilium. There weren't buildings to our sides. A story or two of walls lines our path. Second and Third Platoon had a group of Russian soldiers pinned down and we were flanking them. The Russians had a Knight behind them, firing at the Marines. The CAAT platoon hadn't any trucks left. They were firing their few remaining missiles at the mech.

Fonzie spotted Ivan and halted us. We spread through the rubble, being careful not to make too much noise, and laid down. We aimed in on the Russians that had been giving the rest of the company such a hard time. Fonzie opened fire. They dove for cover and shot back.

"CONTACT REAR!" A Marine screamed.

I looked behind me and another squad of Russians had snuck up behind us. The Marines fired in all directions. A Daedalus screamed from the sky, its exhaust leaving its signature black stream. Without slowing down, it changed from an eagle into a giant silver god, and rammed into the Knight by the Russians. The Daedalus' chest read, *GET SOME*.

Fonzie screamed, "Oh, *Fuck* no!"

"Fucking *right*?" I barked.

"No!" Fonzie was still looking at the soldiers we were to flank, "That fuck Hector is down there!"

"What?" I shot my head around, taking my eyes off of the enemy around me, and looked to the front, "Yup, that's him." Hector was down with the troops firing. "I thought he wasn't an infantry guy."

"I don't give a good goddamn what he is," Fonzie said as he bolted down into the mess of soldiers below.

I turned around to look for Doc. Instead of my friend, I saw an AK's butt stock flying towards my face. I bent my head down and the rifle slammed into my Kevlar. I felt a sharp crack in my neck and fell to the ground. The Russian's momentum had carried him over me. I drew my pistol and shot him in the thigh. He wailed and stumbled to the ground. I put another bullet in his face. Doc was grappling with a soldier on the ground, exchanging blows. Éclair and I pulled the soldier off him and Doc hacked at his throat with his tomahawk.

"C'mon!" I shouted at the two. "Fonzie just saw Hector, he's chasing him down."

"What?" Doc exclaimed in disbelief.

"Who's Hector?" Éclair asked.

"No time, lets go!" We ran away from the platoon after Fonzie. My neck ached, the world was spinning, but I ran towards the enemy. When the rest of the company saw four of us charging the Russians they followed suit and soon there were two companies, one American, and one Russian fist fighting over broken bricks.

Get Some ripped the cockpit hatch off the Knight and threw it to the ground. The Knight jerked back but the Daedalus had its arm in its grip. Get Some pulled the Knight in. The Knight twisted, exposing the pilot to the fighting men below. The Knight's front side was peppered and dinged by the Marines. A river of blood flowed from the cockpit and the Knight stood still.

Hector saw the Fonz charging him. There was fear in his eyes. Fonzie fired a few rounds at Hector, but missed. Hector drew a bead on Fonzie and shot. The bullets hit Fonzie's flack jacket. The force of impact knocked the Fonzie down, but he rolled to his feet without losing momentum, and jumped at Hector like an eagle dives for fish. Fonzie's Ka Bar met Hector's neck.

The Russian fell to the ground, gasping for life, "Let soldiers carry me away. I don't want body rotting in street."

Fonzie stood over Hector with burning hate, "I'm going to feed you to the fucking stray dogs."

The life escaped Hector's eyes and his body went limp. Fonzie spit in Hector's face, "Fucking bitch."

The Daedalus walked through the combat, being careful not to crush the Marines. The Russians retreated to the gates of Ilium. The mech had a long coil of barbed wire wrapped around its foot, dragging behind it.

Fonzie took his Ka Bar and cut holes between the tendon and bones of Hector's ankles. When the mech dragging the wire passed them, Fonzie grabbed the wire and ran it through the cuts in Hector's legs. The Daedalus marched on, dragging the still bleeding, lifeless body.

The fighting stopped. Ivan didn't have anything left to throw at us. The sound of battle rattled lightly in the distance, but for us was silent.

After an hour of sitting there, staring at Ilium's walls I was hunkered down behind half of a wall with a handful of other Marines. "Well, what the fuck do we do now?"

"I don't know," Éclair shrugged. "You've been in there, you know your way around right?" Éclair joked.

"Ha ha."

Lieutenant Toshi handed his radio back to Correa. "The Eighty-Eighth is on the other side of the complex and the Germans and Brits are to the south. Ivan doesn't have a foot in Saint Petersburg anymore."

"Oh, he's out there," Fonzie corrected the lieutenant. "He's lying facedown in a puddle of his own blood, waiting in purgatory's DMV line, with his ticket to Hell."

"So is the city ours then?" Correa asked.

"We have our back to the ocean," Toshi said, "Ivan's not coming from the east. If the Army, Brits and Germans can keep the Russians from marching back in, then we won't have too terrible of a time."

"What about the fortress?" Doc asked.

"That's the only problem," Toshi grumbled. "Intel says that Ilium can self sustain itself for a good year without resupply or reinforcement. And the Pentagon won't let us just level the fucking place because it's a Mech Factory and they want to know how their shit is built."

"Sir, if we do somehow get inside there, won't the Russians burn or destroy everything that could be valuable to us?" Correa asked.

Toshi sighed. "Sergeant, we're talking about the United States Government. Please refrain from applying any sort of common sense to their problem solving."

We all chuckled a little at that.

"But just think about how long and hard it was to take this city," Toshi continued, "We have a long hard war in front of us. We've been here for months, in the largest, debatably, most powerful nation on the planet, a third of the Marine Corps is here, a good chunk of our Army and our allies are two, and we've *kind* of taken a city."

Everyone's face was grim. I lit a cigarette. Éclair and Doc followed suit. Saint Petersburg was beautiful when we got there. Now it was an ashtray of death overflowing with brass, blood, and dirt, wreaking of Satan's fingertips.

The bodies were a testament of the will of nations to send people they don't know, to fight and die for ideas they themselves didn't believe in. The mechs, that laid hunched over or caved into fallen towers of brick, concrete and steel, were like lesser gods strangled by Zeus, cast from heaven.

I stared at the Knight that stood before us. Its pilot's blood stained the front. The mech's engine still hummed and its eye still glowed bright red.

"Lieutenant Toshi, sir," I said, thinking about Ilium and the mech.

"What up Combat Camera?"

"What if we hid some Marines in this mech's cargo bay, if it has one. Then put it on autopilot and have it walk home."

"What are you talking about?" The lieutenant inquired.

"Well, when it got inside, the Marines could pop out, disable whatever defense systems we needed to and let the Division in through the front gates."

Toshi thought long and hard about my idea. "I guess it couldn't hurt to try. But who would go?"

"I've been in there," Fonzie said. "So has Allensworth, Doc Evans, and DeLaGarza."

"Do you think you remember enough about the layout to get to where you need to be?" Toshi asked.

"Not at all," Fonzie admitted. "But it's better than sitting out here with our thumbs up our ass in front of a fortress we're not allowed to level."

"Hell, all we really have to do is get the gates open," I added.

"Well, fuck it." Toshi flung a hand. "I'll go talk to the S2, if any of them are still alive, and get you any intel I can. I'm going to tell the BC about the plan." Toshi looked up at the mech, "How long do you think that thing stays running for?"

"No clue, Sir," I said.

"Well if we take too much more time then Ivan will be suspicious about it walking up. You guys eat, smoke, get ammo, and whatever else you need. Let's shoot for loading Palacios, Allensworth, Evans, and DeLaGarza up in about an hour."

"Aye, Sir," we said.

Éclair patted my shoulder, "Good luck, brother."

"It won't be the worst thing I've ever been through," I said.

Doc snorted a laugh, "*Yeah.*"

"Hey, Éclair." I lit a cigarette. "You got any face paint left?"

19 The Four Horsemen of Troy

DeLaGarza, Doc, The Fonz and I prepared ourselves while the lieutenant was gone. We collected as many AK magazines as we could carry in our pockets and pouches. The Marines from Fox gave us ammo for our pistols. Fonz had four belts of 240 ammo draped over his shoulder.

Doc and I painted our faces green then smeared our hands with black and pressed it to our faces, leaving a dark handprint over our eyes, mouth, and nose. Fonzie and DeLaGarza painted demonic sugar skulls over their faces.

"I thought you weren't Mexican," I poked at Fonzie.

"I'm not, but it looks cool, right?" Fonzie looked like a villainous behemoth with Satan's eyes, and an abhorrent volume of hate seeping through his veins.

"You're the personification of death, Fonz," I told him.

"Yeah, well, the skulls were DeLaGarza's idea."

DeLaGarza gave a single nod and put a black bandana over his forehead. "I'm going to fucking *drink* Ivan's blood when we get in there."

We left our flack jackets and helmets with the platoon; the space we had to squeeze in the Knight was too small to bring them. Plus if we got hit we were dead anyway. For Fonzie and DeLaGarza this was a suicide mission. For Doc and I it would just be immense pain, if we failed.

Éclair gave me an American flag bandana. Instead of red, white, and blue, it was black, green, and darker green. "Thanks, man."

"Good luck brother," Éclair said, offering me a cigarette, stolen from a Russian corpse.

I handed Éclair my camera, "This was one of *your* back ups anyway, right?"

"Yeah," Éclair lit a cigarette. "Just be careful in there."

"Dude, you'll be charging through the gates not too long after me. I'll see you inside."

I wrapped the bandana around my forehead. I pulled two of the black feathers I had fixed to my tomahawk and put them in the knot on the back of my head facing down, over my shoulder.

Éclair turned to back us; "Hey let me get a picture of you guys before you go."

The four of us leaned together and posed with our weapons. Our uniforms were shredded and covered with blood. We looked like beaten, broken monsters who had come back from the dead for revenge. I guess that was literal for two of us.

Éclair snapped the photo and checked to make sure it came out well. "You guys could be the hounds of Hell."

"Are you fucking Devil Dogging me?" I barked.

Éclair smiled, "Yeah."

"Fucker."

Lieutenant Toshi returned with a rucksack over one of his shoulders.

"Good news, Sir?" Fonz asked.

"Eh. The Colonel Amemnon wasn't happy about the plan. He wants to wait and organize a full blown strike, Five Paragraph order everything, and get Division involved. I said to hell with it. I'll take the court martial if it'll get us inside this citadel of shit," Toshi spat.

"Well, Sir," Fonzie started, "The Division only has about a regiment's worth of Marines left. If this doesn't work, what's four more plots in Arlington on top of the thousands of others they're going to have to dig?"

"That's a fucked up way of looking at it Sergeant Palacios." Toshi replied, "but you're not wrong." He pulled a couple of ropes out of his rucksack, some aerial photographs of Ilium and four satchels. "You know how to use C4 right?"

"Yes, Sir," Fonzie handed each of the four of us a bag.

"You got det cord, detonators, and everything else you need in there. If you can't disable the defense systems in there, I want you to blow the fucking gates down."

Fonzie smiled, "Then Fox Company's gonna shove a bayonet up Ivan's ass?"

"You got it," Toshi nodded. "Now do you have any idea what you're going to do when you get in there?"

"Not a damn clue," Fonzie confessed. "But if we don't know what we're doing, Ivan can't beat us to the chase. But do us a favor, Sir."

"What's up?"

"If we start firing in there, start attacking the gate. Maybe it'll throw Ivan off and he'll think we're a decoy."

"Sounds good, Sergeant." Toshi shook our hands. "Semper Fi, Marines."

We gave the lieutenant an Oorah, and started for the Knight. Toshi told the plan to the Daedalus pilot. Our mech took the weapon from the Knight and pulled out its magazine. The Daedalus thumbed out the shells, they shook the earth when they fell. Then the mech ripped out the magazine spring. It lowered its arm and we climbed into the empty magazine well. We were inserted back into the Knight's weapon. We waited for another Marine to climb into the cockpit and set the autopilot.

"Hey, Doc. What if the computer in this thing has an auto kill function and shoots us out of the rifle like human cannonballs," I joked.

"Shut up, Hank."

We were cramped. With the angle we were held at, we were laying down instead of standing on each other's shoulders. The magazine stank of acrid smoke. There was a little air and light coming from the barrel, but it wasn't enough to relieve us. The engine hummed and gurgled. It sounded like a semi truck was having sex with a tank. The Knight's legs creaked and we started to move. The giant lumbered its way along.

"This things taking its time, huh?" DeLaGarza whispered.

"Apparently Ivan's not too concerned about recovering these things," Doc said.

"At least it has something," I said, "and it's a shit load better than being in an AAV."

"Ugh, those things are fucking terrible," Fonzie complained, "I'm fucking happy this thing doesn't swing its arms when it walks."

The mech abruptly stopped. We shut up. We sat there, still, for another hour, sweating, waiting for the Russians to just blow the thing up and leave us in here to burn. The thought of burning, trapped in a metal coffin, revved my heart. *I don't want to be engulfed in fire. I don't remember the aftermath of the artillery shell in Iran, probably because I was dead, but if I stayed conscious for that...* I shook my head and snapped out of it. There was a booming creak outside and the Knight took a few more steps. The sound creaked again. Someone was yelling something in Russian below us. The voices moved closer.

Fonzie whispered in my ear, "It sounds like they're pulling the pilot out."

"Are we inside then?" I asked.

"I think so."

We waited. The mech moved again. This time instead of   creeping along it moved with a sense of purpose. I stuck my head into the chamber and looked down the barrel. The concrete below us wasn't shattered. "Oh yeah, we're in," I whispered to Fonzie. I put a thumbs up over my head and either Doc or DeLaGarza tapped my foot in response. *Thank God this thing fires from the open bolt.*

There was a lot of commotion outside when the Knight stopped. They were arguing about something. None of us spoke Russian; we had no idea what was going on. The argument turned to screaming, then the voices faded away with their footsteps.

We waited until Twenty-Two hundred to venture out. Fonzie peered through the ejection port of our behemoth's weapon. The barrel was still aimed at the ground. Fonzie crawled out, then me, Doc, then DeLaGarza. We used the cooling vents on the giant rifle as a ladder to the deck.

The room was gigantic. There had to be a hundred brand new mechs standing in formation on the other end. The concrete was painted black, the ceilings had to be a hundred yards high. Yellow lights illuminated a working space for the damaged mechs on our side. The pilot was missing from our Knight, but his blood had yet to be washed from the cold metal.

Behind our Knight, a Bishop lay on its back. A mechanic's upper body was crammed into a maintenance hatch. He was barking at the mechanisms inside the iron beast. His hand came out, felt for a wrench and disappeared back into the machine. We crept up behind him, stepping lightly so we weren't heard. Doc pulled out his tomahawk. Fonzie and DeLaGarza grabbed the mechanic's feet and yanked him out. The Russian didn't get a chance to scream before Doc cracked his head open, spilling his brains onto the floor. We shoved him into the compartment and closed the hatch.

We peered around for anyone else, but saw no one.

"I guess they're all asleep," I whispered.

"Where are we?" Doc asked.

DeLaGarza murmured, "We must be underground. There's no space for this on the surface. Look at all these mechs, there's gotta be hundreds of them. Knights, Bishops, Rooks and…" We looked at a line of mechs we hadn't seen before. "…whatever this is."

"They'll probably call that the King or Queen," Fonzie said.

"You mean, Tsar," Doc whispered.

"Why aren't they using these on us?" I wondered aloud.

"They're probably out of pilots," Fonzie said, "I don't think you can just get in one of these and drive it like a pickup."

"Oh well," I said softly, "with half an ounce of luck, they'll never get to use these."

"Yeah," Fonzie jerked his head to the side, "let's go."

We bounded one by one through the mechs' feet, being careful to stay in the shadows and not make noise. We heard a couple of Russians talking idly around us, but they didn't notice as we passed. There was a hatch on the far side of the hangar. Fonzie leveled his 240 to the door and DeLaGarza opened it. No one was behind it. We went through. To our left was a staircase. Fonzie led the walk up with his machinegun slung on his back. The M240 weighed a little less than thirty pounds without ammunition. Most Marines had to carry in on their shoulders. Fonzie, being a descendant of the Cock Strong Warrior Man Gods, handled it with the ease of a pen. He had one hand open, ready to grab, and the other clutched tightly around his Ka Bar. We went into the first door and found ourselves at the top of the staircase.

The lights were out over the room full of tables. Light came in from a large triangular bay window on the other end. We slipped in. In the middle of the room floated a pyramid. Out of each of the corners in its base was a tall onion domed tower. One of its sides had a large, Red Star, the other side had five Red Stars that formed the Southern Cross.

"Why is that on there?" DeLaGarza asked.

"That's where the Virescents are from," I informed him.

"How do you know that?" he asked.

"I married one of them."

"Huh. How is that thing floating?"

"No clue." I peered under it. There was an object reminiscent of a crystal ball, only darker, like translucent coal with stars in it. "Maybe that has something to do with it."

DeLaGarza looked at the evil looking sphere under the pyramid.

"Quit gawking at shit," Fonzie hissed, "try to find a map."

We started looking over the counters and panels for some kind of direction. There were large computers on the walls. They had multicolored diamond buttons, levers, and wheels. On the walls were photos of Russians at parties with Virescents. Some of them were posing, others shaking hands.

"Hey, Fonz," Doc whispered, "I found some documents in a drawer." Doc handed Fonzie the papers. Half of the words were Russian, the other half the Virescent written language. "Think they might be important?"

Fonzie put the documents on a desk. "They probably are, but that's not our job."

I looked out the triangle window. "Check this out," I said, waving the Marines over.

"What is that?" Fonzie asked.

"Looks like a space shuttle," Doc observed, "I mean I've never seen one that looks like that, but it's got the boosters, rockets, and everything."

"It's probably something Ivan built with the Virescents," I muttered.

"Too bad they're never going to get to use it," Fonz said, "Let's blow this popsicle stand. We have a gate to destroy."

We continued through Ilium, trying to stay out of the light. Most of the halls were poorly lit and wide with stanchions. We moved in the shadows, barely even silhouettes, clutching our steely knives, knaves in the night.

Fonzie held up his fist and we froze in the darkness behind the columns. A lone soldier walked through the hall. He had his rifle slung over his shoulder and stared at the ceiling as he walked. Before he passed us, Doc let out a loud sharp fart. The soldier stopped dead in his tracks and looked into the shadows where we hid. He pulled his rifle down to his hands and said something short. He was looking right at us, but couldn't see us. His eyes searched the darkness. He stepped in close, rifle at the ready. The soldier peeked behind the columns. I grabbed the barrel of his weapon. He pulled the trigger, but he hadn't taken the rifle off safe. He growled something in Russian and yanked back. I pulled him back to me and buried my tomahawk into the base of his neck. Doc helped me drag him to the corner where the least light shined. The soldier's final resting place was in the darkness of an evil citadel, built with the power of otherworldly brains with socialist mindsets.

Alongside one of the corridors was a map with a red arrow that we assumed read "YOU ARE HERE," written in Cyrillic. We took note of where we were, and where we were supposed to go, and kept moving about the complex. A ladder in a maintenance room took us to the night's fresh air through a manhole.

It would soon be winter in Russia. The evening's crisp air let us know. I could just barely see my breath. We climbed out of the manhole to an area behind big metal storage boxes.

Fonzie peeked around the corner, then back to us, "we're at the airfield."

"This place has an air field?" DeLaGarza whispered.

"Apparently," Fonzie replied quietly.

"Well, what's the plan?" I asked.

"The front gates should be on the other side of it, but I can't see it through the lights." Fonzie pulled out the photos Lieutenant Toshi gave us of Ilium. He peaked back out at the runway. "Looks like the runway is right between us and the gate."

I looked over at the landing strip. "We're going to have to go around. There's like fifty guys over there." The runway was lit with bright blue lights. Soldiers were fueling and loading mechs. There was a Knight on the tarmac, soldiers with flashlights directed its path. A Rook stood in a small hangar, Russians loaded it with ammunition.

"And mechs," Fonzie said. He glanced at the photos again and put them away. He pulled out his knife, "Follow me."

We crouched around the airfield, staying out of sight. We made it to the other side without incident. The sky was clear and the wind was soft. I could almost see every star in the sky. The moon was nowhere to be seen.

The airstrip's control tower was built into the fortress's wall. A bubble stuck out a few stories up. There were soldiers inside using a substantial amount of communications equipment in dim, red light. Below the glass sphere was a hatch guarded by two men. We hunkered down behind a truck and looked at the tower within the wall. It was only a hundred meters from the gates.

Fonzie scanned the entrance from under the truck. "Think that goes all the way up?" He asked.

243

"Yeah." I replied from beside him.

Doc and DeLaGarza watched for sentries from behind.

"Alright. You and Doc go around to the right and I'll take Garza from this side. We'll take the guards out at the same time."

We split and our pairs circled the base of the tower. I looked at Fonzie from behind the guards and we exchanged a single nod.

In sequence, Fonzie wrapped his arm around a guard's neck and ran his Ka Bar through his chest, while I tackled the other guard and severed the spinal cord in his neck with my axe. The dead guard in Foznie's arm dropped his AK. A burst of fire flew when it hit the deck.

We all stood deathly still, my eyelids touched themselves inside my skull. The soldiers on the tarmac scrambled for their weapons while screaming at each other. Bullets cracked past our heads and chipped away into the concrete wall behind us.

Ilium's alarm blared throughout the citadel. "Goddamnit!" Fonzie pulled up is 240, and started spraying the runway from behind a crate. The other three of us joined in. The soldiers dove for cover.

The door the sentries guarded burst open and a line of soldiers ran out. None of them made it more than a foot before DeLaGarza mowed them down. "Sergeant Palacios!" He screamed.

I grabbed Fonzie's arm, "Fonz!"

"What?" He screamed.

"We gotta get the fuck out of here!"

BOOM!

An explosion knocked us to the ground. My vision went blurry and my ears rang. I looked up over my body.

Doc leaned up on his elbow, "Anyone hurt?" He demanded.

I patted myself down, and was fine. Fonzie and DeLaGarza knelt up. The side of the crate was splintered, but miraculously we were all fine. More explosions blew holes in the ground in a line heading towards the runway.

"MORTARS!" Fonzie screamed.

The Russians coming from the airstrip dove down for cover.

I grabbed Fonzie's arm, "Let's go!"

BOOM!

Another explosion rocked the wall above us. The red control tower bubble exploded. Glass and bits of metal rained down on us. I covered my head with my arms. A Russian soldier fell from the twisted burning hole in the wall screaming, he was completely engulfed in flame. He hit the ground with a thud, but he didn't die. He screamed and rolled on the ground.

Doc aimed his rifle at the wailing soldier. Fonzie pushed it down, "Let him fucking burn."

We rushed over the pile of dead soldiers into the doorway. Fonzie took one of the ammo belts off from his shoulders and reloaded his 240. The mortar team kept upturning the earth outside. We found the stairs and sprinted up the ladder well. We came across the door to the control center. Smoke and fire flowed into the hallway. Soldiers were trying to rest the flames with extinguishers. We killed them without hesitation. I peaked into the room. Red lights flickered over the distorted computers, radio equipment, and shouting soldiers trying to help their fallen comrades in and out of darkness. I pulled out a grenade and showed it to the other Marines. They nodded their heads; I pulled the pin and rolled it into the room.

POP!

Dust rattled off the walls and we continued our run up the inside of the wall. We burst through a door and found a maze of pipes, ladders, and steel grated walkways lit in the color of blood. We hustled up a steel ladder on the wall to the top. We burst through the door at the end. Fonzie opened up with his 240. I was the last one out. We were outside! There was a group of six or eight Russians bleeding to death on the ground. We finished them off with single bullets to the head. Fonzie led us in a sprint to the top of the gates.

There was a guard post on either side of it. We sprayed down the hut on our side as we approached. The other guard hut opened fire. We hit the deck and crawled to the structure on our side. DeLaGarza reached up and pulled the door open, Fonzie laid on the side with his pistol ready to gun down whoever was behind it. The soldiers inside were dead. Bullets still rattled the hut. We were pinned down behind the wall's concrete blocks. Doc and DeLaGarza laid facing behind us, to cover our rear. The fire over our head paused. I reached inside the hut and pulled off the dead soldier's glove. I positioned it on the end of my rifle so that only the middle finger was raised. I raised it over the edge to show Ivan. A burst of bullets cracked over our heads and I pulled it down.

"Hey, do that again," Fonzie ordered.

I shot the hand back into the air. When the Russians shot at the finger, Fonzie popped up, and turned the other guard hut into a steamy mess.

Fonzie and I crammed into the guard hut. "Maybe we can open the gate from here and we don't have to blow it." Fonzie looked over the control panels.

I looked into Ilium. No one was firing at us for the moment. The troops on the ground were scrambling to avoid the steel rain. The mortar fire from the Marines outside still hadn't stopped. "I think Toshi got the whole fucking battalion's mortar teams blasting this place."

"So fucking much for recovering intel." Fonzie clambered over the switches in the guardhouse, pressing every button and flipping every switch. "I don't think this shit's gonna work, man," Fonzie turned his head. "Garza! Get the rope and bring the C4!"

I took my satchel off and handed it to the Fonz. DeLaGarza wrapped one end of the rope around a concrete part of the parapet, then Fonzie wrapped all the C4 satchels over his shoulders and tied the other end of the rope to his belt. We plugged the detonators into the det cord and put them down by the ledge.

"There's too much shit holding these doors up to blow them both down. I'm just going to put the shit on this one's hinges." Said the Fonz.

DeLaGarza and I held the rope and eased Fonzie over the ledge. The Fonz had his feet on the edge of the gate. The satchels hung from his back, the det cord reached from the bags to the guard hut. He looked us in the eye and smiled "Geronimo." We lowered him down, almost to the bottom. Fonzie stuck the first block of C4 in place. We hoisted him up and he placed the second, then third, and fourth sets of explosives. We were pulling up Fonzie, and the Russians started firing at us again from the ground. Fonzie only had his pistol on him. Doc picked up the 240 and started spraying down the Russians. The Fonz fired at the Russians as we hoisted him up. We got him to the top of the wall. He holstered his pistol and grabbed the inside edge. DeLaGarza held onto the rope and I grabbed one of The Fonz's arms. As I was helping up Fonzie, a bullet ripped into his heel, traveled through his body and blew out his opposite shoulder. Blood painted my face, The Fonz went limp and a river of crimson flowed from his wounds.

"NO! FONZIE!" I screamed, pulling him the rest of the way up.

"NO GODDAMNIT!" DeLaGarza shouted.

"DOC! DOC GET THE FUCK OVER HERE!" I laid the Fonz on the deck.

Doc came running, crouching down to avoid fire, "Oh, shit…"

"Ya gotta save him, Doc." DeLaGarza's eyes were already flowing a river of tears.

Doc frantically looked at The Fonz's wounds. "I can't, man," he whimpered. "He was dead before the bullet left is body."

I howled at the top of my lungs. The sky was clear and I could see every crater on the rising full moon's face. I grabbed the 240 and stuck it over the wall. "BLOW THE GODDAMNED GATE!" I pulled the trigger on the machinegun and screamed as a hundred little lead filled demons were sent to possess the enemy.

One of the other two set off the explosives, and with a thunderous clash, the gates of Ilium plummeted to the ground.

It was midnight.

The Daedalus, Get Some, rocketed through the gate. It slid over the pavement firing at the Russian mechs. It went to fight its own battle.

The machinegun went dry. I grabbed the last two belts from Fonzie. "Sorry bro, I need these." I slammed the rounds into the feed tray and held down the trigger. The barrel glowed red from the heat.

Lieutenant Toshi was the first man through the citadel's walls. Screaming through the gate, he lead the charge. More and more Marines flooded into Ilium.

The rounds passed through the barrel. I let go of the trigger. The barrel glowed bright orange and smoked. My breathing was weak from the screaming.

"We gotta go link up with Fox," DeLaGarza yelled.

"What about Fonzie?" I asked, "We can't just leave him here."

"I know, but we can't carry him either."

I stared at The Fonz. There was more blood than I thought a person could have pooled around him.

"Hank, we have to move," Doc said.

I put the 240 next to Fonzie and put my hand on his forehead. I stood up, grabbed my AK, and the three of us descended the wall. When we got to the ground where we had killed the guards, we bumped into a group of Marines who immediately pointed their rifles at us, startled by our appearance.

"Who the hell are you?" Their Staff Sergeant demanded.

"Fox Company, Two-Seven. You?" I demanded.

"Kilo, Three-Five," he replied. "What the hell are you doing without your flacks and kevlars?"

"We just blew down the fucking gate. Which way's Seventh Marines?"

The staff sergeant pointed towards the tower in the middle of Ilium.

"Awesome, thanks." Doc, DeLaGarza, and I bolted towards the tower.

Get Some had been joined by a Panzer in the brawl of mechs. The Panzer was painted black and had tick marks for its kills painted on its shield. It had a picture of a jet with seven ticks, a tank with twelve, eight for mechs, and a flying saucer with six. I didn't know what the flying saucer meant, but I had too much shit going on in my head to give a fuck. The Panzer did have something that looked like a bazooka that was turning the parked mechs into craters in the runway. The mechs were pagan gods battling for control of the universe.

Fighter jets screamed from above. U.S. forces had orders specifically not to bomb Ilium because some fuck in Washington wanted the fortress's secrets. Our fighters were keeping the Russian bombers, who would rather watch Ilium burn than see an American flag over it, at bay.

We found Lieutenant Toshi barking orders to his platoon commanders into the radio Correa had on his back. Fox Company was fighting their way into the central complex.

"Sir," I panted.

"Hey, *outstanding* fucking job, Marines," Toshi shouted over the boiling cauldron of damnation we were burning in. "Where's Palacios?"

"He's dead, Sir," I muttered.

Toshi paused for a second, "I'm sorry."

A roar shook the earth. A pillar of fire erupted to the heavens from in front of the complex. The space shuttle we had seen earlier in the night blasted towards the moon. Its silver hull shined in the darkness. Smoke settled in around the inside of Ilium. It didn't hinder the violence below.

"What the fuck was that?" Toshi screamed.

"I think it was a space shuttle," Doc said, "we saw it earlier down in the hangars. There's an entire other fucking level of shit under us."

"Great," Toshi spat. "That's just fucking great. What the hell else do they have down there?"

"About a hundred mechs," DeLaGarza informed him, "but they didn't look like they were equipped for combat."

The lieutenant grunted, "Well, fight ain't over gents. Get back to it."

After the ship escaped to space, antiaircraft batteries sent red snakes of fire to the sky to swat down our birds.

A Bishop kicked a Daedalus to the ground, crushing its head. Get Some fired its cannon at the Russian mech, causing it to explode into a fiery hunk of twisted metal. The marked up Panzer fired at the Russian infantry.

Fox Company was still hunkered down under lead rain. Doc and I took cover behind a truck that had been flipped on its side. DeLaGarza took control of a squad.

"Glad to see you made it!" Éclair shouted. I didn't realize he was next to me.

"You too man," I gave him one hard pat on the shoulder.

We were about thirty yards from the central building of Ilium. Ivan held most of the property. Get Some grabbed a Bishop's weapon and cleared the way for us. Then blew a few large holes out of the walls.

Toshi shouted, "LET'S GO!" and sprinted towards the building.

The Company followed him. We poured into the structure. The Russians immediately inside, were dazed from the mech's attack. We put bullets and bayonets into them as we passed over and headed deeper into the facility. We slipped on the shell casings and blood on the floor.

The main power had gone out leaving only an occasional spotlight to illuminate the way. The thick concrete walls muffled the war on the other side.

"I think most of them are outside," Éclair said as we crept through the dark, rifles at the ready.

"Yeah, there weren't too many of them when we came through earlier. I don't think the grunts get to come in here," I responded.

"This is creepy as shit."

The smell of sulfur, gunpowder, and death haunted the corridors.

"There's a light," one of the Marines in front of us pointed out.

Bright blue shined through the cracks in a large doorway. A squad broke away to investigate. It took four of us to pull the door open wide enough to fit Marines through.

There were two unarmed Russians inside hurrying to burn documents and hard drives. When they saw us they were overtaken with fear. They trembled for a moment then reached for more things to throw into the fire. Éclair and I shot them.

"How'd I know they were going to destroy the important shit?" Éclair barked, stomping out the fire.

The room was filled with bizarre machinery.

"Hey Doc, when did the alarms stop?" I asked.

"I didn't notice it until you said something," Doc replied.

I looked out the triangular window on the other side of the room. There was a bay below us full of computer terminals and cylindrical water tanks full of the starry coal. Bubbles moved the black orbs around the vats.

"The S2's gonna have a field day with this shit." Éclair lit a cigarette.

"No, shit," Doc mumbled.

"Hey, which one of you's the squad leader?" I asked the Marines in the room.

"I am, Sergeant," a lance corporal answered.

"You might want to radio Lieutenant Toshi about this."

"Aye, Sergeant."

There was a circular platform on one side of the room, large enough for five or six people to stand in. Columns, with enough lights to be a Christmas tree, lined the circle. Attached to it were two coiled poles with silver balls at the top.

The triangle window that overlooked the computer room burst open and AK fire raked the room. We all dove for cover.

"It's just one guy!" A Marine shouted as we fired back.

The shooter wasn't showing himself. He was raising the weapon with his hands over his head to fire into the room.

Éclair and another Marine crawled over the platform with the columns. The rest of us shot over the window to keep the soldier down. Bullets punched through the computer terminals in the other room. Sparks fell from the tops of the vats with the starry coal and the spheres dancing inside. A monstrous humming accompanied the electricity shooting through the air between the coils.

The shooter raised his weapon again and let a burst into our room. Both of the rooms burst into flames.

The squad leader shouted, "Fall back! Get the fuck out of here!"

One by one the Marines bound out through the doorway. Doc and I covered them on their way out.

Éclair and the other Marine were still firing from the platform but the shooter had retreated.

"Éclair!" I barked. "Fuck that guy, let him burn with the rest of this shit!"

Éclair was kneeling down; he grabbed a lever inside of the platform to pull himself up. The lever fell and lightning from the coils above engulfed the platform. The electricity cut the Marine beside Éclair in half from head to foot. Éclair's body started to glow blue. His face was frozen. There was a pounding roar. Éclair and the lightning disappeared together into nothing.

I was in too much shock to move. I stared at the platform where he was, now there was nothing but half of the other Marine.

Doc grabbed the back of my shirt, "Come the fuck on, Hank!"

I gaped at the machine. "What the fuck was that?" I whispered. I don't think Doc could hear me over the fire, noise, and confusion.

"HANK!"

I shuddered walking backwards towards the door, "What the *fuck* was that?" I demanded when we got into the hallway.

"I don't know, dude."

"Where the fuck did Éclair go?"

Doc shook his head. "I..." Doc's mouth hung open, he ran a hand through his thinning hair. "I, uh, fuck. I don't fucking even..." He shrugged. We ran back out into the fight.

20 Iliupersis

When the battle was over Doc and I sat on top of the wall by The Fonz, watching Ilium burn. My eyes watered quietly. I couldn't stop thinking about Fonzie and Éclair, two of my best friends were gone in less than a few hours. I tried to chain smoke my problems away.

I watched the flames about the citadel, soaking in the culmination of the year's blood splattering. We hadn't defeated the mighty Russian Federation, the war was only beginning. All that blood, just for one city with a fortress that held secrets that some cocksucker in Washington wanted on his desk, it wasn't worth my friends to me.

I took off the olive drab American Flag bandana Éclair gave me and fixed it to a pole flying over the guard shack above the gate.

"What do we do now, Doc?"

"Wait for orders."

To Be Continued…

IMAGE LEGEND

ABOUT THE AUTHOR

Tripp, who sexually identifies as an American twin-engine attack helicopter, was genetically engineered in a laboratory in Florida. He cut himself from the womb with a rotary blade so he could put veteran's day on his birth certificate and forever have the day off work. He then ran away to be raised by badgers at the gates of Tartarus. After living by the mantra "If it bleeds, we can kill it," and watching the Battle of Fallujah on TV he promptly joined the Marine Corps as a combat cameraman so he could steal the souls of those killed by the Marines he was with. He deployed to Afghanistan with 2/7 and ¾ in '08, and '09-'10 respectively, then went on a couple of MEUs so he could drink on the ocean and anger sailors by calling their ship a "boat." Tripp spent his decade in the Corps drinking rum, crushing the hopes and dreams of mortals, and chain smoking. He has multiple awards for books he hasn't even written, once deadlifted a battleship, outwitted a sphinx, knows Vicky's secret (it's that she has a penis), is an award winning photographer, and at all times has been the best guitar player in the barracks. Did I mention he's handsome and has a glorious mustache? He's a great storyteller, specializing in fairytales and bullshit. About the only thing he doesn't have is a TV show based on his books (looking at *you* Netflix.) He hopes that you enjoyed this book, but if you didn't it doesn't matter. He already has your money and is currently spending it on strippers, cigarettes, and alcohol.

58864968R00175

Made in the USA
San Bernardino, CA
30 November 2017